REDUCED TO RUBBLE

She was about to become gigolo bait in a dark garage, with a Dodge Ram grille pressing into her butt.

She had never been so turned on.

Or so disgusted with herself.

He could reduce any woman to rubble, she told herself in an attempt to regain her sanity—or at least her dignity. He was trained in the art of pleasure.

It was the wrong thing to think, because the word "pleasure" in conjunction with Wyatt wrung a shameful moan from her throat.

"God, you're the sexiest woman I've ever met," Wyatt said roughly, moving impossibly closer.

The heat of him set her on fire. Kasidy let out a little whimper. She wished she could call it a protest, but she knew she'd be lying.

Something had to give, she thought desperately, or she was going to let him have his way with her right there on the hood of his truck.

CRITICS RAVE FOR SHERIDON SMYTHE!

COMPLETELY YOURS

"A delightfully fast-moving and witty romance."
—*RT BOOKclub*

"*Completely Yours* is a winning combination of humor, romance, and intriguing characters."
—*Romance Reviews Today*

"A well-written and sexy novel."
—Roundtable Reviews

MR. COMPLETE

"Sprinkled liberally with laugh-out-loud scenes, and not one but several yummy hunks, this fast-paced story will keep you engrossed to the last page."
—*Romantic Times*

"Humorous and hunk-heaven, Sheridon Smythe spins a delightful tale."
—*The Midwest Book Review*

"This will become many a fan's favorite...it will make you a fan of her hot, steamy, and completely wonderful romances!"
—A Romance Review

HOT NUMBER

"*Hot Number* is a fast-moving story with loads of sexual pressure and plenty of hot scenes....[a] light and humorous tale."
—*RT BOOKclub*

"An engaging romance... For a thoroughly entertaining read, I recommend *Hot Number*."
—*Romance Reviews Today*

"*Hot Number* moves at a fast pace, and gives us lots of chuckles...a great read that any fan of contemporary romance won't want to miss."
—A Romance Review

COMPLETELY IRRESISTIBLE

SHERIDON SMYTHE

LOVE SPELL NEW YORK CITY

LOVE SPELL®

May 2006

Published by

Dorchester Publishing Co., Inc.
200 Madison Avenue
New York, NY 10016

ISBN 0-505-52668-9

*This book is dedicated to my
oldest grandchild, Kasidy Raeann.
As a gifted child, Grandma has no doubt
you're going to make an impact on the world.
At seven, you're already, incredibly, an avid reader,
which warms my heart. Someday you'll be
reading my books, and that, my darling,
is what makes it all worthwhile!
Grandma Sherrie loves you!*

*Thanks again to the Haverkampf family
for contributing to my inspiration in
creating Dillon and Wyatt.
God bless you!*

PROLOGUE

"Good God Almighty! Kassy! Get in here!"

Kasidy Evans bumped her head on the undercarriage in her haste to slide out from beneath the car. Her heart was pounding as she leaped to her feet and took off at a dead run toward the screened-in front porch.

There were two things her fraternal grandmother rarely did; she rarely shouted, and she rarely took the Lord's name in vain.

In one breath, she'd just done both. It had to be bad.

Heart attack, Kasidy thought, jerking open the screen door and barreling inside. Or maybe a stroke. Heedless of her oil-slicked hands, she burst into the living room and came to a skidding stop on the waxed linoleum floor.

Not a heart attack.

Not a stroke.

Not unless Nana Jo was trying to keep up a good front by reading her newspaper while struggling for her last breath.

The second most stable person in her life was sitting in her worn easy chair with the paper spread out on the cluttered coffee table. The only thing preventing her spectacles from sliding off her face was the slight upward curve of her nose.

Kasidy stood with her mouth agape, chest heaving from the wicked scare her grandmother had given her. "Nana? Did I just hear you say—"

"Never mind that," Nana Jo interrupted, waving her hand in the air. "Listen to these headlines, and you'll know what I was shouting about. 'During a press conference held yesterday at the estate of the late Amelia Hancock, estate attorney Drucilla Jacob announced a fifty-thousand-dollar reward to the person or persons with information leading to the whereabouts of her estranged granddaughter. Anyone with information should call Attorney Jacob's office.'"

It was a moment before Kasidy could sound properly unconcerned.

First she had to swallow a big wad of fear.

She'd been raised on stories of how mean and vicious Grandma Hancock could be. "So? The old witch is hunting me from the grave." She walked nonchalantly to the sofa and sat down before her weak legs betrayed her. "Nobody knows what I look like, or what name I'm using. They can't catch me. They never caught Mom and Dad, and they can't catch *me*."

"Of course they can't, honey."

The soothing note in Nana Jo's voice scared Kasidy more than the headlines. "I should call Dad. He'll want to know the wicked witch is dead."

Nana Jo put a hand on Kasidy's trembling knee.

Kasidy's calm front hadn't fooled her. "Sweetheart, he still can't go back to Atlanta, not as long as there's a chance Amelia kept that evidence against him. Whoever inherits the estate will surely find it."

And when they did, Kasidy thought, her fists clenched in anger, her father would be hunted down and killed by the Slowkowsky family.

Unless . . . unless *she* found it first! Kasidy sucked in a gasp as the idea expanded. She looked wildly at her fraternal grandmother. "I'm going to get that evidence and destroy it!"

Her grandmother's eyes went wide. "Oh, honey! You can't go there! There's a bounty on your head. Every bounty hunter and amateur P.I. will be looking for you!"

Kasidy smiled grimly. "And I'm going to be in the last place anyone would think to look." She rose and wiped her greasy hands on her stained jeans. "Tell my customers I'll finish their cars when I get back."

And she *would* be back. There was absolutely nothing in Atlanta that would make her want to stay.

CHAPTER 1

"Maybe she left you all of her sex toys."

Refusing to be goaded on this solemn day by his twin brother, Dillon, Wyatt Love folded his arms and tried to ignore him. Normally *he* was the one doing the agitating, but it was fast becoming obvious that something had riled Dillon, prompting him to take on the role of agitator.

"Did she have one of those rooms? You know . . . with manacles on the walls and a hidden video camera?"

Wyatt's jaw ached from clenching it. He had thought Dillon, who was normally uptight, yet level-headed, was the one person he could count on not to tease and torment him about being included in a deceased client's will.

"How about whips and chains? Was she into the kinky stuff?"

That did it. Wyatt turned his furious gaze on his twin. "Are you still mad at me for switching your kids? Is that what this is all about? Because if it is, I gotta tell you, Kaden looked a hell of a lot cuter in

4

that pink frilly dress than Jada." When Dillon's eyes narrowed, Wyatt couldn't stop his mouth from curving. Jada and Kaden were Dillon's one-year-old twins. "I wish you could have seen your face when you changed Jada's diaper and found out she was a boy. Admit it. For just a moment there, you thought Jada had grown an extra appendage overnight."

"It was *not* funny," Dillon said through gritted teeth.

"You're right. It wasn't funny. It was hilarious. Especially when he peed in your face. Really, bro, you need to lighten up."

"Maybe I will . . . when you *grow* up."

"Excuse me," a feminine voice said from behind the sofa where Wyatt and Dillon sat waiting for the attorney.

Wyatt nearly jumped out of his skin. He'd been feeling creeped out from the moment the housekeeper had led them to the massive study of his recently deceased client, Amelia Hancock.

They both stood, and the woman behind the sofa blinked in shock. Wyatt couldn't get a good look at her face because of the cap pulled low on her forehead, but there was no mistaking the curvy outline of her figure in the tight-fitting coverall she wore. Flashing her a wicked smile, he explained unnecessarily, "Twins."

The woman cleared her throat, but the low, husky tone of her voice didn't change. "I see that. Um, I'm from the phone company. I need to check the lines in here."

"*You* work for the phone company?" Wyatt realized his mistake the moment he saw her shoulders stiffen.

Beside him, Dillon snickered. "What I meant was, did you know that Mrs. Hancock . . . has passed?"

"I heard. Sorry for your loss." She indicated the clipboard in her hand. "Should I reschedule?"

Wyatt wished she'd remove her cap so he could see her face more clearly. And her hair. It was either very short, or she had stuffed it beneath the cap. Either way, he had a hunch he'd like the feel of it. "Um, what exactly were you scheduled to do?"

"New line. She's got static . . . *had* static." She pulled an object from her belt. "I just need to plug in this receptor, and then I can get out of your way."

"Hey, that looks like a baby monitor," Dillon said, "with duct tape wrapped around it to hold it together."

The woman shrugged. "I suppose it does. May I?"

"Be my guest." Wyatt admired the cute curve of her butt in the coverall as she walked to an outlet and plugged in the receptor. Her face remained in shadow as she scribbled something on her clipboard.

"Thanks," she said, heading for the door, still scribbling.

"My pleasure," Wyatt murmured, wishing the meeting was over so he could follow her out and chat her up, find out if she was available. There was something about that sex-roughened voice and stubborn little chin that made him think of hot sex on a stormy night. Was she a local? Married? Interested?

Dillon jabbed him in the ribs. "Way to go, Bozo."

"How about *you*? 'That looks like a baby monitor with duct tape,'" Wyatt mimicked derisively. "As if she'd be using a baby monitor to check a phone line."

"If you weren't so busy teaching cross-dressing 101 to my kids, maybe you'd see the resemblance, Mr. Gigolo of the Year."

Wyatt held on to his temper. "Mr. Complete is a respectable escort company, and I'm a respectable escort, not a gigolo."

Dillon's brow shot up to a taunting angle. "Oh, yeah? Is that why the old lady put you in her will, because you 'escorted' her? Tell it to the press, little brother."

Despite the fact that he knew Dillon was teasing him, Wyatt felt his face grow hot. What if the old broad *had* left him something substantial? What would people think? More important, what would they believe?

"Sorry I'm late."

The cold voice belonged to Drucilla Jacob, Amelia Hancock's attorney. She was a buxom, middle-aged woman with ice blue eyes and a heart to match. As Wyatt looked into those frigid eyes now, he knew he had his answer, at least where Mrs. Jacob was concerned.

Her contemptuous gaze flicked from Wyatt to Dillon, then back again. She wasn't impressed by their identical looks. "Which one of you is Wyatt Love?"

Although Wyatt was tempted to shove Dillon forward and run for his life, he refrained. Just. "Um, I am. I escorted Mrs. Hancock on occasion—"

"None of my business," Mrs. Jacob interrupted to say briskly—and with open contempt. "I'm—I *was* Mrs. Hancock's attorney, not her mother. Her sex life was her own business."

Her sex life? Wyatt was speechless with shock at

7

the woman's rude, judgmental comment. He looked at Dillon and found that Dillon looked just as shocked. Anger slowly seeped in, shoving embarrassment aside. Wyatt seldom lost his temper, but when he did it wasn't pretty, and usually left him feeling awful afterward. He had a feeling this time might be an exception.

His voice was soft and outwardly pleasant as he drawled, "Too bad you two weren't closer. The three of us could have had some fun." When color rushed into the attorney's cheeks, Wyatt felt a vicious satisfaction that would have shocked his mother. "In fact, if you're not doing anything after the meeting, I've got a couple of home DVDs you might enjoy watching."

"Wyatt," Dillon warned beneath his breath.

But Wyatt wasn't finished. "Maybe after you see what I can do, we can talk business. Obviously, with Mrs. Hancock gone, I'll be looking for another old lady to suck dry."

Mrs. Jacob's outraged gasp echoed around the room.

Without missing a beat, Wyatt went into graphic—and fictional—detail about his imaginary sex life with the seventy-year-old widow.

"Eeew!" Kasidy gasped, jabbing at the OFF/ON button on the baby monitor until it crackled into silence. She dropped the monitor onto the plush carpet in disgust. She was in the library, shamelessly eavesdropping on the meeting in the next room.

Only it had turned ugly.

No, not just ugly; *disgustingly* ugly.

So the hunk that had stared at her butt had been her grandmother's boy toy. Kasidy wiped her sweaty hands on her coveralls, brushing aside the regret that tried to creep in. To think she had been *attracted* to the creep—gigolo—whatever he was! She'd heard about his type, although she'd never actually met a real gigolo face-to-face.

From the sound of it, Wyatt Love wasn't the least bit ashamed of his profession, either. Too bad, she thought, reaching for the monitor again. It wasn't often she met a guy who could make her knees weak the way he had done when he spoke to her.

And those eyes . . . those gorgeous bedroom eyes.

Kasidy covered her hot face and groaned with embarrassment. Of course he had bedroom eyes! That's where he spent the majority of his time. Thank God she'd found out before she had done something humiliating, like flirting with him.

Shaking her head and smiling ruefully, Kasidy turned the monitor back on and slid down the wall to the floor, listening intently.

"Once we did it on the roof. I had shingle burns on my—"

Desperately, Dillon kicked Wyatt in the shin.

The pain finally broke through Wyatt's fury. He yelped and glared at Dillon. "She deserved it. You know she did."

"Yes, she did, and you got even. Now can we get on with the meeting? Kaden's getting his first haircut this afternoon." Dillon looked smug. "No more switcheroo for you."

"Whatever." Wyatt was slow to anger, and slow to

cool. He focused a wintery gaze on the attorney, who looked as if she'd swallowed a green persimmon—whole. "Sorry about that. I got carried away." With the devil still prodding him, he managed to look wistful. "She was some kinda woman."

Mrs. Jacob drew herself up. "Are you finished?"

Wyatt lifted an inquiring brow. "Unless you'd like to hear more?"

"No!"

"Then I'm finished. You may start the meeting." With as much dignity as he could muster, he settled himself on the sofa. When Dillon remained standing, Wyatt snagged his belt and pulled him backward. "Sit down, will you? The meeting has started."

"Thank God," Dillon whispered. "I was about to start believing you myself."

The flustered attorney pulled out a chair and sat behind the massive desk that dominated the room. "This won't take long. Amelia was very clear about her instructions concerning her estate. As you probably already know, she has offered a reward for anyone with information on her granddaughter. If her granddaughter is found, or decides to show up on her own, she will inherit the entire Hancock fortune." Mrs. Jacob paused and looked at a spot over Wyatt's head. "In the event she isn't found or doesn't claim her inheritance at the end of six months, the estate will be divided among"—the attorney consulted her papers—"Larry Edmond Hancock, Curly Cartwright Hancock, and Moe Bartholomew Hancock. On the event of *their* deaths, her estate will go to a charity of your choice, Mr. Love."

Wyatt and Dillon gasped simultaneously. Before

either could form a verbal response, the attorney continued.

"Mrs. Hancock has requested that you, Mr. Love, assume the job as caretaker of the estate until her granddaughter is found, or the six months are up. You'll receive one thousand dollars a week for the position."

"That's insane!" Wyatt blurted out.

Mrs. Jacob smiled thinly, apparently misunderstanding him. "I'm sure it isn't what you're accustomed to. I'm equally sure you'll find a way to compensate."

Dillon's hand landed on his arm, holding him down. Wyatt gritted his teeth. He'd never hit a woman, of course, but he'd wanted to get closer when he told the pompous woman exactly where she could stick her snide comments.

To Wyatt's relief, Mrs. Jacob began gathering her papers and placing them in her briefcase. He couldn't wait for her to leave so that he could mutter every cussword he'd ever heard. Maybe he'd even invent a few of his own.

She was at the door before she spoke again. "Oh, I'm sure you're anxious to meet Amelia's babies, so I'll send them in."

"Babies?" Wyatt said, blinking at her.

"Babies?" Dillon sat up straight on the sofa, looking as confused as Wyatt. "What is she talking about?" he whispered to Wyatt.

Wyatt frowned. "I have no idea. Despite what the old bat thinks, I've only been in this house once, and that was to take a piss."

"You'll need to find someone to care for them," the attorney said.

Her smug expression made Wyatt distinctly uneasy. "Babies? Mind telling me what the hell you're talking about?"

"Larry, Curly, and Moe. They need constant supervision. I'm afraid Amelia spoiled them."

Wyatt and Dillon stood together.

"Larry?"

"Curly?"

"Moe?" Wyatt felt on the edge of another explosion. "Would you please explain? Because I can't believe you're actually trying to make a joke."

"Oh, it's not a joke." The attorney smiled to reveal perfectly capped teeth. She looked exactly like a shark to Wyatt. "I'll have the housekeeper bring them to you." Her hand paused on the doorknob.

Wyatt felt his balls shriveling. He could have sworn the air in the room dropped ten degrees. The woman was evil. Pure evil. She was probably a barracuda in the court room. Hell. Scratch that. She was probably *Freddy Krueger* in the court room.

"You might, um, want to be careful. They've been a little jumpy since Amelia was burglarized last year."

When she disappeared through the door, Wyatt let out a huge breath. Dillon echoed the sound.

They barely had time to draw it in again when they heard a thundering noise in the hall. The sound grew louder. The tiny hairs on the back of Wyatt's neck rose.

The door crashed open. Three large shapes barreled in their direction. A blur of red. A blur of white. A blur of black.

Poodles, Wyatt thought as he absorbed the shock, throwing up his arms to shield his face. Enormous

12

poodles. Poodles that growled and bared sharp teeth. Poodles that didn't look as if they were going to stop before they leaped on him and—

"Heel!"

The sharp command didn't come from the wicked attorney, whom Wyatt suspected was laughing her way to her car. It didn't come from the housekeeper, either, he saw as he lowered his arms, for she was nowhere to be seen.

It came from the curvy phone woman in the snug overalls.

He wiped the sweat from his brow, staring at the frozen trio of poodles less than a foot from the sofa. He could almost hear Dillon's heart pounding alongside his own. His voice was a shameful croak as he said, "Whatever the phone company is paying you, I'll double it."

"Amen," Dillon whispered. "What *are* they?"

"Show poodles," their savior said. She swept off her cap. A cascade of honey blond hair spilled over her shoulders.

Wyatt's mouth went dry.

"Lucky for you two they're highly intelligent and easy to train."

"Yeah, lucky for us," Wyatt said faintly. Her eyes were green. A deep, beautiful green.

And then the phone girl smiled, and Wyatt's world turned upside down.

CHAPTER 2

She was in.

She was in!

Kasidy pressed a hand over the nervous quivering in her belly as she surveyed the items she'd thrown in her battered suitcase. T-shirts, jeans, shorts, and a couple summer dresses just for emergencies. That should do it.

Nana Jo snagged a T-shirt and began folding it. "I can't believe someone would pay good money for you to babysit a trio of poodles." Nana Jo slanted a narrow-eyed, worried look at Kasidy. "Sounds fishy to me. Tell me more about this Wyatt guy."

"I've told you all I know, Nana." Kasidy added her toothbrush, hairbrush, and a package of disposable razors to the suitcase. She'd made some cash from oil changes, so she knew she could buy anything she might have forgotten.

"He's good-looking?" Nana Jo asked, folding yet another T-shirt before slipping it back onto the pile of clothes.

"Yes. Very." Kasidy ignored the shiver that stole

14

down her spine. Wyatt Love had been more than good-looking; he'd been drop-dead gorgeous, oozing sex appeal . . . "Which I'm sure most gigolos are," she added a little too forcefully. She managed a convincing snort of contempt. "I have to hand it to the old witch, she knew how to pick 'em." *Boy, did she ever*. Kasidy suppressed the urge to fan her suddenly hot face.

This time it was Nana Jo's turn to snort. "That woman . . . imagine rolling around in the sack with a guy young enough to be her grandson."

"I have a harder time imagining *him* wanting to," Kasidy said on a disgusted note. Never mind that she was more disappointed than disgusted. Why did the only man who had ever interested her have to be a flippin' gigolo? Even worse, her grandmother's boy toy?

Nana Jo gave up trying to keep the clothes straightened and sat on Kasidy's single bed. "Kasidy . . . I don't want you to go."

Seeing the concern on her grandmother's face, Kasidy plopped down beside her. They had spent many happy hours sitting on that bed, talking about boys, cars, parents . . . she had always been able to talk to Nana Jo about anything during the many summers she'd spent with her. She wasn't about to change now. "I've got to do this, Nana Jo. For Daddy." Her eyes misted as she took her grandmother's hand. "And for Mom. She always knew that Daddy missed Atlanta, and felt guilty about it. She told me as much before she died."

"Well, it wasn't *her* fault," Nana Jo said, her brown eyes flashing with a spark of temper. "It was that wicked mother of hers, believing my Albert wasn't good enough for her daughter. If she'd left well enough alone, she wouldn't have had to miss out on you."

Kasidy couldn't resist an impish grin. "I don't think she would have liked me much." She held out her hands, palms down. "I'm not into tea parties and piano lessons."

Nana Jo grabbed Kasidy's hands and peered at the stained, ragged nails. She tsked-tsked. "Of all the trades to teach you . . . let me see what I can do about these nails. You look a fright. We don't want anyone getting suspicious about the phone company girl turned dog sitter, do we?"

Laughing, Kasidy rose and followed her grandmother into the kitchen, a cheerful place where she had spent many happy afternoons helping her grandmother make lemonade and bake chocolate-chip cookies. "Right. There are a lot of phone lines in that big ole fancy house, but I don't think I could have stretched the work more than a week without arousing suspicion." She nearly bumped into Nana Jo as her grandmother stopped in the kitchen doorway.

Nana Jo turned around, her expression suddenly serious. "Kas, I just want you to know that if you decide to take your inheritance, I'm behind you. As far as I'm concerned, that woman owes it to you."

With a grimace, Kasidy gave Nana Jo a light push to get her going again. She was hoping her grandmother wouldn't see the flush that rose to her face. "You know I can't do that, Nana. Mom would come back to haunt me."

"She wouldn't," Nana argued. She pulled out a

chair at the kitchen table and waved to Kasidy. "I think she would understand."

"I don't." Kasidy's voice rang with conviction. "Look what money did to them—us. Daddy had to keep changing jobs. Mom had to keep making new friends. I had to keep changing schools *and* friends. If Grandma Amelia hadn't had money, she wouldn't have been able to keep hunting us." She gave her head an emphatic shake. "Nope. I don't want it, and I don't need it. That may sound crazy to some people, but to me taking that inheritance would be the height of hypocrisy."

But Nana Jo wasn't convinced. "You could buy yourself a new car."

Kasidy didn't have to feign outrage. "What? And give up Arnold? Are you kidding?" Arnold was her '67 El Camino. "Daddy and I built that thing from the ground up. I wouldn't trade that car for a new Cadillac—fully loaded."

"You could have your own garage, then. Now that Amelia's dead, you won't have to worry about staying in one place too long."

"If I wanted my own garage, I could get a small business loan, and if I wanted to go to college—and I know that's what you were going to say next—I could work my way through like millions of others do." She winced as Nana Jo smeared toothpaste on one of her nails and began to scrub vigorously with an old toothbrush. Nana Jo had learned the trick from *her* grandmother.

Injecting a serious note into her voice, Kasidy said, "I really don't want the money, Nana. It would seem too horribly disloyal to Mom. Besides, when I don't claim it, it will eventually go to a good charity. Maybe that will in some way make up for all the heartache Grandma Amelia caused Mom and Dad."

Nana Jo looked up. "And you," she added.

Kasidy shook her head. "I had you, and Mom and Dad. That was all I needed."

Changing hands, Nana Jo went to work on the other one. "Sweetheart," she reminded her gently, "when other girls were going to proms and dances, you were rebuilding carburetors with your dad."

"And what's wrong with that?" Kasidy wanted to know, honestly. "I was just too much of a tomboy to be interested in boys. Lots of girls are tomboys. It's not like I'm gay." No, she definitely wasn't gay, she thought, remembering the weakness in her legs when she'd caught Wyatt Love watching her. "I just haven't had *time* for men."

"You're twenty-five, Kas." Nana Jo tugged on her hand and pulled Kasidy to the kitchen sink to wash the toothpaste off. She began scrubbing Kasidy's fingers as she spoke. "You're forgetting. This is *me* you're talking to. I know why you never dated much. You didn't want to get attached to someone you would eventually have to leave behind."

Drat. Her grandmother had her there. And because she knew her grandmother almost as well as her grandmother knew her, she knew what was coming next.

"Now that Amelia's gone, you don't have to run anymore. You could settle down."

Kasidy was silent as Nana Jo dried her hands and gave her nails one last inspection. Then, quietly, she

18

confessed to the one woman in the world she could tell anything. "I don't know if I can stop running, Nana."

Nana Jo flipped the towel over her shoulder. "Well, it's something for you to think about while you're dog-sitting and snooping through your grand-mother's house."

"Sleuthing," Kasidy corrected with a grin. "I prefer to call it sleuthing."

Trying to look stern—and failing—Nana Jo said, "Well, just don't get carried away with all that illegal stuff your father should never have taught you. I don't want to have to drive down to Atlanta and spring you out of jail. God knows I did enough of that when *he* was younger."

"Yes, ma'am."

"And watch out for that guy, Wyatt. I've read about those guys. They live and breathe sex."

Kasidy sucked her bottom lip between her teeth. She didn't have a problem believing that one. The man definitely looked as if he knew exactly what to do to a woman to make her melt at his feet.

"Not that I don't think you should *have* sex," Nana Jo continued, always up front with Kasidy about these matters. "I just want you to be selective."

Straight-faced, Kasidy said, "Nana, I've had sex before."

Nana Jo scowled. "You talking about that idiot mechanic, Calvin? Honey, from what you told me, he not only didn't know where to put it, he didn't know what to do with it when he got it there."

By the time Nana Jo was finished, Kasidy's face was hot. Yes, they talked about everything under the sun, but that didn't mean she was always comfortable with the subject. "He was bad, wasn't he?" Twenty seconds, tops. She'd barely had time to feel the pain of losing her virginity. The experience hadn't left her exactly yearning for more. That's when she had decided she wouldn't have sex again until she found a man who could actually make her want to. Otherwise, what was the point?

"Don't worry, Nana," Kasidy said, hugging her grandmother. "I may look as if I just stumbled out of a cotton patch, but I've got a brain and I know how to use it. Besides, there's no way I could ever be interested in Grandma Amelia's boy toy."

Absolutely, one hundred percent, *no way*.

Wyatt had always wondered how the other half lived. The movie stars, the rich tycoons . . . wealthy widows. But if someone had told him a week ago that he'd one day find himself soaking in a hot tub in the luxurious backyard of a mansion, sipping eighty-year-old Scotch and smoking an imported Cuban cigar while anticipating his dream girl's arrival, he would have laughed out loud.

Grinning to himself, Wyatt took a drink of Scotch, then pulled on the fine cigar.

And had a coughing fit that lasted a full two minutes.

With a rueful sigh—and tears running down his face—he put out the cigar and set the Scotch aside in favor of a frosted bottle of Root Beer from the cooler beside the hot tub. "You can take the man out of the country," he gasped out, "but you can't take the country out of the man."

As if to mock his dry observance, the three canines that had become thorns in his side started howling.

It wasn't dog abuse, he told himself sternly, to lock them up in the ridiculously large bedroom Amelia had decorated doggie style. The damn room was a canine's dream castle, with satin pillows and every doggie toy imaginable, and a fifty-two-inch television that stayed tuned to the Animal Channel. *As if.* Wyatt, finally catching his breath, managed to snort without coughing.

He'd tried to win them over—really tried. His friends didn't call him "Dr. Love" for nothing. He was a great problem solver, especially when it came to relationships. People flocked to him for advice.

But apparently his talents didn't apply to the canine world.

The three stooges, as Wyatt secretly called them, hated him. It was that plain and that simple.

Finding pieces of his favorite leather sandals all over the staircase had been the last straw. First it had been his Mark McGuire baseball cap—signed by the great guy himself, thank you very much. Then the state-of-the-art cell phone he'd just gotten for his birthday from his mother, never mind that he knew damn well she couldn't afford one, much less two, since she'd stuck to her steadfast rule of always getting Wyatt and Dillon the same thing. Wyatt thought the rule was now silly, since they had both just turned thirty. They no longer fought over toys. Well, there *was* that one time. . . .

Then, early this morning when he'd crawled into the big king-size bed in the master guest bedroom, as

Louise the housekeeper called it, weary to the bone after tending bar at the honky tonk he and his brother owned, his bare knees had landed in a huge, cold wet spot in the middle of the bed.

There hadn't been a leak in the roof above his bed, either. No, it hadn't taken him long to realize that not one, but *three* canine bladders had joined forces for this new form of torture.

The object of his daydreams, Kasidy Evans, had informed them the poodles were highly intelligent. Just *how* intelligent? he'd found himself wondering.

Intelligent enough to arrange an "accident" one night when he came downstairs for a midnight snack? It would be easy enough for one of them to trip him. No one would ever be the wiser.

Wyatt sat up so fast he sloshed water over the sides of the hot tub. A horrible possibility occurred to him. What if they hated Kasidy, too? What if they had only been *pretending* to like her the day she'd saved him and Dillon from certain death?

Oh, he knew if he told people his suspicions they would laugh themselves silly—especially his twin and his mother—but Wyatt had seen those canine eyes gleam with malice and calculation on more than one occasion since moving into the mansion five days ago.

They were evil. The flip side of the slapstick comedy team they were named after. The three evil stooges. Triplet cujos.

He was so deep in thought, it took a moment for him to realize the doorbell was ringing—and the howling had stopped.

Hastily, he rose from the water and turned, reaching for the pile of clothing he'd left close by, a pair of khaki shorts and a T-shirt, his standard summer wardrobe. He was naked—and why not? The housekeeper had the day off, his dream woman wasn't due for another day, and he'd forgotten to bring his swim shorts.

Wyatt froze, staring in disbelief at the bare spot where his clothes had been. He followed a trail of wet paw prints leading away from the hot tub, and let loose a string of curses that would have made his mother head for the soap.

CHAPTER 3

After the third knock, Kasidy might have decided there wasn't anyone home, if not for the sudden shouting she heard coming from inside. She pressed her ear to the door, catching the word "mutts" and "kill you with my bare hands" before she took the initiative and tried the door.

It was locked. Using the handy tool she kept in her pocket, she quickly sprang the lock and swung the door open. If challenged, she could always claim that it hadn't been locked.

She looked upon a sight that would be forever etched into her woefully inexperienced mind.

Wyatt Love was playing tug-of-war with one of the poodles, while the other two were busy playing tug-of-war with one another—and what appeared to be his shorts.

She blinked several times to make absolutely certain her mind wasn't playing tricks on her. Then she rubbed her eyes for good measure.

Nope. She was definitely not hallucinating.

There, in the great, gleaming marbled foyer of her

grandmother's mansion was her future employer, Wyatt Love, as naked as the day he was born.

Gloriously, shamelessly, gut-clenchingly naked.

Kasidy grabbed the open door for support as the bottom dropped out of her stomach. Yes, she'd seen naked men before. Calvin, for one, and she'd walked in on her father once as he was stepping out of the shower.

Okay, so she'd only seen *two* naked men in her life, except on television and in magazines. None of that could have prepared her for the knee-weakening, liquid heat that inflamed her body at the sight of Wyatt.

Naked.

Hugely naked. All tanned muscles and sinew and strong thighs and . . . and . . . Kasidy gulped, unable to stop staring at his groin. Until now, she'd had no idea how woefully inadequate her first lover had been.

"Thank God, you're here," her naked employer shouted, jarring her out of her dream state. He gave a vicious yank on what appeared to be a T-shirt, dragging the poodle across the slick floor. The poodle, in return, yanked hard and backpeddled, regaining ground as he pulled Wyatt with him. The dog's low growl sounded remarkably victorious.

Face flaming, Kasidy jerked her gaze upward. Every instinct urged her to turn and flee, to get away from this gorgeous, sexy, naked man. He was dangerous. Tempting. Mouth watering.

Out of her league.

A gigolo. Disgusting boy toy. Sex for hire. Quickly, silently, Kasidy repeated the litany in her mind, until the moisture returned to her mouth and dried up elsewhere, and she was able to speak without revealing just how turned on she was by the sight of him. Later, she would give her untrained libido a sound talking-to.

Right now, she had an employer to impress.

Dropping to her knees, she slapped her hands against her legs. She injected a note of excitement into her voice that she knew the dogs would respond to. "Come here, boys!"

Almost comically, the dogs dropped their prizes and turned to look at her, noticing her for the first time. In a mad scrambling of long legs and hanging tongues, they raced to her.

Laughing, Kasidy allowed them to push her backward as they subjected her to a slobbery dog bath that only a dog lover could enjoy.

"Do *you* need help?" Wyatt asked.

He sounded close. Kasidy pushed a black dog snout back so that she could read the bone-shaped dog tag on the collar. "No—Curly, down boy—I think I've got it under control." She gave the red dog a gentle shove. "Sit, Moe. Back, Larry." Whining, they reluctantly did as she ordered.

Only then did Kasidy look up at Wyatt, relieved to see that he had gotten dressed while she was getting the dogs under control.

Well, almost.

She quickly looked away again, her voice gruff as she said, "Um, you have a hole in your, um, shorts." And something she was trying desperately to forget was peeping through . . . unless he was trying to shock her? Kasidy shot him a sharp glance, ready to blast him if she caught him smirking.

But the bonafide blush on his handsome face proclaimed his innocence. The embarrassment—liberally mixed with disgust—in his voice reinforced it. "Sorry." He put a hand over the hole, then held out his other one to help her up. "If you think my shorts are bad, take a look at my T-shirt."

Kasidy did—briefly. One quick glance at patches of tanned, smooth muscle and skin was enough for her. Her pulse picked up as he turned to show her the damage to the back of his T-shirt.

Apparently he didn't feel the breeze drifting through the open door, or he would have noticed that his left butt cheek was bare from another big rip.

A very tight, very muscled, very superfine butt cheek. In fact, it was also a very *tanned* butt cheek, which immediately evoked the erotic image of Wyatt spread-eagle in a tanning bed.

In self-defense, Kasidy closed her eyes. She didn't even realize she had also clenched her hands until she felt her short nails bite into her palms. Because of the way she'd lived with her parents—always having to be alert and one step ahead of the men her grandmother Amelia had hired to find them—Kasidy had learned to trust her flight instincts.

They'd never been stronger than they were at that moment.

But she couldn't run. She was here, and she was in. She had to find the evidence against her father. It would be her gift to him, for being the best damned father any man could be.

"Are you okay?"

Kasidy opened her eyes to find Wyatt facing her again, his hand still covering his groin. She looked into his green eyes, framed by golden lashes so thick they looked artificially enhanced, and managed a nod.

"Because you look a little . . . agitated," Wyatt added with a slight frown. He cast a dark look at the three dogs lounging behind them. "If you think this job is too much, I'll understand. Believe me," he added sourly. "My brother's one-year-old twins are angels compared to these guys."

"I can handle them just fine," Kasidy said. It was Wyatt she wasn't sure she could handle. Or his body, rather. She couldn't imagine someone in his profession interesting her in any other way. He probably wouldn't know a piston from a spark plug.

His sex appeal was his meal ticket.

But he wouldn't be turning that appeal on her. He only knew her as a blue-collar worker desperate enough to ditch her job with the phone company in favor of better paying work dog sitting. Not exactly his type. Now, if he knew who she *really* was, she figured he wouldn't hesitate to turn on the charm. Considering his occupation, he'd likely try to convince her to claim her inheritance in the hopes he could weasel his way into her life as he had her grandmother's.

"Well," he said with a husky little laugh that made Kasidy's insides quiver. "I'm glad you came a day early, but I'm sorry if I shocked you. I was in the hot tub when the doorbell rang, and those mutts had taken off with my clothes." He ran a hand through his blond hair, ruffling it in a way that made Kasidy itch to smooth it. "I don't know how they got out of a locked room—"

"You had them locked in?" Kasidy interjected before she could censor her words. This was her employer. She had to remember that. It wouldn't do her father any good if she got fired before she found the evidence. "I mean, that would explain why they took your clothes."

Wyatt looked surprised instead of skeptical. "You think?" He scratched his chin thoughtfully. "Yeah, I guess that makes sense."

His sudden, rueful grin caught Kasidy off guard. For a split second, she thought of him as human.

But only for a second.

"I'm not accustomed to people—or animals—not liking me," Wyatt went on, sounding so sincere and genuinely perplexed, Kasidy almost believed him. "I've given them snacks, taken them for walks. Tossed the ball. Scratched their backs." He gave a bewildered shrug. "In return, they've eaten my favorite sandals, demolished my cell phone, ripped to shreds my autographed baseball cap, and whizzed in my bed."

"Something's bothering them," Kasidy said. He was too handsome for his own good, she was thinking. If he'd just back off so she couldn't feel his body heat, maybe she could concentrate on the conversation. He smelled faintly of chlorine and a musky cologne she'd never liked.

Until now.

On Wyatt, it was a mating call.

Down, girl.

Wyatt grabbed his T-shirt and held it out, holes

and all. He raised an amused brow. "You think? Question is, *what* is bothering them? Because I'm an animal lover, and it's really hurting my feelings that these guys hate me."

"They don't hate you."

"Well, I don't like to argue with a professional, but you're wrong there. They definitely hate me."

"I'm not a professional," she corrected. "I spent the summer working for a dog trainer, cleaning out kennels, grooming, things like that." She shrugged. "I picked up a few pointers."

"And thank God you did," Wyatt said fervently. He glanced around, then back at her, his expression questioning. "Your luggage?"

"Oh, it's out in my car. I didn't know where I should park."

"Come on, I'll show you where the garage is and get your luggage."

Bristling, Kasidy said, "I can carry my own luggage." Intending to prove her point, she followed him outside. She stopped short when he did. His low, appreciative whistle had her nipples puckering alarmingly.

"Oh . . . my . . . God. She's beautiful!"

It took a moment for Kasidy to realize he was talking about her car. Relaxing, she said shyly, "1967 model. My dad and I restored him."

He shot her an inquiring, amused glance. "Him?"

"Yes, him. Arnold." Blushing, Kasidy moved around him to get her lone suitcase from the backseat. When she withdrew, he was popping the hood.

"I hope you don't mind. I gotta get a look at this

30

baby." Even before he lifted the hood, he was saying, "I'll bet it's got a 396."

"You'd win that bet." Kasidy's legs were weak as she went around to stand beside him. Together, they stared at the motor, his expression rapt. But Kasidy wasn't thinking about the motor. She was thinking how much trouble she was in.

Not only did he have a to-die-for body, he was also knowledgeable about cars.

It just wasn't fair.

"I don't know if I can stay, Nana Jo."

Dillon, who had found the front door locked and was making his way around the house to the back-yard, paused beside a trellis of ivy to listen.

He recognized the voice of the phone girl, the one Wyatt had hired. The very woman who had caused his brother to look as *he* had felt when he'd first met his wife, Callie.

Floored.

Dazed.

Shot.

There were many, many definitions, but it all boiled down to Cupid and his arrow—and the fat little guy's extremely accurate aim.

Shamelessly—and gleefully—Dillon eavesdropped.

"No, no! Nothing bad has happened . . . I just don't know if I can stay in the same house with Grandma Amelia's boy toy."

Dillon sucked in a sharp breath and held it. Grandma Amelia? Boy toy? He was hit with two re-alizations in quick succession.

31

SHERIDON SMYTHE

Kasidy was Amelia's long lost granddaughter.
And she believed Wyatt was Amelia's boy toy.
"Why? Well . . . I'm just not very comfortable
staying in this big house alone with him. I don't really
know him, and the dogs' room is downstairs—"
There was a pause. Dillon crept closer to the corner of the house.
"Yes, she actually has a room for her dogs, Nana. I
think she was crazier than we thought. Anyway, with
me being downstairs in the maid's room, I don't have
much opportunity to look around. No, I haven't
changed my mind about taking the inheritance. I
don't want any part of it, or her disgusting gigolo.
Let it go to the dogs, like the lawyer said."
Dillon covered his mouth to stifle a gasp. So the
equipment he'd thought resembled a baby monitor
that day in the study must have been a bonafide baby
monitor. Kasidy had been listening in the next room.
How else would she know Amelia planned to leave
her money to her dogs if the granddaughter failed to
show? The news hadn't been made public. Also, she
believed Wyatt had been her grandmother's gigolo,
and Dillon couldn't think of another reason she'd
think that unless she'd been listening when Wyatt un-
leashed his fury on the narrow-minded lawyer, telling
the old battle ax in explicit detail about Wyatt's
imaginary sex life with Mrs. Hancock.
But the biggest question for Dillon was . . . why
didn't Kasidy want to be alone with his twin brother?
Dillon knew Wyatt enough to know that he would
never push himself on a woman. He wouldn't have
to. He would woo her and charm her into his arms.
Dillon couldn't let Kasidy leave. If she was the

woman for his brother, then it was his responsibility to give them a chance to connect. He rubbed his jaw thoughtfully, plotting how he could keep Kasidy at the mansion, dog sitting of all things.

She had told her "Nana" that she didn't want to be alone with Wyatt. Well, then he'd have to make sure she wasn't.

Creeping back the way he'd come, Dillon made it to his SUV and quietly left. He had a lot of calls to make, and very little time to complete them. He chuckled gleefully as he realized he had the opportunity to pay his twin back for the trick he'd pulled on Dillon with his wife, Callie. All along, Wyatt had known Callie hadn't come to Atlanta to do a review on his club for a travel magazine, yet Wyatt had kept that small, but very important detail from him.

Tit for tat.

A very *big* tit for tat.

Oh, yeah. This was going to be big-time fun.

Payback wasn't a bitch. It was a goddess.

CHAPTER 4

When Wyatt answered the door and saw his twin standing on the threshold, he tried not to sound impatient. "I didn't know you were coming over," he said, casually barring the door. He had set out steaks to thaw for grilling on the patio, hoping to lure Kasidy from her room. She'd been glaringly absent since her arrival.

Dillon looked grim-faced as he held up a bulging sports bag. "Callie and I had a fight. She said I need to give her some space."

Wyatt tried to conceal his dismay. "Can't you stay at my apartment?"

He twin shook his head. "No can do. Mom noticed some mouse droppings the last time she cleaned your place, and called an exterminator. Nobody can go in there for forty-eight hours."

"Mom's house?"

"She's having all new pipes put in, remember? After working in a noisy bar all afternoon and half the night, the banging would drive me crazy."

34

Running out of options, Wyatt got desperate. "How about a hotel?"

"Too expensive." Dillon looked hurt. "Look, if you don't want me to stay, I can find somewhere else to crash. No problem."

As his brother turned toward the door, Wyatt swallowed a curse and said, "No, no. It's not a problem. I've got a dozen spare bedrooms." Bedrooms he'd been hoping to explore with Kasidy at a later date.

Dillon sighed his relief and offered him a grateful smile. "Thanks, bro. Don't worry. You won't even know I'm here."

Fat chance, Wyatt thought sourly. Before Dillon could head upstairs to pick out a room, Wyatt's pager went off. Exasperated, he checked the number. "It's Mrs. Scuttle. Damned dogs ate my phone. Can I use yours?" Mrs. Scuttle was a feisty elderly lady who worked at the escort service, Mr. Complete, as secretary. There wasn't an escort there who didn't fear her anger, yet they all loved and cherished her. "I can't imagine why she's calling me," Wyatt muttered, taking Dillon's phone and punching in her number. "She knows I'm not on the schedule this week."

"She's almost eighty," Dillon said. "Maybe she forgot."

"I *dare* you to suggest that—oh, hi, Mrs. Scuttle. How are you?" As Wyatt listened intently, his hopes for a romantic evening with Kasidy dwindled to a tiny, pathetic spark. By the time he hung up the phone, his brother had disappeared up the winding staircase, and Wyatt had promised the secretary he'd come right over.

Hell.

He snapped the phone closed and started to shove it into his shorts pocket. On second thought, he pulled the phone out—it would probably be just as tempting as the one the mutts had demolished—and set it on the hall table by the door.

Since birth, Wyatt had never been able to resist tormenting his twin. Someday, he thought with a rueful chuckle, Dillon was going to pay him back big time for all the pranks he'd pulled.

Letting himself out, Wyatt found himself looking forward to that doubtful day. If it meant his brother would loosen up a little and have some fun, it would be worth it. Besides, with the extra grand a week he was making living the rich life, he could replace both phones with no problem.

He was so going to enjoy this.

Dillon rubbed his hands together and chuckled with glee as he watched the steaks his brother had thoughtfully left out sizzle to perfection on the grill.

Deciding to share his good fortune, he'd called a meeting and let friends and relatives in on his little secret. They had all agreed to help execute Dillon's plan.

Finally, after thirty years of enduring Wyatt's pranks and flat-out mischief making, he was going to extract his sweet, sweet revenge. And the best part was that his twin would never see it coming. Even their mother had agreed that Wyatt had it coming to him. Of course, the prospect of seeing her last single son settled went a long way toward gaining her cooperation.

Speaking of his future sister-in-law . . . Dillon glanced at his watch, then checked the steaks. They were ready. He'd hoped Kasidy would wander out on her own, but it didn't look as if that was going to happen. Now that he knew who she really was, he couldn't wait to find out why she didn't want anything to do with her inheritance. Whatever it was, Dillon mused, glancing at his opulent surroundings on his way to Kasidy's downstairs room, it had to have been bad to make her spurn all of *this*. And why was she here, if she didn't plan on claiming the estate?

It was a fine mystery he planned on helping his twin solve . . . without Wyatt's knowledge, of course. No, he wanted his brother to focus on wooing the reluctant heiress. Wyatt didn't need his mind cluttered up with mystery and money.

Pausing in front of Kasidy's closed bedroom door, Dillon wiped the smug smile off his face and knocked lightly. The door opened abruptly, startling Dillon.

"Well," she drawled, one arm braced casually against the open door. "I hardly recognized you with your clothes on."

Dillon almost swallowed his tongue. "Pardon me?"

Her face turned scarlet. "You're not Wyatt," she stated, then covered her hot face with her hand. She peeped at him between her fingers, her voice muffled and thick with embarrassment. "Can you please pretend you didn't hear that?"

Recovering quickly, Dillon flashed her an endearing grin. "On one condition; that you tell me how you managed to see my brother naked on your first day at the job."

Kasidy hesitated. Then, apparently deciding Dillon

was harmless, she grinned back at him, revealing a dimple in her left cheek. "Deal." She sniffed the air. "Do I smell something cooking? I'm starving."

"You do indeed. Do you mind having dinner with an old happily married man?"

"Only if his happily married wife doesn't mind," she retorted lightly, taking his proffered arm. "Dillon, right?"

"Right." And then, because Dillon couldn't resist, he added, "I'm the oldest by five minutes."

Her laughter rang out, simple and spontaneous. "I believe it. You seem much more . . . mature than your brother."

A woman after his own heart, if it hadn't already been taken. She'd make a great sister-in-law, and he knew instinctively that the women in his life would love her. She had a tough, don't-mess-with-me look in her green eyes, but Dillon was shrewd enough to note the shadow of vulnerability she tried to hide.

Her beauty lay in her simplicity. She had straight, honey-blond hair and a petite, yet curvy body. Her nails, Dillon saw at a discreet glance, were short, but clean. As far as he could tell, she wore very little makeup.

But then, she didn't really need it.

She walked with the confident stride of a tomboy, but there was nothing tomboyish about her curves, or the strain her breasts put on the stretchy material of her T-shirt.

Dillon cleared his throat, steering his thoughts back to safer waters. He'd been assessing Kasidy in a clinical way, but he doubted Wyatt would agree. He hadn't forgotten how jealous he'd been of Callie when Wyatt talked about her.

They had reached the patio before Kasidy popped the question Dillon had been expecting her to ask. Good. She had excellent self-control. Or maybe that was bad.

"Where's Wyatt?" She took a seat in a lounger, watching him as he pulled the steaks from the grill with a pair of titanium-tipped tongs he'd found in the kitchen.

"He had to check on Mrs. Scuttle. She's the secretary at the escort service where he works."

"He's an escort?"

Dillon bit his lip to keep from blurting out that he knew she knew. "Yes. He works for a reputable company called Mr. Complete." When she didn't laugh or make a sarcastic comment about the company's name, Dillon took that as a good sign. Either she was being polite, or Wyatt had already gotten under her skin.

Placing the steaks on a platter, he took them to a patio table he'd already set with plates, napkins, and wineglasses. "I'll just get the salad," he said.

She got out of her lounger in one fluid, graceful move. "I'll go let the dogs out while Wyatt's gone." Her lips twitched. "They can't seem to behave around him."

Dillon perked up at that. He shot her a naughty smile. "My heart bleeds for him."

Laughing, she flung over her shoulder as she walked away, "I can tell!"

When she returned a few moments later, Dillon

took one look at her face and nearly dropped the salad bowl he'd been about to place on the table. "What's wrong?"

She shook her head, looking pensive. "Nothing. It's just that . . . when I let the dogs out, they headed upstairs."

"Ah . . ." Dillon nodded his understanding. "You think they're looking for Mrs. Hancock?" The flash of pain Dillon saw in her eyes was quick and fleeting, but he recognized it.

"Yes . . . I don't know. Maybe. I'm sure they miss her."

"I'm sure they do. Did you know her?"

Kasidy shot him a startled, wide-eyed look as she took a seat at the patio table across from him. "Who? Mrs. Hancock? Um, no. I'm not originally from Atlanta. Did you? I mean, I guess you probably did, since Wyatt knew her."

The slight disgust in her voice didn't go unnoticed. But the devil in Dillon let the comment slide. He could have told her the truth, but he doubted she was ready to believe it. Besides, it was more fun this way. At least for now. "Actually, I think she was a fairly new *client*, so I didn't get a chance to get to know her." Before she could ask another question that Dillon would have to shamefully manipulate in the name of fun, he hurried on. "You promised to tell me how you managed to see my brother naked."

Her expression relaxed as she told him. Before she finished, Dillon was literally choking on laughter. Tears ran down his face. He grabbed his napkin and mopped them up, but more quickly took their place.

His laughter ended abruptly when he caught sight

of the red poodle charging out onto the patio, followed by the white one, then the black.

The first one held the remains of his cell phone.

The black one proudly toted a single running shoe, already badly chewed.

But the third dog . . . what the third dog carried made Dillon's heart stop. It was the remains of the vintage edition *Playboy* featuring Pamela Anderson that he was auctioning off on eBay. Last time he checked, the bidding was up to two hundred dollars.

"What the hell?" Dillon roared. His chair crashed behind him as he jumped to his feet.

Kasidy hastily moved to stand between a furious Dillon and the innocent-looking dogs. "Now, Dillon," she said in a voice meant to soothe. "They can't be blamed for acting out. They're probably just missing Mrs. Hancock."

In the face of her cool logic, Dillon managed to get his temper under control. It wasn't fair, he thought darkly, still glaring at the dogs. His revenge was supposed to be sweet.

Wyatt was the one who was supposed to suffer.

Wyatt was suffering plenty.

"That's not a blouse, you dolt!" Mrs. Scuttle screeched at him.

He dodged a jar of cold cream in the nick of time. It hit the wall behind him with a resounding thud before falling soundlessly to the carpet. He held out his hands in surrender, dropping the offending garment. "I'm sorry!"

"You should be. That's a lace *teddy*, not a blasted blouse."

A lace ... *teddy?* This was not a conversation Wyatt ever expected to be having with an eighty-year-old woman. Cautiously, he kept a wary eye on the secretary. He'd found her sitting in a chair in her bedroom with her support-hose-clad leg propped up on a footstool, wearing a bandage around her ankle.

"Never mind the blouse. Just find my swimsuit. I think it's in the top drawer."

Wyatt wasn't born yesterday. He knew that he shouldn't ask, but he had to. "Swimsuit? What will you need with a swimsuit?"

A box of Q-tips came whizzing past his right ear. "I sprained my ankle, you idiot! I didn't have a stroke! That fancy place where you're staying has a heated pool, doesn't it?"

"Yes, but—"

"Well, then. Warm water is good for arthritis. Besides," she declared with deadly seriousness, "I need to work on my tan."

It was not an image Wyatt cared to evoke. "Oh." Desperately, he searched for a miracle. He spotted a fish tank with one solitary goldfish swimming around. "Who will feed your fish while you're gone? And water your plants?" *Please, God. Give me a way out,* Wyatt prayed.

"You will, or someone else will," Mrs. Scuttle snapped. "I've got more friends than I can shake a stick at, so that shouldn't be a problem." Her arthritic fingers closed tightly around the remote control.

Wyatt braced himself.

But apparently the secretary didn't care to risk

damaging something so important. She laid it aside as if to rid herself of the temptation.

And promptly picked up an empty teacup. "Are you going to finish packing? It's gettin' close to my bedtime. I want to be settled into my new room before nine."

Resigned to his fate, Wyatt found Mrs. Scuttle's heavy swimsuit and stuffed it into her suitcase.

There was no way out. Mrs. Scuttle would be staying at the mansion until her ankle healed. How was he supposed to romance Kasidy with Mrs. Scuttle screeching orders and his brother breathing down his neck?

Not to mention those mutts. . . .

So much for the good life.

He should have known it was too good to be true.

CHAPTER 5

Kasidy was settling the dogs in for the night when she heard a commotion. Curiosity got the best of her. She cracked open the door and peered out.

She gasped, belatedly slapping a hand over her mouth. She needn't have worried; the struggling woman in Wyatt's arms was making too much noise for her to be heard even if she had called out to them.

The woman was eighty if she was a day. Wearing a pink housecoat that matched the dozens of sponge rollers in her hair, the woman continued to struggle and screech at Wyatt. She boxed him soundly in the head more than once, but Wyatt refused to put her down.

"I told you, I can walk, you nitwit!"

"You're not walking upstairs," Dillon told her sternly. "You could do more damage to your ankle, and at your age—"

Kasidy saw the warning look Wyatt shot his brother, but it was too late. The woman renewed her struggles, her face turning an alarming shade of red. This time she focused her fury on Dillon, who looked as if he'd swallowed a very large, very bad-tasting pill.

"Let me down so I can throw something at him, Wyatt! Did you hear what he said? He thinks I'm too old to tango, does he? Let me down so I can show him a thing or two!"

"He didn't mean it," Wyatt said, his voice soothing and affectionate despite the red hand prints on the side of his face where the elderly lady had walloped him. "Be still so I can carry you upstairs to your room. Pretend you're Scarlett O'Hara and I'm Rhett Butler. You know, you kinda remind me of Scarlett . . ."

To Kasidy's amazement, Wyatt's obvious bullcrap worked like a charm. She felt her stomach lurch as the elderly lady, apparently dazed by his sweet talk, wound her arms around his neck and bussed him a sloppy kiss on his cheek.

"Bless you, Wyatt. I knew there was a reason you're my favorite." She shot Dillon a triumphant look. "Dillon, you'll have to wait your turn. This *old lady* only has the strength for one man at a time tonight."

Holding a hand over her rolling stomach, Kasidy quickly shut the door. She couldn't listen further without getting physically sick. Her grandmother wasn't even cold in her grave, and her boy toy had already brought another woman into the house.

It was disgusting.

And Dillon . . . she had thought he was nice, but now she didn't know what to think. The woman had implied that she—she slept with *both!*

A cold nose pushed against her palm. Kasidy looked down to find Moe staring up at her with black, brooding eyes.

In his mouth was a book, pockmarked with teeth imprints, but otherwise in good condition.

"I see it, but I don't believe it," Kasidy whispered, taking the book from Moe. It was an obviously well read edition of *101 Dalmatians*. Kasidy turned the book over in her hands, trying to find a single spot that wasn't marked by dog teeth. "My grandmother read this book to you every night, didn't she? You didn't understand a word she said, but you listened to the sound of her voice."

As if he had understood her, Curly whined and thumped his tail against the giant satin pillow that served as his bed. Moe returned to his own pillow.

All three dogs stared at her expectantly.

Feeling foolish, but curiously choked up, Kasidy took a seat in the rocking chair—the mystery of its presence solved—and opened the book.

She swallowed the lump in her throat and began to read. Niggling doubts began to creep in. How could a woman who cared enough to *read* to her dogs be the tyrant Kasidy had always thought her grandmother to be? Were the dogs a result of her eccentricity, or were they simply a comfort to a lonely old woman who missed her only child, and longed to see her granddaughter?

Kasidy brought her disloyal thoughts to a grinding halt. She slammed the book closed and jumped to her feet, startling the dogs. They whined and thumped their tails. "Sorry boys," she said, taking a deep, shuddering breath. "I've got to get out of this house. Good night."

Apparently, "good night" was the magic word, for they settled back down on their pillows and closed their eyes. Kasidy didn't know why they had focused their aggression on Dillon and Wyatt, but she wasn't a dummy; these dogs were very well trained.

After the disgusting scene she'd witnessed tonight, Kasidy figured they were even smarter than she'd first thought.

Amelia Hancock's garage was a mechanic's wet dream.

Big enough to house six vehicles with room to spare, it was equipped with a lift, an air pump, and about every tool a mechanic could ever want or need. Kasidy had a strong suspicion that at one time her grandmother had employed a full-time mechanic to service the vehicles.

Now there were only two vehicles, aside from her own and Dillon's SUV. She assumed Wyatt had left his vehicle parked in front of the house, since she didn't think the luxury Cadillac and the BMW belonged to him.

But then again, he *had* been her grandmother's boy toy, and if the wicked witch had pampered her gigolo as well as she had pampered her dogs, then it was believable.

Kasidy walked around the silver BMW slowly, thoughtfully. No, she couldn't imagine Wyatt in the classy car. He was too earthy. It wasn't his style.

Neither was the Cadillac, but Kasidy could easily envision her grandmother riding in the back, barking orders to the driver. Hunkering down, Kasidy surveyed the concrete floor beneath the Cadillac, checking for fluid leaks. To her disappointment, the concrete was clean.

She did the same beneath the BMW, with the same disappointing results. Without much hope, she checked under Dillon's SUV. She could still smell the newness on it, so she wasn't expecting a leak.

Rising from her crouched position, she was about to turn away when she noticed a fresh, oily stain on the concrete in the empty space beside her El Camino. She frowned. Where Wyatt had parked his vehicle, perhaps? Bending down, she touched it with her fingertips, then brought it to her nose.

Brake fluid. Not good.

The sudden whine of the garage doors startled Kasidy. She looked frantically around for a place to hide. After what she'd witnessed, she didn't think it was a good idea for her to talk to anyone tonight.

Spotting a creeper leaning against the garage wall, she raced to it and quietly set it on the concrete. With the ease born of experience, she lay down on it and swiftly rolled herself under Dillon's SUV.

Damn. She'd forgotten to turn out the lights!

With her heart thumping painfully against her chest, Kasidy waited and listened as Wyatt—she assumed—pulled his vehicle inside the garage, revved the motor like every other male she'd ever encountered, then cut the engine.

She was dying to see what he was driving.

What did a gorgeous, earthy, T-shirt wearing gigolo drive these days?

She passed the time by trying to guess. An SUV, like Dillon's? No. Too big. Too new. A low-riding Porsche? Possibly, but rather rich for a T-shirt— wearing man.

The garage door whined down. The lights inside

the garage went out, leaving Kasidy staring into blackness. A few moments later, Kasidy heard the door leading into the garage open and close.

It was safe to venture out. Safe to see what Wyatt was driving. Safe to satisfy her curiosity about a man she shouldn't even be thinking about.

By the time she emerged from under the SUV, her eyes had adjusted to the dark. She could make out the shapes of the cars, and there wasn't a car made that Kasidy couldn't identify, day or night.

She stared at the bulky shape of the Dodge Ram pickup, wishing she hadn't given in to her curiosity.

A man after her own heart. Dammit.

"I'll show you mine if you'll show me yours."

The soft, sexy voice came from directly behind Kasidy, right near her ear. She felt his warm breath feather her neck, and her knees went weak. She closed her eyes and prayed the concrete floor would open up and swallow her.

His hands landed lightly on her arms. He turned her around, then guided her backward until she felt the warmth of the truck grille against her butt.

He came in close, pressing his hard body against her, causing her breath to hitch in her throat. She knew she should stop him. She knew his touch should make her want to hurl her dinner at him.

"How did you know?" she whispered, trying to read his expression in the dark—and ignore the jut of his erection against her belly.

Impossible, though, to ignore. Impossible not to melt into him, press herself shamefully against him. How could she? How could she feel this way about him, knowing what she knew? It was sick. It made *her* sick.

"I have an acute sense of smell," he said, his voice alarmingly husky. His hands moved up her arms until they framed her face. His thumbs went to her lips like a blind man searching for a target.

Kasidy held her breath, while her body did a nuclear meltdown that would take years to recover from. She quivered in places she didn't even know it was *possible* to quiver.

"You always smell like coconut," he whispered against her mouth. His own breath had become ragged.

Her hand lotion, Kasidy thought in a daze. Nana Jo bought the cheap stuff in big bottles, then dispensed them into smaller bottles she could carry around with her.

Because of cheap, coconut-scented hand lotion, she was about to become gigolo bait in a dark garage, with a Dodge Ram grille pressing into her butt.

She had never been so turned on.

Or so disgusted with herself.

He could reduce any woman to rubble, she told herself in an attempt to regain her sanity—or at least her dignity. He was trained in the art of pleasure.

It was the wrong thing to think, because the word "pleasure" in conjunction with Wyatt wrung a shameful moan from her throat.

"God, you're the sexiest woman I've ever met," Wyatt said roughly, moving impossibly closer. He shifted until his erection fit snugly between her legs.

The heat of him set her on fire. Kasidy let out a little whimper. She wished she could call it a protest, but she knew she'd be lying.

Something had to give, she thought desperately, or

she was going to let him have his way with her right there on the hood of his truck.

Screw that. She was going to *beg* him to have his way with her. On his truck hood. In the back of her El Camino. On the concrete. She didn't really care at this point.

Shameless.

Disgusting.

Slutty.

Who cared? She was twenty-five years old. If she wanted to have mind-blowing sex with a gigolo who had slept with her grandmother, well then—

It was the "something" she'd been waiting for.

Her voice cracked as she said, "Shouldn't—shouldn't you be getting back to your lady friend?"

She felt him pull back slightly, and fought to keep from yanking him back to her. She couldn't see his expression, but she sensed his puzzlement.

"Mrs. Scuttle? She's out like a light every night at nine, and thank God for that. I don't think my ears could have stood another pounding."

He sounded amused. Kasidy felt sick. Finally. She both welcomed and hated the feeling. "Why—why is she so mean to you?"

"Oh. That. She's like that with all the escorts, even my boss. He keeps her on because she's a damned good secretary, despite her temper, and because she'd have to go into a nursing home if she didn't work. It's her greatest fear, so we've all vowed it will never happen, even if we have to care for her ourselves."

Kasidy's mouth fell open in shock. "She's the secretary?"

"Yeah. Didn't Dillon tell you where I went tonight?"

Kasidy wondered if her face was glowing. Dillon *had* told her, but when she'd seen Wyatt carrying an elderly woman, she hadn't connected the dots because it hadn't occurred to her—and probably wouldn't have in a million years—that the secretary would be an eighty-year-old hothead in pink rollers.

She felt him stiffen suddenly, and knew without a doubt that he'd just realized what she had thought.

Wyatt's full-blown arousal died an instant death.

Slowly, he stepped back from the sensual woman who had been moaning in his arms only moments ago. Moaning, yet believing he'd just left the bed of an eighty-year-old woman.

He was too humiliated to let her know how much it hurt, and too proud to openly deny her assumption. Before he could recover from that blow, another realization slammed into him.

If Kasidy believed Mrs. Scuttle was his . . . that he was involved with her, then she very likely believed he'd been Amelia's gigolo.

Which meant . . . she'd probably thought Mrs. Scuttle was Amelia's replacement.

Wyatt felt ill. He was angry, too, but the hurt kept his temper in check. "I, um, should get back to the house," he said, unable to keep the chill from his voice. "Mrs. Scuttle might need me." He didn't give a damn what she thought about that. He *would* be there if Mrs. Scuttle needed him, but not in the way Kasidy's nasty little mind implied.

"Wyatt . . ."

He waited, willing to accept her apology on the grounds that she didn't know him. After a few moments of damning silence, Wyatt walked away.

CHAPTER 6

Okay. So maybe the old lady he'd carried upstairs wasn't his new keeper.

He was still a gigolo.

Kasidy kicked at the worn leather sandal she had removed, then groaned when she saw that she'd left a scuff mark on the cream-colored carpet. She was furious because she felt awful, when she knew damned well she had no reason to feel awful.

A gigolo was gigolo was a gigolo.

She blew out a sigh, glancing around the bedroom where her grandmother's former maid—or several, who knew—had lived in splendor. The room was three times the size of any room Kasidy had ever lived in. The heavy oak bedroom furniture upholstered in white and cream was the kind that lasted through generations, not the yard-sale stuff they'd always bought.

Kasidy had yet to sit anywhere but the cream satin chair beside the big, four-poster bed, and even then she was perched gingerly on the edge with her hands in her lap.

She was afraid that if she touched anything, she would leave a grease print. Nana Jo was forever complaining about her getting grease on her clothes, or the towels, and sometimes the furniture.

Wyatt had been hurt. No doubt about it.

Because she didn't want to think about it, or feel sorry for him, or feel bad about what she'd said, Kasidy tried to concentrate on something else.

Anything but the awful hurt she'd heard in his voice.

She hated to hurt someone's feelings. It was the biggest reason she'd never given her parents any trouble. Of course, she'd been a daddy's girl from the moment she was born. That was the day her daddy had ended his life of crime. For her, he'd told her, and for her mother, who had given up so much by leaving her pampered, wealthy lifestyle.

Checking her hands for grease spots—although she had scrubbed them twice—Kasidy very carefully laid them on the arms of the chair. She eased back until her head hit the backrest, and closed her eyes. A faint smile curved her mouth as she thought about the secret sessions she'd had with her dad growing up, the ones her mother never knew about.

He'd taught her how to pick a lock, crack a safe, and hot-wire a car. She knew how to scale a two-story house, and enter and leave without a trace. She knew the difference between costume jewelry and the real thing at a glance. He'd coached her on how to invent a believable story without warning, something Kasidy was now certain her mother wouldn't have approved of.

That little talent had come in handy the day a

stranger had approached her on her way home from school. She'd been twelve at the time, and they'd been living in the same town for a record-breaking two years. Her father had a great job as a mechanic. Her mother was happy, and Kasidy had made a friend—a *best* friend—a first for her.

She hadn't wanted to leave, hadn't wanted to trust her instincts about the man with the dog, but when he'd started asking her personal questions about her family, Kasidy had known what she had to do. She'd invented a cheery, believable story about being the youngest child of a preacher. She had even invited him to church, telling him they were having revival all week and whoever brought the most visitors won an electric ice cream maker.

Because her father had taught her well, the private investigator had believed her and left her alone. Kasidy had mulled over the incident for two days before guilt drove her to confess to her parents.

They'd moved that night, leaving everything but their personal belongings. It was the night she really truly began to hate the grandmother she'd never met. Because of Amelia Hancock and her obsession with finding them and breaking up her parents, Kasidy hadn't been able to say goodbye to her best friend, Angelina Lateaf. And since she wasn't allowed to contact anyone from her past as long as Amelia was alive, Kasidy had never seen her again. She sometimes wondered what Angelina was doing now. Was she married with kids? Gone to college? Had she cried when Kasidy didn't show up the next day to walk with her to school?

Hoping to make it up to his daughter, her father

had started taking her with him to his new mechanic job, and teaching her everything he knew. He became her new best friend, and Kasidy had never told him that it wasn't the same.

What if she'd had sex with Wyatt in the garage?

Just like that. She'd hesitated a second in her thoughts, and he was back.

Kasidy let out an aggravated huff and dared to tuck her feet beneath her in the chair. So what if she'd had sex with him? That didn't make her like her grandmother. At least she was closer to Wyatt's age! And she wasn't buying him things . . . paying him for sex.

Oh, why in hell did he have to be a gigolo? Kasidy moaned her frustration and buried her hot face in her hands. Even now, she couldn't stop thinking about him, feeling his hands on her, his hard body pressed against hers. Wondering what he'd feel like inside her.

He hadn't kissed her, and she had wanted him to more than she'd wanted anything in a long while.

More than she wanted to find the evidence against her father, so that he could finally stop looking over his shoulder and return to his hometown?

Disgusted with herself all over again, Kasidy leaped to her feet and began pacing. She had to play nice, so she could have the run of the house, but not *that* nice. Be trusted, so that if Wyatt caught her snooping, he'd believe whatever story popped into her head.

She would apologize to Wyatt and offer her friendship, yet make it very clear that she didn't want to muck things up by becoming involved with her employer.

Yes, that was the ticket. A nice, clean solution to an embarrassingly naughty problem. She was honest enough with herself to admit that she lusted for Wyatt Love, but smart enough to realize that hooking up with him would put a sizable dent in her self-respect.

And since she was being honest with herself, she admitted that it wasn't the gigolo part that bothered her the most—after all, it was just lust, not love that she felt for him—it was the fact that he'd been her *grandmother's* gigolo. Heck, she had two hundred dollars in her backpack she'd gladly give him, just to see if he was as good as he looked.

She put a hand over her quivering stomach. Yep. Take her grandmother out of the equation, and she'd drag Wyatt back to the garage in handcuffs, if she had to. Maybe not very romantic to most, but she wanted to have mind-blowing sex with him surrounded by the familiar smells of gasoline, oil, and new leather.

With the heat of his truck engine searing her behind, and the squeak of shocks bouncing on the—

"Lordy, lordy," Kasidy breathed, stunned at her shameless thoughts.

How was she going to be friends with him, when she couldn't string a coherent thought together without a lustful fantasy thrown in?

Heaven help her.

Wyatt hadn't slept very well, so he was having trouble opening his eyes as he stumbled into the kitchen in search of coffee. After only a week of the housekeeper's freshly ground one hundred percent

Columbian, he knew he'd have a hard time going back to instant.

But it wasn't a cheerful Louise he found at the massive cook stove, it was Dillon. He was, however, wearing Louise's apron.

Slack-jawed with shock, Wyatt surveyed the disaster that had once been a gleaming, everything-in-its-place kitchen. Now it was covered in dirty pots, the cabinets nearly invisible beneath a massive pile of ingredients, cookbooks, and utensils.

"Hey, sleepy head," Dillon said, catching sight of him standing in the doorway. "Coffee's on. Should be ready in a minute."

"What are you doing?" Wyatt managed to get out.

Both Dillon's eyebrows rose. "Pretty self-explanatory, bro. I'm cooking."

"Where's Louise?" *And my wonderful coffee, and those delicious apple pancakes she makes?*

"She quit."

Wyatt staggered to a chair and plopped down. This wasn't happening. "What? Why?"

Dillon shrugged. "I don't know. Might have had something to do with the fact that Mrs. Scuttle wanted eggs Benedict." He used a spatula to point to a laundry basket full of delicates by the door. "Her Majesty also wanted those hand washed."

Bug-eyed, Wyatt followed the spatula. He shook his head. "Louise wouldn't have quit because of that." When Dillon's gaze slid suspiciously away from his, Wyatt narrowed his eyes. "What else did Mrs. Scuttle do?"

"She, um, might have hit her . . . with a roll of toilet paper." Before Wyatt could respond, Dillon hurried to explain. "See, Louise heard a crash in the bathroom and thought Mrs. Scuttle had fallen. Mrs. Scuttle didn't take too kindly to Louise barging in on her in the middle of . . . well, you know."

Still . . .

"A roll of toilet paper? That wouldn't hurt," Wyatt mused out loud. He'd been hit with a lot worse.

"Maybe it was the bar of soap afterward," Dillon supplied helpfully. "Or could have been the soap dish. I think it was made of brass."

"She threw a brass soap dish at Louise?" Wyatt was now beyond shock. He knew Mrs. Scuttle's temper, but a brass soap dish?

"Well, I think she threw the soap at her, and the soap just happened to be stuck to the brass soap dish. You know how soap does when it gets wet—"

"She's lost her mind," Wyatt interrupted to say decisively. "I think we should all face facts and get her some help."

Dillon turned the flame down under the skillet and faced Wyatt, casual and way too innocent-looking for Wyatt's piece of mind. "That's a pretty strong accusation for someone you've only known a week, bro."

"Not Louise!" Wyatt roared, standing. He could feel the blood pounding in his veins. His twin was being deliberately obtuse, and that was *his* M.O. "Mrs. Scuttle! I'm talking about Mrs. Scuttle." Before his brother could answer, Wyatt heard a loud banging directly overhead. Almost simultaneously, the doorbell began to peal.

Grabbing his hair, Wyatt looked at the ceiling,

then at Dillon, dumbstruck. "What the hell is that noise?"

"Which one?"

Wyatt glared at Dillon. If he didn't know better . . .

"The banging noise coming from upstairs. I think I recognize the doorbell."

"Oh." Dillon had to raise his voice to be heard. "That would be Mrs. Scuttle. I gave her a pan and a wooden spoon so she could let us know when she wanted something." When Wyatt continued to glare at him, Dillon shrugged. "Hey, you didn't want her trying to come downstairs on that bad ankle, did you? She could fall and break her neck or something."

The "or something" sounded good to Wyatt. Muttering, "I'll get the door, you get the crazy," he stomped out of the kitchen. His fantasy come to life was swiftly turning into a nightmare. Amelia's "babies" thought he was Satan, his brother and the crazy secretary had moved in, Kasidy believed he'd been Amelia's lover, and—

He jerked open the door, his jaw clenched tight.

—and his little sister and two of her college friends were standing on the threshold, smiling at him as if they were auditioning for a toothpaste commercial.

"Surprise!" Isabelle cried, throwing her arms around his neck and sending him reeling backward into the house.

He caught her instinctively, picking her up as he'd always done when she jumped into his arms. But though she was still petite like their mother, she packed quite a punch when she jumped. He glanced at her bright blue eyes, then her shoulder-length blond hair. "You got your hair highlighted," he said. "Why aren't you at college?"

"Spring break, silly!" Isabelle wiggled free and gave him a playful punch in the stomach. "Mom told us about your cool new job taking care of this cool mansion."

"And the cool pool," one of her friends—Brandy, Wyatt remembered—chimed in.

"And the cool tennis court," Natasha added, following Brandy inside and shutting the door. "And the cool hot tub."

It was then that Wyatt noticed the sports bags each of the girls held. Another one sat beside the door. His entire body seized in a groan of dismay. No. *No no no no no.* Not happening. Couldn't be.

But Isabelle said the fated words. "Mom said you wouldn't mind us staying here. The plumbers said the water would be off for a couple days."

What would three more houseguests hurt? Wyatt thought savagely. And then, because he was a glutton for punishment, he said, "I suppose Mom's on her way."

"That's right!" Isabelle beamed at him. "She heard your housekeeper quit, so she volunteered to help with the cooking when she's not studying or going to class."

"How did she know Louise quit?"

"Dillon told her, silly, when he called to find out how to make eggs Benedict. Does it matter which room we take? We swear we'll be low maintenance. We'll even share a room."

Brandy raised a timid hand. "I know how to clean the pool."

"I know how to run the dishwasher," Natasha offered shyly.

Too bad they didn't know how to become invisible, Wyatt thought darkly as he watched them take off upstairs to pick out their room. He was immediately ashamed of his thought. He hadn't seen Isabelle since Christmas because she went to Michigan State. Of course, he didn't see much of her when she *was* home. He was either working at the bar, or working for Mr. Complete, and she was always off with her friends.

But this was different. He was technically on vacation for the next two weeks from both jobs to get used to his new *third* job, which definitely wasn't going as he'd planned.

Nothing was. If Dillon wasn't such a die-hard stick in the mud, Wyatt might entertain the idea of his brother setting him up.

Nah. Not Dillon. He would never take the time and energy to plan such an elaborate hoax, and he would never leave Callie to handle the twins alone. But if he had . . . he was definitely succeeding in irritating the absolute hell out of him.

Forcing himself to unclench his hands and his jaw, Wyatt decided he needed an outlet for his frustration before he blew. A swim sounded good. It would cool him off and give him a chance to work out his anger.

Glancing down, he decided his shorts would do just fine. He figured he had about thirty minutes before Isabelle and her friends decided on the right bathing suits and hit the pool—just enough time for a good swim.

Wyatt heard the splash before he cleared the patio

doors. He let out a low curse, thinking someone had already beat him to the pool, then stopped short. He blinked, then blinked again.

No way. How many shocks could a guy take before noon?

It was the black dog—Curly, Wyatt remembered—diving to the bottom of the pool to retrieve something. In amazement, Wyatt watched as the poodle swam strongly to the surface, then clawed at the side of the pool until he gained leverage and pulled himself over. The moment the dog started shaking water from his coat, Kasidy's clear, gut-punching laughter rang out.

His gaze immediately swung to her. The breath left his lungs in a hot whoosh.

"Let me have it, boy," she crooned, taking the bone-shaped toy out of Curly's mouth. She snapped the toy open, removed a doggie snack, and gave it to Curly. "Good boy, Curly. Anyone else want to try?"

Wyatt's throat worked. If he could have spoken, he knew he would have volunteered and made a fool out of himself, just to hear those throaty, provocative words, "Let me have it, boy."

Kasidy wore a simple white one-piece bathing suit, yet she managed to look sexier than any woman Wyatt had ever seen in the skimpiest of bikinis. And why was that? He wondered, unable to look away from the perfection of her body. Why was *she* different? What made her so special? Why did she get under his skin the way she did?

Why did she have the power to *hurt* him, as no other woman had?

She looked up, then, and noticed him standing on

the marbled patio. Her smile slowly faded. Wyatt's mouth went bone dry as she began to walk toward him. She possessed the strong, confident stride of a tomboy, which made her breasts bounce in a very *un*-tomboyish way.

He prayed for strength.

CHAPTER 7

This is ridiculous, Kasidy thought, praying he wouldn't notice that she wasn't quite steady on her feet as she approached. How could she be, when her kneecaps felt as if they'd been replaced with silly putty?

She's seen hundreds of naked chests in her life. There was absolutely no reason the sight of Wyatt's gleaming, bronzed chest should make her legs want to fold like wet noodles beneath her.

Absolutely no *logical* reason.

Just for sanity's sake, she stopped a good fourteen inches from him. She stood there, feeling her breath rush in and out of her lungs as if she'd been running. Felt water droplets trickle between her breasts as if they were made of ice, and knew, as only a woman instinctively knows, that if he touched her, those drops would start to sizzle.

Saw his gaze lower, and realized that he'd seen the drops, too, and was following their progress with a healthy male appreciation that made Kasidy feel like a healthy, *horny* female. When he slowly licked his lips, desire streaked through her lower belly and into her groin.

She wanted to clench her thighs—right around the hard, thick length of him. As a result of her lustful thoughts, a huskiness she couldn't control thickened her voice. "I, um, hope you don't mind the dogs in the pool. I think Mrs. Hancock took them for a ritual morning swim. They brought me out here this morning."

Wyatt looked a little shell-shocked, but Kasidy didn't think the dogs had anything to do with it. Unfortunately, she knew exactly how he felt.

"No . . . that's okay." He cleared a frog from his throat. "After all, it's their pool."

Remembering that she wasn't supposed to know, she blinked her confusion. "What do you mean, it's *their* pool?"

A wry grin curved his lips—as if he were thinking of a private joke—then disappeared. "Mrs. Hancock left her estate to her dogs in the event her next of kin isn't found. I'm just a trustee."

How much did he know? Kasidy wondered, searching his expression. He gave nothing away, so she went fishing. "Her next of kin is missing?"

Wyatt nodded. "Her granddaughter. I don't know all the details, but apparently they've been estranged for some time."

A profound understatement, Kasidy thought, realizing that Wyatt was either a very good liar, or he knew next to nothing about the family history. "Mrs. Hancock didn't confide in you?" Kasidy boldly asked.

That wry grin of earlier returned with a hint of

coolness as he said, "No, she didn't. Contrary to popular belief, Mrs. Hancock and I didn't have a close relationship. I was only her escort on occasion."

By the skin of her teeth, Kasidy managed to choke back a disbelieving laugh. Did he really expect her to believe him? Well, she might have if she hadn't heard him with her own ears describe in lurid detail the nature of his "relationship" with her grandmother.

But now wasn't the time to challenge his lies. She had to apologize, convince him that she was willing to be friendly, to a certain point. Under the guise of checking on the dogs, Kasidy twisted around, subtly wiped the distracting moisture from her breasts, then turned back to face him.

Their gazes met. Heat popped and sizzled between them. Kasidy's knees went weak again as she realized that he knew what she had done—and why.

Okay. So the gauntlet was down between them. He knew that she wanted him; she knew that he wanted her.

It was lust, a lust she didn't plan on giving into. He was her grandmother's ex-lover. It was sick. Just plain sick.

Before she lost her nerve, or got sidetracked by the dark, sultry gleam in his sexy eyes, Kasidy looked away and said breathlessly, "I owe you an apology for last night." She felt him shift closer, and was exasperated with her body as it tingled in anticipation.

Softly, in a voice that shivered over her damp skin like a cool breeze, he asked, "Which part? The part where you stopped me from taking you on the hood of my truck?"

Their gazes collided again—his slightly amused

and a lot angry; hers shocked and dismayed. Desire speared through her again, this time hotter, sharper than before. Dang him and his talents!

"A gentleman would never—" she didn't get any further. The breath left her lungs in a surprised whoosh as he pulled her against him, his mouth only inches from her own.

"Who in Sam Hill said anything about me being a gentleman?" he demanded roughly. "Lady, you got me confused with someone else."

He yanked her closer still, until she could see his irises, and realized with a jolt of shock that he wore contacts.

"From the moment I saw you in those coveralls, I've wanted you so badly it makes my teeth ache to look at you."

It was useless to try to stop her body's reaction to those brazen, lust-inducing words. Her nipples sprang erect and stayed that way. In a nearly sound-less whisper, she said, "It's just—just lust."

"Is it?" Wyatt sounded very doubtful, almost smugly so. "Then why don't we find out, if you're so sure?"

Kasidy licked her lips. "Because you're my em-ployer." It sounded weak and silly to her own ears, considering the temperature between them, so she wasn't surprised when Wyatt laughed. She stared at the strong column of his throat and found herself wondering why she bothered to argue. Apparently her body was fully capable of making its own choices.

"Because I'm your employer—or because you be-lieve I was Mrs. Hancock's boy toy?" The last he delivered on a harsh note that left Kasidy in no doubt about how much her assumption had hurt him.

Trying to sound dignified when she felt anything but, Kasidy drew herself up to her full height of five feet six inches. "What I believe doesn't really matter. I work for you. Nothing good ever comes of getting involved with one's employer."

He let her prudish delivery hang provocatively in the air between them. Then he smiled a smile of pure devilment. But Kasidy was street-smart enough to see the lingering anger behind it. She knew she had to choose her words carefully if she was going to get back into his good graces.

She tried the soft approach. "Wyatt . . . I like you. It would be stupid of me to deny it." She bit her bottom lip and attempted a regretful look, which wasn't hard, since she *did* regret the fact that he'd been involved with her grandmother. "But I like this job, and I don't want to do anything to mess it up." At least not until she found what she was looking for.

For a long moment, she forced herself to meet his gaze with level innocence. Curly finally came to her rescue, nudging her hand with a wet nose. In his snout he held the toy bone. Kasidy eased out of Wyatt's grip, inwardly relieved when he let her go without a struggle.

Another moment or two of that boiling hot look and she'd have been a goner.

"I told her flat out that I was Mrs. Hancock's escort, and nothing more," Wyatt said to Dillon later that evening. "She didn't believe me. I could see it in her damned sexy green eyes."

All Dillon could say—with a smug grin on his face was, "Sexy green eyes, huh?"

They were in the storeroom of the bar Dillon had named The Love Nest, of all things, surrounded by cases of hard liquor, beer, and stacks and stacks of mirrored tiles that had once graced the far wall behind the dance floor. Thank God Dillon had come to his senses and taken the mirrors down, realizing that folks didn't want to view themselves while dancing a drunken two-step.

In a fit of frustration, Wyatt lifted his foot and kicked the door the rest of the way shut.

There was a wounded shout from the other side.

Wyatt yanked the door open, saw that he'd clipped the nosy noses of Lou, the bartender, and Fish, the bouncer, and growled, "That's what you get!" before slamming it shut again.

He turned to find Dillon watching him with one lifted eyebrow. "What?" he demanded, glaring at him.

Dillon shrugged. "You hurt their feelings. After all, they were privy to each and every one of *my* humiliations when I was wooing Callie."

"That's different," Wyatt snapped, still glowering at his too-smug brother. The idea slithered in again, and he wondered if Dillon had actually set him up. But no . . . he just couldn't imagine his uptight brother involved in such an elaborate scheme.

"Different how?" Dillon asked, tongue in cheek.

"Different in that you were falling in love with Callie. I'm just trying to . . . trying to . . ." Wyatt hated floundering, and he quickly discovered he hated to hear his brother laugh.

"Get into her pants?"

"She wears shorts. Short shorts, and tight T-shirts," Wyatt ground out. "And yes, I just want to get her into my bed. Hell, since when did lusting after a woman mean you had to fall in love with her?"

He found out very quickly that he shouldn't have asked.

"Since you met your soul mate," Dillon said glibly, adding a smug chuckle that sounded like nails on a chalkboard to Wyatt.

"Bull shit. I don't even *know* her." Wyatt stared at Dillon, then laughed and shook his head. "You're crazy. You think just because you met your soul mate in Callie, that it's naturally going to happen to me the same way. Well, you're wrong, bro. I could never fall in love with a woman who thinks I sleep with old ladies for money."

"Lydia thought the same thing about Luke," Dillon pointed out, referring to his now happily married boss and his wife. "It didn't stop him from falling in love with her."

Wyatt kicked at a box and had to swallow a pained cry to save face. "Well, I'm not Luke, and Kasidy has no reason to think that about me. She doesn't even know me."

"You keep mentioning the fact that you two don't know each other. Have you considered the possibility of *getting* to know her before you bonk her on the hood of your truck?"

If looks could kill . . . Wyatt ground his teeth and prayed for patience. He was getting the uncomfortable feeling that his twin—who was normally on the receiving end of his laughter—was enjoying his torment a little too much. "If I had known you were going to throw that in my face, I wouldn't have told you about it."

"Oh, but I'm so glad that you did."

Dillon's leering grin almost got him killed. Wyatt had to clench his fists and count to ten. Then he went and blurted out something else he immediately regretted. "I don't seem to have much control when I'm around her."

"Ah-ha!" Dillon crowed, standing up for his victory shout. He jabbed an excited finger at Wyatt, who was beginning to fear his brother had lost his mind. "When, my dear twin, was the last time you couldn't control yourself around a woman?"

Dead silence filled the small storeroom as Wyatt attempted to stare down his exuberant brother.

As usual, his contacts lost him the battle. "Go to hell," he snarled, for want of a better comeback. When he yanked open the door, Lou and Fish fell forward, just like in the movies. Feeling totally justified, Wyatt stuck out his leg to ensure they kept on heading for the floor.

Dillon had never felt so fantastic in his life. Okay, so maybe when his twins came squalling into the world . . . but other than that, there was no contest.

Wyatt was in love!

But the best part—the absolute *best* part—was that Wyatt not only didn't have a clue he was in love, he didn't know that Kasidy was Amelia Hancock's granddaughter. Finally, *he* had a secret from Wyatt that was going to make Wyatt's life a living hell for a very entertaining while.

There was, however, a downside. He missed Callie,

and he missed his babies, Jada and Kaden. And, according to Wyatt, Kasidy had made a pact with herself about sleeping with her grandmother's boy toy.

Dillon shuddered, sympathizing with her. Not that Wyatt had been Amelia's boy toy, but that Kasidy believed he had been. Hell, even *he* had started believing Wyatt when he spun the lurid tale to shock the attorney that day in the study.

He would have to do something about that, and soon. Wyatt would get nowhere fast as long as Kasidy believed the worst about him.

With his mind turning, Dillon pulled out Callie's cell phone and punched in a number. He waited, silently urging Mrs. Scuttle to pick up. He'd had a hell of a time convincing her to carry a cell phone in the first place. He knew he'd be lucky if she'd overcome her stubborn nature and answer it.

Finally, a strident voice bawled into his ear, "Well! Speak your piece, you numskull! You know I hate these blasted things. They give you brain cancer."

Prudently keeping the smile from his voice, Dillon said, "That was quite a show you put on last night. I think you convinced her."

"That wasn't a show, you idiot. I didn't appreciate you making remarks about my age."

"I'm sorry." Dillon's voice dripped with sincerity. "Will you forgive me?"

After a lengthy silence, Mrs. Scuttle huffed and said, "You slick dog, you. I guess I forgive you. What do you want?"

Eying the closed storeroom door, Dillon lowered his voice and said, "I think it's time to start dropping hints about Wyatt's relationship with Mrs. Hancock to Kasidy."

"You mean last night didn't convince her?" Mrs. Scuttle yelled, nearly deafening Dillon.

Dillon held the phone an inch from his ear. "No, no. That convinced her. Too much. Now we need to convince her that Wyatt wasn't involved with Mrs. Hancock."

"You mean now we need to convince her that he *wasn't* having sex with her?"

Swallowing a sigh, Dillon said, "Right. He wasn't."

"I know he wasn't, you nitwit!"

"I know that you know," Dillon soothed. "Now we just need to convince Kasidy."

"How we gonna do that," Mrs. Scuttle bawled into the phone, "after the nasty stunt he pulled on that lawyer shark?"

Good question, Dillon thought, constantly amazed at how sharp Mrs. Scuttle was at the ripe old age of eighty. "Has she been in to see you yet?"

"Kasidy?"

Dillon rubbed his nose. He was convinced that when Mrs. Scuttle was being obtuse, it was a deliberate attempt to test his patience. "Yes, Kasidy."

"Oh. I thought you were talking about that pervert housekeeper, Louise."

He had to hide the phone against his chest so that she wouldn't hear his laughter. He was fairly certain Mrs. Scuttle wouldn't appreciate it. "Um, no. I wasn't talking about Louise, and I believe that was an accident, Mrs. Scuttle. The housekeeper thought you had fallen."

"Were you there?" Mrs. Scuttle screeched, her strident voice sending a shard of pain through his head.

"No, I wasn't." Dillon could only hope to high heaven nobody was standing in the hall outside the secretary's room. Or even on the same floor.

"I didn't *think* so. I'm telling you, the woman had a wicked look in her eye . . . I'm not crazy, so don't you go thinking it."

"I would never," Dillon promised, holding his crossed fingers behind his back. "Back to Kasidy . . ."

"Oh. Yeah. She's a cute thing, isn't she? I think she'll give Wyatt a run for his money."

"That's what we're all hoping for." Dillon chuckled to himself, remembering the murderous look in Wyatt's eyes earlier. Oh, revenge was sweet . . . sweet . . . sweet!

"So you want me to start working on her?"

"I thought you'd never ask." If anyone could do it, it was Mrs. Scuttle, Dillon thought with great affection.

Well, as long as she kept that temper in check. Dillon didn't think Wyatt's little spitfire would take too kindly to having objects chucked at her head.

CHAPTER 8

Kasidy caught the remote deftly in her right hand. The impact stung, as did the unsuspecting action.

Behind her, Wyatt caught the jar of Vicks VapoRub that quickly followed.

Grimly, he said to Kasidy, "Leave us alone for a minute, would you?"

Totally confused, Kasidy tried to defend herself. "I didn't mean to offend her. I just asked her if she would like to use the wheelchair I found in the closet downstairs." Never mind what she was doing in the closet in the first place. She hoped Wyatt was too distracted to wonder.

Not taking his stern gaze from the irate elderly woman's, Wyatt said, "It's okay. You didn't do anything wrong, Kasidy. I'll explain later."

Perversely, Kasidy felt sorry for Mrs. Scuttle. Wyatt looked madder than hell. She lingered, afraid to leave them alone. "I'm, um, sure it was an accident, Wyatt."

"The hell it was," Wyatt said pleasantly. He held up the Vicks VapoRub for emphasis. "And this? Was that an accident, too? Imagine that, two accidents in a row."

She grimaced at his sarcasm, reluctantly edging toward the door. The moment it shut behind her—nearly clipping her bottom—Kasidy turned around and put her ear to the door. She let out a strangled gasp when she felt a hand on her arm.

Dillon put a finger to his lips in silent warning, then leaned next to her.

Together, they listened.

Wyatt set the remote and the jar of salve on the nightstand, then stood back, patiently waiting for Mrs. Scuttle to speak.

He didn't have to wait long.

She shot him a burning, half-guilty look before staring at the covers. "I don't need a dad-gum wheelchair," she muttered, plucking nervously at the covers.

He remained silent.

After five beats, she became more agitated. "That little girl hurt my pride." It was as close to an excuse for her behavior that she could manage, Wyatt knew.

He folded his arms across his chest and continued to stare sternly at her. It was a new feeling for Wyatt. Normally, he quivered in fear of the secretary, but she'd gone too far in forcing his housekeeper to quit. The fact that he'd caught her threatening Kasidy had been the last straw. Very softly, he said, "And Louise?"

Mrs. Scuttle shot him a scorching look from beneath her gray eyebrows before she turned her gaze to the satin ribbons on her flannel gown. "She walked in on me while I was taking a poop."

Good, Wyatt thought with inward relief. The fight was going out of her. Maybe he'd get to leave the room without any new scars. Knowing that any sign of weakness could be fatal, Wyatt remained firm. "And what did Kasidy do that was so wrong? Sounds to me like she was trying to help."

"Maybe she was," the secretary grudgingly admitted. "But it struck me the wrong way. I'm not helpless, you know. I can walk, when my ankle ain't sprained. I don't need a nursing home."

Melting like putty, Wyatt relented. He sat on the edge of the bed and took her gnarled hand in his own, surprised at how cold it was. He made a mental note to trick her into getting a checkup soon. Gently, he said, "Of course you don't need a nursing home. But Kasidy doesn't know you like we do, does she, hmm?" When the secretary nodded, looking ashamed, Wyatt squeezed her hand. "How many times do we all have to tell you that you'll never, ever have to go into a nursing home, as long as we live and breathe?" When she remained stubbornly silent, he jiggled her hand until she looked at him.

He saw the raw fear in her eyes, and it nearly made him cry.

"Among the dozen or so of us, do you not believe that we can take care of you, if the need arises? We love you. I mean that, from the bottom of my black heart."

"Your heart's not black," she whispered in a wavering voice. She sniffed and shot him a shy glance. "Why?"

Her simple, stark question jolted his heart. Wyatt closed both hands over hers and squeezed tight. "I told you. Because we all love you."

"But I throw things," she whispered dejectedly.

"We love you anyway. However," Wyatt continued, injecting a note of sternness back into his voice, "we also like to eat around here. So, if you could possibly control your urges to throw things, I would appreciate it."

She perked up, sensing forgiveness. "I can't always control it, you know. I try. I try hard."

"Try harder." Wyatt leaned forward, hesitated, then said in a whisper he was certain nobody but Mrs. Scuttle could hear. "Kasidy's special."

Mrs. Scuttle came alive at that. She beamed at him, then reached out and patted his cheek. "That she is, Wyatt. That she is. I promise I won't throw anything else at Kasidy."

"Or the hired help," Wyatt prompted with a warning look.

"Okay." The secretary blinked rapidly behind her magnified glasses, a sure indication she was becoming agitated. "As long as you don't hire any more perverts."

Knowing defeat when it slapped him in the face, Wyatt hid his impatience and nodded. "Deal. Now, why don't you get some rest? We're having spaghetti for supper. I'll bring some up when it's done."

With her beaming face etched in his mind, Wyatt left her and made for the door.

Just as he reached it, something light, but sharp hit the back of his head.

He whirled around to find Mrs. Scuttle regarding him with a smug, unrepentant grin. Glancing down, he spotted the box of tissues on the floor.

"What?" she barked. "You didn't say anything

about not throwing things at *you*. I gotta have an outlet, don't I?"

This time Wyatt remained facing her as he let himself out.

"Go ahead," Kasidy urged gently. "Pet him. He won't bite." Holding her breath—because she wasn't as certain as she sounded—Kasidy watched as Mrs. Scuttle put out her hand and tentatively laid it atop Moe's head.

She had picked Moe, the red poodle, because he seemed to have the best disposition.

When Moe licked the elderly woman's gnarled hand, Kasidy nearly wept with joy. "See? He's as gentle as a kitten."

"And so soft. I never had a dog. My husband was allergic."

Kasidy felt a pang of empathy. "Your kids must have wanted a pet."

"No kids, either." Mrs. Scuttle shot her a mischievous grin that totally endeared her to Kasidy. "He was allergic."

"You're kidding."

"Yeah, I'm kidding." Her grin faltered, then faded. "I couldn't have children, but he stayed with me anyway. He told me that he loved me enough for a whole passel of children."

"How sweet." Kasidy meant it. She couldn't imagine anything more romantic than a couple who knew the power of their own love.

"Dillon loves Callie that way, even though they have kids."

"Twins, right? Jada and Kaden." When Moe

pulled on the collar she held, she let him go. He climbed gently on top of the bed and lay beside Mrs. Scuttle. She giggled like a schoolgirl and began stroking his head.

"Luke and Lydia were like that, too," Mrs. Scuttle said after a long, companionable silence.

"Luke and Lydia?" Kasidy was intrigued by anyone she thought remotely connected to Wyatt, and this woman was definitely connected, so it stood to reason that Luke and Lydia were, too.

"Yeah. Luke's my boss. When he met Lydia, now his wife, she thought he was a conniving, heartbreaking gigolo."

The elderly woman didn't seem to notice that Kasidy stiffened.

Mrs. Scuttle cackled as if remembering a hilarious moment. "Lydia thought he was plain ole sex for hire, she did. She set out to trap him, believing one of his men was responsible for breaking her aunt's heart."

Caught up in the story for reasons she wasn't prepared to share with the secretary, Kasidy urged her onward. "So what happened?"

"They both landed in jail," Mrs. Scuttle announced, chuckling gleefully at Kasidy's shocked expression. "This nosy detective mistook him for a prostitute, and got Lydia for soliciting."

"No!" Kasidy was genuinely shocked. How embarrassing would that be?

Mrs. Scuttle took her hand, and Kasidy noticed how cold it was. She automatically started rubbing the elderly woman's hand in her own to create heat.

"Yes, indeed. The escorts and I—"

"The escorts?"

"Yes, the other escorts that work for Luke, sweety. All good men, men I would trust with my life. We bailed Luke out and had a high time doing it." She paused, looking sly as she added, "I had the cop in the station cowering behind the counter, threatening him with a paperweight."

"You didn't!" Kasidy was suitably impressed. And just a little jealous. It was obvious the old woman loved the escorts, that they were all a close-knit group, like family. Kasidy had never been a part of any group.

"I did. He was making fun of my Luke, calling him a man whore and such." She sucked a thin bottom lip between her teeth in a hissing motion. "I showed him a thing or two, let me tell you. My escorts are respectable men. Why, most of them are married, for heaven's sake!"

As Kasidy pondered the information, the secretary grabbed her hand and pulled her closer, sounding earnest.

"When the rich woman who owned this place croaked and left Wyatt in charge, there were people who thought the worst," she confided, sounding outraged on Wyatt's behalf. "Ain't that horrible, them thinking that, without no evidence at all? It's disgusting, is what it is! Wyatt owns half the bar with his brother, and makes good money as an escort. Why would people think he'd have to sell himself to get what he wanted? It's a shame, isn't it?"

The way Mrs. Scuttle put it, it was, but Kasidy couldn't forget Wyatt's lurid, detailed description that day in the study when she'd been listening in. By his own admission, he had been Amelia Hancock's lover.

Poor Mrs. Scuttle was just a naive fool who didn't know any better.

Outside the secretary's room, Kasidy ran into the other new houseguests, Wyatt's little sister and her friends. Wyatt had warned her, but nothing could have prepared Kasidy for the friendly exuberance that burst on her like a tidal wave.

"Oh, my God!" Isabelle screamed, her blue eyes big and round as they stared at Kasidy. "You're gorgeous, just like Wyatt said!"

Kasidy, unaccustomed to compliments, blushed. She tried to backtrack, but the girls moved forward as one, surrounding her and circling her as if they'd found the new Gia. All this fuss over a dog sitter? Nervously, Kasidy introduced herself, although she didn't think there was much need. What else had Wyatt said about her?

"Kasidy," Isabelle repeated almost reverently. "What a beautiful and usual name." The girl's eyes literally sparkled. She pointed to her friends. "Brandy and Natasha. They go to Michigan State, too. Brandy's my roommate."

"Nice to meet you," Kasidy said politely. Inwardly, she felt a pang of jealously. Friends. Something a lot of people took for granted.

"Can we take the dogs for a walk?" Isabelle asked. "I think it would be so cool to walk down the street with them. A poodle for each of us."

Kasidy hesitated. Isabelle was likable, but was she also responsible? Picking her words with care, she began, "The dogs are my responsibility, so I don't think—"

"Didn't Wyatt tell you I'm going to be a vet?" Isabelle burst in. "I spent last summer assisting Dr. Legrow, a vet here in town."

"She's very good with animals," Brandy added, stuffing her hands in the back pockets of her low-riding jeans.

Kasidy longed to be a part of their group, to be part of a circle. What would it be like to have a girlfriend to confide in? Someone to share secrets and heartaches, triumphs and failures?

She had Nana Jo, but it just wasn't the same as having a friend closer to her own age.

"Well, what do you think?" Isabelle persisted. "Will you trust us?"

"Yes," Kasidy said, praying she'd done the right thing. She had to cover her ears to mute the sounds of their happy squeals as the girls raced downstairs to the "doggie" room. She hadn't had time to explain that Moe was taking a nap with Mrs. Scuttle.

When she dared to take her hands away, she heard the insistent peal of the doorbell. Where was Wyatt, or Dillon? Sighing, she trod downstairs to answer the door.

The sight of the hunk on the threshold took her breath away. Dark-eyed and dark-haired, he looked as if he'd stepped right out of a soap opera. Kasidy couldn't stop staring at him. He was, simply put, one hell of a hottie.

He smiled, slow and easy and strangely without conceit, as if he knew exactly the effect he had on her. "Hi. You must be Kasidy. I'm Ivan."

Kasidy stared down at the hand he held out. She shook herself out of her daze and took it, more chagrined than relieved when her body didn't react. "You've got me at a disadvantage," she said politely. "You know me, but I don't know you."

"I work for Mr. Complete," he explained. He darted a glance over her shoulder, his beautiful smile fading. "I need to speak with Dr. Love."

"Dr. Love?" Kasidy parroted. There were two Loves in the house—make that three, including Isabelle. Which one did he mean, and why was he calling him or her "Dr."? "Um, I'm not following you."

"Wyatt," Ivan said. His smile was completely gone now. "I'm in trouble with my old lady, and I need his help."

"His help?"

Ivan slapped a hand to his forehead. "Ah. I get it. You don't know about Wyatt's, um, hidden talents."

Hidden talents? Kasidy tried to look casual as she reached out and grabbed the door for support. How many talents could you possibly fit inside a hunk's body? Gigolo . . . escort . . . entrepreneur . . . trustee . . .

Sex machine.

And now this. Whatever "this" was.

"Thank God he doesn't charge for his services," Ivan was saying with a chuckle, oblivious to her dazed state. "We'd all go broke. Is he around?"

"Um, I'm not sure." Kasidy massaged her brow. She wasn't accustomed to so much drama, and wasn't certain she was cut out for it. "I was upstairs talking with Mrs. Scuttle just now, then Isabelle and her friends wanted to take the dogs for a walk—"

"Good," Ivan interrupted, stepping around her. "They're breaking you in right." He gave her arm a sympathetic pat after delivering that enigmatic comment. "Don't worry, I'll find him myself."

Still confused, Kasidy watched him walk away. The man definitely knew how to wear an old pair of jeans, she mused. She started to shut the door, but someone on the other side put pressure against it.

Kasidy let out a startled squeak as the door flew out of her hands. A woman stood on the threshold. There was a bit of gray in the short blond hair that framed a young-looking face, and her smile seemed vaguely familiar. She carried a suitcase and a grocery sack.

"Hi. I'm Mary Love. You must be Kasidy."

Did everyone in Atlanta know she was here? Kasidy wondered with a streak of alarm. And then it hit her. "You're their *mother?*" she squeaked out.

Mary laughed as she came inside and set down her suitcase to get a better grip on the grocery sack. "The one and only. Is that sympathy I hear in your voice, sweetie? Because if it is, you and I are going to be great friends."

Sympathy? Certainly. Shock? Definitely. Somehow, she hadn't pictured Wyatt's mother as a petite, young-looking woman with a warm smile and friendly eyes. The gray hair she'd undoubtedly got . . . raising twins *and* Isabelle. It was a wonder she had any hair at all.

"Can you point me in the direction of the kitchen, Kas? I need to get the sauce on for the spaghetti. The boys like it homemade, but Izzy hates onions, so I cook the onions until they disintegrate and tell her she's imagining things."

Still reeling from the "Kas" thing—only family called her that—Kasidy led the way to the enormous kitchen. A thousand questions raced for first place in her mind. What did Mary think about Wyatt's relationship with her grandmother? Did she even know? Did any of them know? Why was Mary here? And what was with the "Dr. Love" thing?

But the biggest question, the one that concerned her the most was how in the hell was she supposed to search the house when it was quickly filling up with people? People, no less, who seemed to know her on sight.

What was Wyatt saying about her?

She felt like a very tiny bug under a very big microscope.

So much for staying low.

CHAPTER 9

Kasidy had already searched the entire attic by the time she heard someone calling her name. She'd cried over dusty photo albums filled with pictures of her mother as a baby, a child, and later as a beautiful young woman.

One photo album, much older than the rest and smelling of mildew, had chronicled the life of the grandmother she'd never known. Feeling inexplicably guilty, she'd hurried through it and then quickly put it aside.

She'd found no sign of the videotape her grandmother had claimed to have.

Now she was hot, dusty, and hungry, but reluctant to return to the madhouse downstairs. She'd been an only child of parents who, out of necessity, had allowed only a surface familiarity with the people they met. They'd had friends, but not the kind of friends they dared confide in. Constantly aware they might have to pick up and move at a moment's notice, they never allowed themselves to get attached to anyone outside their little family.

As a result, Kasidy knew she was woefully dysfunctional when it came to friendships or serious relationships. In fact, just being under the same roof with this many people made her as skittish as a bobcat on a hot tin roof—with a hunter on his trail.

She longed to talk to her father, but she and Nana Jo had decided it would be best to keep him in the dark about her plans until she had something definite to tell him. Kasidy closed her eyes, imaging the look on his face when she presented him with the evidence and told him he no longer had to run. With the proof destroyed, he wouldn't have to worry about the powerful Slowkowsky family coming after him for a twenty-six-year-old slight—okay, so maybe *slight* was a little too mild a word for turning state's evidence against your employer.

If she succeeded, he would be free to return to Atlanta for the first time in twenty-six years. Free to use his real name once again. Free to bring her mother's ashes back and distribute them over a field of wildflowers growing on the outskirts of town. The field was still there—Kasidy had checked on her way in.

"Kasidy? You up there?"

Liquid heat bloomed in her belly at the sound of that familiar, deep, drawling voice.

Wyatt.

How had he found her? What excuse would she use to justify being found in the attic?

Her eyes were on the door when Wyatt came into view. Her heart was pounding hard, but she forced herself to appear relaxed against the dusty sofa she'd found hidden under a pile of blankets.

He saw her and paused. His brows shot upward,

and his lips curved. "I know my family can be overwhelming, but are they really *that* bad?"

The perfect excuse, already voiced and everything. Kasidy swallowed a happy little sigh and tried to look sheepish. "Not bad . . . just . . . just—"

"Scary?" Wyatt supplied, his grin widening.

She shook her head, her own lips twitching. "I was thinking more along the lines of *exhausting.*"

Wyatt appeared to consider her words, still amused. "Hmm. Yes, I can see how they might be exhausting, especially Isabelle. She's spoiled rotten, you know."

"Pretty obvious."

"Blatantly obvious," Wyatt agreed. He topped the stairs and came to sit beside her on the sofa.

Suddenly, the sofa wasn't big and comfy, but small and electrified. Amazing how quickly his mere presence could rearrange the atmosphere, Kasidy mused.

Lacing his hands behind his neck, he leaned back and let out a sigh. "I don't know what's going on. It seems there's some weird conspiracy going on to keep me from, er, having any peace."

Kasidy didn't know what to say to that mystifying comment, so instead she asked, "Did Ivan find you, *Dr. Love?*"

He turned his head sideways and shot her a naughty smile that made her stomach somersault about fifteen times in rapid succession. It left her downright dizzy.

"Yes, he found me, but that puzzles me, too. The last time I gave him advice, it backfired on him. He said he'd never trust me again."

"Okay, if you were trying to arouse my curiosity, it worked. What happened last time?"

Wyatt propped his sandaled feet on a box. "He inadvertently implied to his wife that her butt was getting bigger. To rectify the huge mistake, I suggested he buy her lingerie a couple of sizes smaller than she normally wears. My reasoning was that she would think that was how *he* saw her in his mind."

Kasidy had to bite her lip to keep from laughing outright. "But it didn't work."

"Nope. She thought he was hinting that she lose weight so she could get into the lingerie. Ivan got to try out the new sectional they'd purchased a few weeks earlier."

"For how long?"

"Four nights."

She winced. "Ouch."

"Yeah, ouch. He didn't talk to me for a week. I guess I don't blame him."

"So this Dr. Love business . . . that's what it's about? You give fighting couples advice on how to get to the making-up stage?"

"Yep."

"Yet you've never been married?"

"Nope." He shrugged his broad shoulders. "I didn't go looking for the title. It just sort of found me."

"Amazing." Kasidy didn't attempt to hide her wonder.

He looked askew at her. "Skeptical?"

She nodded. "Yep. I mean, that's like a baby doctor writing a book on how to raise kids when he doesn't have any. How could he possibly know?"

He pretended to be offended. "Hey! I've had relationships."

"Oh, yeah?" Kasidy had never enjoyed arguing with anyone more, she realized. "How many?"

"A few."

"Serious ones?" She held her breath, hoping to appear casual, instead of hanging on to his every word. The man's ego was big enough, thank you very much.

Wyatt wanted to lie—she saw it in his eyes. Instead, he smiled ruefully and said, "Okay, I've had one serious relationship."

"Live in?"

"Six months. She got tired of my jokes."

"Yeah, right." Kasidy rolled her eyes. "I'll bet *you* were the one who got tired first." She couldn't imagine a woman getting tired of Wyatt.

His eyebrows rose. "Have you been talking to my mother?"

"No. I mean, I talked to her, but not about you."

"It's my turn to ask questions. Turnabout's fair play."

Kasidy braced herself.

"How about you? How many serious relationships have you been in?"

"I don't go around calling myself Dr. Love," Kasidy hedged.

He didn't fall for it. "How many?"

There wasn't a doubt in Kasidy's mind that she could fall back on her father's teachings and tell a big whooper that she knew he would believe.

But this time she couldn't. This time, she didn't want to. Besides, what could be the harm in telling him? He didn't know who she was and wasn't likely to figure it out. So she heaved a big, courageous sigh and blurted it out. "None."

She'd stunned him. He was staring at her, waiting for the punch line. Well, he'd have to wait a hell of a long time, because there wasn't one.

Finally, he must have realized that she wasn't going to change her answer. His eyes darkened. Slowly, he brought his hands down from behind his neck and settled one arm along the back of the sofa.

She felt the very tips of his fingers in her hair. She shivered.

"Are you teasing me, Kasidy?" he asked softly.

"No."

"Are you gay?"

She punched him in the stomach, lightly. "No!" Then, flushing, she added, "You should know that by now."

He waited a beat, then said, "Are you trying to tell me that you're a virgin?"

"No!" Her face got hotter. "I've had sex, I just haven't had a serious relationship. You don't have to love someone to have sex." The moment the words were out, she wished them back.

Too late. Wyatt was wearing that naughty, knee-weakening grin again. "That's exactly what I was trying to tell *you*." He cupped the back of her neck and applied pressure, trying to bring her face to his.

Kasidy hung back. They were in an attic, alone on a sofa. She didn't trust her own willpower—which was sadly lacking when it came to resisting Wyatt's sex appeal. "I'm not having sex with you, Wyatt." Well, she could have sounded a bit more forceful, she realized.

"So you keep telling me," Wyatt murmured, his gaze focused on her mouth. Inch by inch, he kept bringing her closer. "I want to taste you. Your lips are so damned kissable."

Oh, why couldn't he say something crude? Then she'd have a better chance of resisting him. Besides, she wanted to kiss him, too. They didn't have to have sex. Kissing didn't necessarily lead to sex, right?

She watched, hypnotized by the heat in his gaze, as his mouth came closer and closer. Just as their lips were on the verge of touching, panic seized her. She shoved him away and bolted for the door. This was wrong. He'd been her grandmother's boyfriend!

The old-fashioned doorknob she grabbed felt cold against her hot palm. She twisted, but the knob only gave slightly either way. It was locked! Desperately, she jiggled it to and fro, wishing Wyatt wasn't behind her so that she could use the handy tool in her pocket.

Wyatt's warm breath washed over her neck, making her shiver. She froze, her heart pounding hard.

"Kasidy," he whispered in her ear, his voice warm with amusement and a touch of concern. "I'm not going to attack you, silly."

Of course he wasn't, Kasidy thought, closing her eyes in despair. But she couldn't guarantee that *she* wouldn't attack *him!*

Dillon found Callie in the laundry room, sitting on the washing machine as it shook and wiggled beneath her. She shot him an accusing look.

"I asked you to level this stupid thing weeks ago," she said, her voice jiggling with the washer.

His heart missed a beat as he studied his wife. A wisp of dark hair had fallen from her ponytail over her brow. She had an orange stain—sweet potatoes or peaches, Dillon mused—on her T-shirt over her left breast, and more on her navy shorts. Her feet were bare, and as Dillon's heated gaze fell to her toenails, he recalled with a rush of desire the night he'd applied the hot pink nail polish for her. It was what happened afterward that had him hyperventilating.

Slowly, he let his gaze travel back up her body to her face. His lips lifted in a crooked grin. "I missed you too," he said softly, advancing in her direction.

She threw up both hands, trying not to smile. "Hold it! You leave me here alone with the twins, and you think you can just waltz in here and expect me to leap into your arms?"

"Yes," Dillon said without conceit. His brow shot up. He'd almost reached her. "Isn't that exactly what you're going to do?"

Instead of answering, Callie leaned forward and wrapped her legs around his waist. The next few moments were silent as they kissed. Finally, she lifted her head and sighed. "God, I missed you!"

A husky chuckle rumbled through his chest. "I've only been gone twenty-four hours."

"That's twenty-four hours too long," Callie said with feeling. "Jada and Kaden have been running through the house looking for you. They think you're hiding."

Dillon drew his hands along her ribcage and around, cupping her breasts. He swallowed a moan. As badly as he wanted to see his children, he was a man who knew his priorities. "Are they asleep?"

96

"Better." Callie smiled and leaned into his caress. "Luke and Lydia took them to the park. How long have you got?"

"Mmm. An hour or two at the most. Maybe less, if Kasidy and Wyatt start making noise."

Callie narrowed her eyes at the mischievous glint in her husband's eyes. She knew that look. "What did you do, Dillon?"

A grin exploded on his face. "I locked them in the attic." He laughed at her shocked expression. "Hey, they needed some time alone, darlin'."

Still looking at him as if he were a stranger, Callie shook her head. "You're really getting into this, aren't you? And it's not fair, you know. *You* get to have all the fun. *I* have to stay home and get plastered with baby food, and keep the washer from dancing into the hall."

Dillon's smile faltered. "Well, it's not all fun and games, sweetheart. Those damned dogs hate me." Quickly, he told her about the destruction of his precious *Playboy* magazine, the toothbrush, and his shoes. By the time he finished, Callie was laughing and clutching her side. "It's not *that* damned funny," he growled playfully, tickling her.

She shrieked and grabbed at his hands. "Uncle! Uncle! Okay, I'll stop laughing. I swear." She went boneless against him. Her voice was muffled against his shoulder as she said, "Are you absolutely positive she's the one? Because if you're not sure, then you're going to owe me."

"I'm positive." He stroked her back, inhaling her sweet scent. She smelled like peaches . . . and heaven. Without hesitation, he let her in on a little secret.

"Wyatt confessed to me that he couldn't control himself around her."

Callie shot upright, her eyes wide. "Oh my God. He *is* in love, isn't he? But how do you think he'll react when he finds out she's the granddaughter?" She frowned thoughtfully. "You know, some men are intimidated by wealthy women."

"She doesn't want the inheritance," Dillon reminded her.

"That's insane. If she doesn't want it, she could give it to charity or something. I wonder why she's there, if she doesn't want the money?"

"I don't know, but I intend to find out."

Sighing, Callie began to nuzzle his neck. "How long are we going to be separated?"

"Not any longer than we have to," Dillon murmured, growing aroused by her heated lips against his skin. "I don't think he's suspicious, but just as a precaution, I'm going to send Isabelle over tomorrow night to babysit."

The washing machine stopped abruptly. Callie allowed Dillon to lift her away. She struggled to remember the thread of the conversation. "Why?"

"I think you should pay Mrs. Scuttle a visit, and reinforce our story. Make a scene. Slap me or something."

The idea intrigued Callie. "You really think Wyatt will fall for it?" She sounded doubtful. Wyatt knew how much in love they were. In fact, he'd known before *they* had figured it out.

Dillon chuckled gleefully. "Trust me, honey. A rock the size of our house could fall on Wyatt, and he'd still never believe I was behind this. I'm too up-tight, remember?"

"Mmm." Callie trailed her hand between them and cupped his hard length. "Not on my watch, you aren't," she murmured. "Take me to bed, Dil."

"I thought you'd never ask."

"I'm not asking."

"Oh. My bad."

"Speaking of bad . . ." She tightened her legs around him and moaned.

Dillon didn't need to be told twice.

CHAPTER 10

"This house is full of people—uninvited people—and not a soul has noticed us missing," Wyatt grumbled, checking his watch again.

An hour. He'd been cooped up in an attic with a woman who set his world on fire for a solid . . . torturous . . . frustrating hour.

He'd promised he would keep his hands and lips to himself.

What had possessed him to make that insane promise? Had it been the naked vulnerability he'd seen in her eyes? Or had it been the fear in her expression?

Or was he just stupid?

Since when did kissing equal sex?

Wyatt sighed to himself. He knew the answer to that one. Since he'd met Kasidy, that's when.

The tempting, luscious blond bombshell on the sofa cleared her throat.

"Maybe we should make some noise," she suggested.

Before Wyatt could think, his eyebrows shot up suggestively. She blushed, and he silently cursed his

100

lack of control. By her own admission, Kasidy wasn't very experienced. He needed to keep that in mind. The trouble was, remembering that particularly provocative fact made him want her even more.

He was damned either way.

With extreme effort, he pulled his eyebrows back down. "My mother's in the kitchen—three stories down—and my sister and her friends are walking the dogs. That leaves Mrs. Scuttle, who can't hear worth a flip, although she won't admit it."

"And your point is?"

Wyatt had to smile at her cheeky question. "My point is, making noise would be useless." Unless, of course, they were making noise while they were making love. Then that wouldn't be useless. It would be very arousing.

"Tell me more about your family," Kasidy prompted.

He watched as she pulled her knees to her chin and regarded him with sultry green eyes. She was a mystery, and he yearned with every fiber of his being to delve below the surface and discover her secrets.

Each and every one of them. Especially the erotic ones.

That was it, he decided wryly. Kasidy was turning him into a lecher. A bonafide, dirty young man. But then, she already believed he was.

His smile was slow, with hidden secrets of his own as he said, "Mom's in college. She's going to be a teacher. Dad died when we were teenagers, so she's getting a late start on her career. Dillon and I manage a bar, and I work as an escort for Mr. Complete part-time."

"What's it like, being an escort?"

Wyatt hid his surprise at her question. Did he dare to hope she was beginning to believe that she might have been wrong about him? He shrugged. "It's fun, for the most part. Occasionally, I get a contrary client who can't be pleased." He almost bit his tongue, cursing to himself. No matter what he said, it was the wrong thing, and he could tell by the way she swiftly lowered her lashes to conceal her expression that she had definitely drawn her own conclusions.

An old, familiar anger reared its ugly head. He was beginning to think it was useless trying to convince her that he wasn't a gigolo. Maybe he should just concentrate on seducing her and to hell with her narrow-minded opinion of him.

"How about you?" he asked, struggling with the urge to give the devil his due. "The information on your application didn't list an emergency number."

Her expression remained veiled as she said, "Pretty much the same story. My mother died when I was a teenager. My dad's still alive. No siblings, though."

He caught the wistful note in her voice and managed a wry grin. "Don't tell me that you envy me. Having an identical twin is a pain in the butt."

Her brow rose. "Is that why you wear contacts, because you have an identity crisis?"

Wyatt let out a low, sarcastic whistle. "Wow. You've missed your calling. You should have gone into psychiatry."

This time her chin shot out. "Maybe I did. You don't know anything about me."

Her defensive comment sparked Wyatt's anger again, even as it sparked his curiosity. He shuttered his own expression. Tit for tat. "That's right, I don't. And unless you Googled me on the Internet, you don't know me, either. You might *think* you do, but you don't." His voice softened on the outside, but hardened on the inside. "In fact, I can safely say that you haven't gotten one single thing right about me yet."

Just as softly, she said, "Is that right?"

Even more softly, Wyatt said, "That's right."

Without realizing how they got there, Wyatt became aware that they were sitting nearly nose to nose in the middle of the sofa, like two children on the verge of a brawl. The air between them seemed to crackle with electricity.

Never, ever, had a woman gotten under his skin the way Kasidy was doing. Anger, desire, intrigue, mystery . . . she evoked emotions rusty from disuse.

Her lips were shiny with moisture. Wyatt licked his own and whispered, "Truth or dare."

Her eyelashes fluttered up, revealing her confusion. "What?"

"Truth or dare," Wyatt repeated. "I believe it's a popular game at slumber parties."

She blinked at him. "I wouldn't know. I've never been to a slumber party."

Wyatt didn't bother hiding his shock. His younger sister had practically invented the expression "slumber party," so it was difficult for him to believe that he was sitting beside a woman who'd never been to one. "For Pete's sake," he blurted out. "Have you been living in a convent?" He watched with interest as a flush darkened her cheeks.

With a careless shrug, she looked away. "My parents were very strict. Besides, I wasn't into that girlie stuff."

Her bravado didn't fool Wyatt. He felt a tug at his heart strings for the yearning she couldn't completely hide. "I don't mean to knock your parents, but—"

"Then don't," she snapped, whipping her head around to glare at him at close range. "You don't know them. They had their reasons for being so protective of me."

"Such as?" Wyatt demanded, still thinking about the little girl who'd never been to a slumber party.

"They—" She pressed her pretty lips closed, heaved a deep sigh, then said, "They had their reasons, okay?"

"Have you always been this prickly?"

"Yes."

"Have you always been so narrow-minded and quick to judge?" To Wyatt's great satisfaction, the question stumped her. She even looked a tiny bit ashamed.

"I'm not narrow-minded," she muttered.

"Oh, yeah?" When she tried to look away, Wyatt broke his promise and took her face in his hand, gently forcing her to look at him. Then he broke another promise—one to himself. "Then why can't you consider the possibility that you're wrong about me?" He saw immediately that he didn't have to spell it out for her; she knew exactly what he was talking about.

For a long moment, she simply stared at him, as if debating her response. Finally, she disengaged his hand and leaned back. She put her knees back to her chest. "Because I heard you that day," she said slowly, reluctantly. "You described the disgusting details of your . . . *relationship* with Mrs. Hancock to that lawyer."

Wyatt was so stunned by her revelation, he couldn't speak.

But he could laugh. And laugh he did, until tears streamed down his face and his side began to hurt. He tumbled from the couch and onto the floor, still laughing.

That's where his mother found him when she burst into the attic.

"Wyatt David Love!" Mary admonished, hands on hips. "I've been looking everywhere for you. The temp service sent someone over to take Louise's place." She stepped aside to reveal the woman standing behind her.

Wyatt stopped laughing. He rolled to his feet in one smooth motion, gaping at the curvy brunette regarding him with dark brown eyes.

She was wearing a miniskirt and a halter top, and high heels. *Red* heels, to be exact. The hooker red matched her lipstick and her nail polish.

It was a joke. It had to be a joke.

Then he opened his big mouth and said, "*You're* the housekeeper?"

Mary shook her finger at him. "Watch your manners, Wyatt."

Behind Wyatt, Kasidy muttered sarcastically, "Yeah, watch your manners, *Lover Boy*."

The brunette stepped forward, her gaze literally eating him alive. In a smoky voice, she drawled, "I'm very good at what I do, Mr. Love."

Wyatt was still waiting for his mother to burst into laughter and yell, "Gotcha!" when Kasidy rose from the sofa and came into his line of vision.

Her jaw was set, and her eyes brimmed with scorn

as she looked from the brunette to Wyatt. "Sounds like a match made in heaven," she said, then stalked from the attic with her head held high and that stubborn little chin leading the way.

"Son of a bitch," Wyatt ground out, then headed after her.

Mary hooked his arm along the way, stopping him. "Let me go talk to her."

He looked into his mother's eyes, searching for amusement, or guile, anything to indicate she was in on the joke. Dismayed, he realized she was serious. "But you don't know what she's mad about," he said.

His mother's brows shot upward. "Wanna bet? Had we been wealthy, do you think I would have let your father hire someone who looked like her?" She glanced at the brunette, who frowned and opened her mouth to argue. Mary shushed her. "Take my advice. Send her back and request someone older . . . and uglier."

"Hey, that's not fair!" the brunette protested. "I can't help it that I'm gorgeous."

Wyatt knew his mother was right. He knew he should send the sex kitten back and get someone more like Louise, someone less threatening.

But he was damned tired of trying to convince that stubborn little narrow-minded spitfire that he wasn't what she thought he was. It was becoming more and more obvious that she *wanted* to think the worst of him.

So he would give her the worst. What did he have to lose?

* * *

Kasidy took out her list and checked off the attic. So far she'd searched the dogs' room, her own room, the hall closet, and now the attic.

She had a lot of rooms left, but the most likely place was the one room she couldn't get to—her grandmother's room. It was locked, not that the lock posed a problem. Getting the time to pick that lock and get inside without anyone seeing her was the problem.

The fact that it was kept locked indicated to Kasidy that her grandmother's safe was in that room. Why else would Wyatt keep it locked?

A knock at the door made her jump. She quickly hid her notepad beneath her butt. "Come in," she called, praying it wasn't Wyatt. She didn't want to see him or talk to him until she got a grip on her jealousy. Sheesh. A dead giveaway. As if the man's ego wasn't big enough!

Kasidy held her breath as her bedroom door slowly opened.

When she saw that it was Mary, she exhaled in a relieved rush.

"Do you have a moment?" Mary asked, shutting the door behind her.

"Yeah." Kasidy grew nervous again. This was Wyatt's mother. Was she coming to berate her about upsetting her son? The thought made Kasidy flush with humiliation. As she watched, Mary sat on the bed and kicked her knee up, making herself comfortable.

She shot Kasidy a friendly smile. "I don't know where to start."

Since Kasidy didn't have an inkling, she kept silent.

"I guess I should start with the day you met Wyatt

and Dillon, in the library during the reading of the will."

Kasidy stiffened.

Mary's smile widened. "Oh, yes. I know all about it. It's almost impossible for the boys to keep secrets from me."

Boys? Kasidy begged to differ. But she didn't.

"And you might find this hard to believe, but normally I don't interfere in their love lives. But this has gone on long enough."

Kasidy blinked in confusion. She had to ask. "What's gone on long enough?"

"You believing my son is a gigolo, and that he was Mrs. Hancock's lover."

Before she could swallow it, a gasp escaped Kasidy. Mary plowed on before Kasidy could respond.

"It's okay, I understand perfectly how and why you believe this. You heard it straight from the horse's mouth, so to speak." Mary sighed. "What you don't know is that Wyatt's very touchy about the subject of his line of work. It's about the only thing that can make him blow his stack, and when Wyatt gets angry, he's slow to cool. His pride gets in the way. That's what happened that day in the study. That cow of a lawyer made a few comments about his relationship with Mrs. Hancock, and Wyatt went postal on her, deliberately shocking her with lurid, *fictional* details of his alleged sex life with Mrs. Hancock. Dillon told me about it, and when I realized what you believed, I figured the only way you could be convinced otherwise is to hear the truth from someone else."

That would definitely explain Wyatt's uncontrollable laughter. Before she could get too excited at the prospect of being wrong about Wyatt, Kasidy said cautiously, "You're his mother. What if that's the story they told you, because that's what they want *you* to believe?"

Mary spread her hands. "What would it take to convince you? Are you just stubborn, or are you really that narrow-minded?"

Her question stung Kasidy. She bit her bottom lip, choosing her words with care. She liked this woman, and wanted her to understand. "I'm sorry. I don't trust easily."

"You've been hurt."

Kasidy shook her head. "Not in the way you're probably thinking." She wished she could trust Mary enough to talk to her about her grandmother, but she knew it was too risky. After she found the tape and destroyed it, she could sing like a canary.

In the meantime, she would have to make do. Mix fabrication with a little truth to make it believable. "My dad made me a lot of promises that he didn't keep." *Please don't ask more questions*. Kasidy didn't want to keep lying to Mary.

"Okay, that would explain the reason for your distrust of men." Mary hooked her hair behind her ear and patted an imaginary wrinkle from the satin comforter on the bed. Finally, she looked at Kasidy again and said bluntly, "But that doesn't explain why you don't believe a middle-aged mother of three who knows for a *fact* that her son is not a gigolo, or a boy toy, or whatever you want to call it."

"It doesn't matter."

"It matters to Wyatt, and it matters to me."

"I don't want to get involved with . . . anyone," Kasidy said with a hint of desperation. Who was she trying to convince?

"Honey," Mary said gently, and without conceit, "if Wyatt wants you, Wyatt will have you."

Stunned, Kasidy simply stared at Mary.

Mary laughed at her expression. "I'm sorry, I shouldn't have shocked you, and I should have been more specific. I meant that if he's in love with you, then you don't stand a chance."

"What if I don't love him?" Kasidy blurted out, then flushed to the roots of her hair. Talking to Mary wasn't the same as talking to Nana Jo. This was Wyatt's *mother*.

"You will," Mary said with amused conviction. "Based on what I hear from his past lady friends, he's completely irresistible." With that, she rose from the bed and walked to the door.

When she reached it, she turned. "I think it's only fair to tell you that Wyatt intends to keep the brunette on as a housekeeper—to make you jealous. You've wounded him, Kas, and Wyatt's like a big ole bear when he gets wounded." She winked at Kasidy. "Now you know something that he doesn't."

CHAPTER 11

Grand Central Station. That was exactly what Wyatt decided the mansion should be called as he strode across the foyer to answer the door—again. Maybe he should take half his pay and hire himself a damned butler.

It wasn't until he saw Callie standing on the threshold, and noticed her red-rimmed eyes, that Wyatt realized he hadn't asked his brother what their fight was about.

Dr. Love was definitely falling down on the job.

"Callie!" Wyatt took her hand and tugged her inside for a gentle, brotherly hug. He pulled back and searched her solemn face, frowning at the bruised shadows under her eyes. "What's up with my favorite sister-in-law, huh?"

Callie smiled wanly. "I'm your *only* sister-in-law, you big goof."

He shot her a naughty grin. "That you are, but you're still my favorite. Are you here to see Dillon?"

Wrong question, Wyatt realized as he watched her eyes cloud over and her mouth turn down. He mentally kicked himself for being so wrapped up in his own life that he'd forgotten the people he loved.

All for a stubborn, narrow-minded spitfire who made him want to tear open his shirt and beat on his chest like an enraged gorilla.

"I'm not here to see *him*," Callie said with a telltale little lift of her chin. "I'm here to see Mrs. Scuttle."

"What's going on, Callie?" He wrapped an affectionate hand around her arm to keep her in place. "What has my brother done this time?"

Callie grimaced. "He hasn't told you?"

Wyatt wallowed in good old-fashioned shame. "Um, I haven't had time to ask him."

"Well, he probably won't tell you anyway," Callie said tartly. "He'll be too embarrassed."

Now Wyatt's curiosity was piqued. "Tell me what?"

"Uh-uh. You won't hear from me. If you want to know, ask *him*. I don't care if I ever speak to him again."

Leaving Wyatt gaping after her, she headed for the stairs. It took a moment for Wyatt to wonder how she knew where to find the secretary, but then he realized any number of people could have told her, since a large number of people now shared the house with him.

Deciding now was as good a time as any to find out what was going on between Callie and Dillon, Wyatt went in search of his brother. He'd last seen him in the kitchen, helping his mother clean up after dinner.

The new housekeeper, Bridget, had been sitting at the table filing her nails. He was definitely going to have to have a word with her, as well. When she'd stated she was good at what she did, Wyatt suspected the brunette hadn't been talking about housekeeping.

Why would the temp agency send over a *Baywatch* babe, instead of the middle-aged professional he'd asked for? It was almost as if . . . nah, Dillon wouldn't stoop that low just for kicks. Besides, if Callie's forlorn expression was anything to go by, Dillon had bigger fish to fry.

Mary was drying the last dish when Wyatt walked into the kitchen. Frowning, he glanced around in search of Dillon. Hearing voices from the pantry, he headed in that direction.

"Wait!" his mother cried.

The sound of a dish breaking startled Wyatt more than his mother's urgent shout. He stopped in his tracks, staring at his mother in surprise. "What?"

"Um, I wanted to talk to you," she said, sounding suspiciously nervous as she bent to pick up the broken pieces of the plate she'd dropped.

"Can it wait?" Wyatt looked toward the pantry just as Dillon and Bridget emerged. They were laughing together. *Laughing* together. His twin. The one who had to be coaxed into laughter. His brother, the one with the wife and two kids.

Dumbfounded, Wyatt stared at the blood-red nails curled intimately around Dillon's arm. He was still staring when the couple caught sight of him.

A guilty flush rose up along Dillon's cheeks. Bridget, however, didn't look a bit guilty. She looked more like the cat that ate the canary. Smug and . . . sated.

Two astounding realizations occurred to Wyatt in that frozen instant of time.

Dillon had been in the pantry with the sex kitten, while his wife was upstairs visiting Mrs. Scuttle.

And his *mother* had known about it. Had even tried to cover for him.

Had the world gone mad?

At least now he had a strong—and disgusting—inkling of the trouble between Callie and Dillon. And now he knew why Dillon hadn't told him.

Wyatt pointed a shaky, righteous finger at Bridget, then to the back door. "Out!" he yelled. "You are fired!"

"But—"

"Out! Out! Out!"

Some of the rage he was feeling must have shown on his face, for Bridget shot a hasty glance at Dillon, then hightailed it to the back door. It slammed hard behind her. From the corner of his eye, Wyatt saw his mother jump at the sound.

Good. She *should* feel jumpy.

To Dillon, he growled, "Have you lost your mind? Callie's upstairs with Mrs. Scuttle, and you're down here with—doing God knows what with that—that man-eater!"

Dillon had recovered, apparently. He folded his arms and said calmly, "We were talking, bro. Just talking."

But Wyatt wasn't listening. He whirled on his mother, who blanched, but held her ground. "And you!" He pointed an accusing finger at her. It was still trembling, he noted. "You knew he was in there with that—that floozy!"

"Housekeeper," Mary dared to correct, albeit in a

small voice. "She's a housekeeper, ordered to *your* specifications."

Wyatt felt his eyes bulge. "I did *not* order a *Baywatch* Bimbo! I ordered a woman with experience"—he glared at Dillon when Dillon snickered at that one—"in housekeeping," he finished in a roar.

"Lower your voice," Mary ordered, sounding more like herself, instead of the shameless mom she'd been moments ago.

Since Wyatt felt on the verge of a stroke, he attempted to do just that. But not because he wanted to. Oh, no. He wanted to keep shouting and accusing. How could Dillon do this to Callie? How could their own mother be a part of it?

"Look, Wyatt," Dillon said. "I think, in light of what you think you know, that I should tell you—"

"Tell it to Callie," Wyatt snarled. "And go home with your wife. You're no longer welcome here." He glared long and hard at his mother, but didn't quite have what it took to order his own mother out of the house. "Shame on you," he said instead, and stalked from the kitchen.

He was fed up, he decided as he stomped his way to Kasidy's room. Fed up with lies and secrets and madness and stubborn wenches believing the worst about him.

When he reached her bedroom door, he pounded on it hard enough to make the door quake beneath his fist.

A startled Kasidy opened it just as he was about to pound again. Her big green eyes regarded him warily.

She *should* be wary, Wyatt thought savagely. He

grabbed her arm and began to pull her in the direction of the front door. "You're coming with me," he said. "We're going to have this out once and for all."

Kasidy tried to wriggle loose from his grip. "Stop! Wait! Where are you taking me?"

Without looking around, Wyatt jerked open the front door. He nearly barreled into Greg, a blond giant of a man who worked for Mr. Complete. Muttering a curse, he glared at the poor, unsuspecting Greg.

"Let me guess. You and Ramon had a fight and you need a place to stay. No problem. Take your pick of the rooms, and I'll get back to you later."

Not bothering to wait for an answer, he pulled Kasidy along through the door, around the stunned Greg.

"Where are you taking me?" she asked again, this time with a hint of desperation.

"To the garage, where we can talk in private," Wyatt snapped. It was about the only place not overrun with friends, dogs, and relatives.

"No! Not the garage!" Kasidy wailed in a panicky voice. She renewed her efforts to break free.

Wyatt stopped, turned around, and hoisted her in his arms.

The kid gloves were off: This time, he was going to make her listen.

"Well, *that* was an unexpected development," Dillon said, struggling with laughter. His gaze met his mother's, who was biting her bottom lip, obviously torn between pity and amusement.

They both lost it at the same time.

"Oh my God," Dillon gasped out, clutching his middle. "He actually thought I was messing around with Bridget!"

"Yes," Mary said between gasps of laughter. "And he thought *I* was covering for you!"

"What's going on?" Greg asked from the kitchen doorway. "I just watched Wyatt cart some woman off like he was Tarzan or something."

Greg's bemused comment sent Dillon and Mary off into new gales of laughter, so it was some moments before Dillon could satisfy Greg's curiosity. He caught the dish towel his mother pitched to him and wiped his streaming eyes, trying to compose himself.

Chuckles still escaped him as he explained, "I was coaching the actress we'd hired to pretend to be the new housekeeper when Wyatt caught us in the pantry and drew his own nasty conclusions."

"He thought you and she were—" Greg scratched his head. "That doesn't sound like Wyatt."

"No, it doesn't," Dillon agreed, grinning at Mary. "But he's not thinking too clearly right now, thanks to Kasidy."

"Kasidy would be . . . the blonde he was carrying off?" Greg asked, a slow grin curving his mouth. "Man, she sure was freaked out."

Over their laughter came the sound of something crashing to the floor.

The sound came from above, from Mrs. Scuttle's room.

Dillon sobered, glancing at the ceiling.

"I wonder what that was?" Mary mused out loud.

"Sounded like someone fell," Greg said.

"Crap," Dillon muttered, racing from the kitchen.

He took the stairs two at a time, aware that Greg and Mary were on his heels. Without knocking, he barged into Mrs. Scuttle's room.

Callie stood in the middle of the room, staring at the closed bathroom door as if it was the portal to hell. She glanced at Dillon. "I think she might have fallen," she said, looking worried. "Someone should check."

"Yeah," Dillon agreed. "Someone should check it out." It just wouldn't be him. He turned to Greg.

Greg shook his head. "Uh-uh. Not me. I'm not going in there."

Mary didn't give them a chance to focus on her. "No way."

Downstairs, a door slammed. They all heard Isabelle's clear, spontaneous laughter, followed by the excited barking of the dogs.

Dillon shot his mother a hopeful look.

She frowned. "She's just a baby, Dil. You should be ashamed."

"Young people heal quicker," Callie suggested, not looking Mary in the eye.

"She could hold a pillow in front of herself," Greg volunteered shamelessly.

With an exasperated sigh, Mary stalked to the bathroom door and knocked. "Mrs. Scuttle? Are you okay in there?"

It was a long, suspense-filled moment before Mrs. Scuttle replied, her voice uncharacteristically low. "No, I'm not okay. I'm stuck."

"Stuck?" Mary shot the others a puzzled look. "Stuck in what way?" She stumbled back as the secretary bawled through the doorway.

"I'm stuck in the blasted toilet, you nitwit!"

"Oh, Lord," Callie breathed.

Her heartfelt sentiment was echoed by the others.

Kasidy feared her legs wouldn't hold her when Wyatt finally put her down. She wavered unsteadily, reaching out to catch the side mirror of his truck to support herself. "Why did you bring me out here?" she asked, wondering if he could hear the frantic pounding of her heart.

Or smell the lust that must be coming off her in pungent waves. He couldn't possibly know that making love in the garage was one of her fantasies . . . could he?

Wyatt leaned against Dillon's SUV and folded his arms. "Because this is where I kissed you for the first time. Maybe the place is charmed."

Charmed. Kasidy took a deep breath. That was *one* way to put it. She searched for moisture in her mouth and found none.

She had a sneaky feeling she knew where it had all pooled.

"Kasidy . . . that day in the study. I made up those lies to shock the lawyer. She'd made me mad with her nasty insinuations. Mrs. Hancock was eccentric, yes, but she was a fine woman. She gave thousands of dollars a year to Hope House, a homeless shelter funded by a friend of mine, not to mention other various charities. She single-handedly supported one of the humane societies in town, and in the last ten years, she put seventeen underprivileged kids through college."

Kasidy wanted to cover her ears. She didn't want

119

to hear *nice* things about her grandmother. Wyatt wasn't describing the woman she knew; he was describing a stranger. A stranger who, even in death, couldn't leave her family alone.

"Because I *did* admire her—greatly—I shouldn't have said those things about her," Wyatt said with quiet regret. His earlier anger seemed to have vanished.

Now he just sounded plain old weary.

"In any case, I wasn't her gigolo, or her lover. In fact, she made no bones about the fact that she had given her heart away a long time ago."

The revelation jolted Kasidy. Her grandfather had died before Kasidy was born. "You mean . . . her husband?" she asked. As far as she knew, her grandmother had never remarried.

His teeth gleamed in a quick, lethal smile. "Nope. She married *him* for his money. As for the mystery man who stole her heart, she never mentioned him by name."

Although she had other, more pressing things on her mind, Kasidy had one more question she needed to ask Wyatt. "If you two weren't that . . . close, why do you suppose she put you in charge of her estate?"

His husky laugh kicked her heart into overdrive.

"Amelia had a weird sense of humor. She knew what people would think, and she knew how much that bothered me. This is her idea of a joke."

Kasidy shifted her butt against the truck and crossed her ankles. She felt suddenly very, very shy and not at all certain she was equipped to handle the hunk of man in front of her.

But she was going to try. Oh, yeah. She was definitely going to try.

"I, um, guess I owe you a big fat apology," she said, staring at his chin. He had a strong, square jaw to go with his wide, sensuous mouth.

"Yeah, I guess you do." When she stiffened, he chuckled and held out his arms. "Come here, you little spitfire."

She licked her dry lips and hung back. Her body wanted to leap into his arms and get down to business, but her inexperienced mind still had hurdles to get over. What did she know about satisfying a man like Wyatt? What made her think—that she *could?*

"Kasidy?"

She heard the question in his low, deep voice, but didn't know how to answer. "I'm, um, afraid I might disappoint you," she mumbled in a voice barely above a whisper.

"You could never disappoint me," he said.

She heard the scuff of his sandals against the concrete, and braced herself for his touch. Did he know how much she wanted him? Did he? Did he have the slightest idea how badly she wanted to shed her inhibitions and jump in with both feet?

He reached her, stretching his arms around her waist and tugging her gently to him until they stood hip to hip, thigh to thigh, chest to chest.

Then he rested his chin on top of her head and sighed as if he'd waited his entire life to do just that.

Kasidy began to tremble.

CHAPTER 12

"It's not tight enough."

"Can you do anything about it?"

"I don't know." Kasidy wiggled around, grunting from the effort. "I don't think it's big enough. Can you get me a bigger one?"

"I don't know. I don't think I *have* a bigger one. Do you think we should give up?"

"No way. I'm too close. You can't leave me hanging like this, so will you please look? If we can't make it work, I'll be thinking about it all day."

"What if it doesn't fit?"

Kasidy stuck her head out from under the Dodge truck to give him a reassuring smile. "Then we'll keep trying until we find one that fits. One way or another, I'll stop this leak."

It wasn't the conversation Wyatt had had in mind when he dragged Kasidy to the garage, but it was definitely fascinating.

A woman who could work on cars. How lucky could a guy get? He found the big wrench she needed and brought it to her, hunkering down so that he could watch her in motion. The drop light they'd found in the small storage room illuminated the underside of the truck—and Kasidy. He could see the outline of her nipples straining against the T-shirt, and the beads of sweat gathering on her upper lip.

He was slightly chagrined to see her arm muscles come into play as she strained to tighten the brake line. Either she worked out, he mused, or she did this kind of work often. He suspected the later, since she was perfectly, wonderfully soft in all the right places. Well, all the places *he* had touched, anyway.

There were plenty more he planned on testing when the time was right. When he'd felt her trembling against him, something warm had blossomed inside him, mellowing his anger and frustration. By her own admission, she was inexperienced. By her own admission, she was afraid she'd disappoint him. For those two reasons alone, Wyatt knew he could not rush her.

When she wanted him as much as he wanted her, when she was ready and willing, then they would make love. In the meantime, he would woo her the old-fashioned way, because he'd realized something tonight: Kasidy was an old-fashioned girl.

From what she'd told him, she'd been cheated out of a normal childhood. Wyatt decided he wasn't going to cheat her out of her first romance. He wasn't ready to call it love, not yet, but he no longer liked the word "lust" in conjunction with what he felt for Kasidy.

It was something in between.

Perversely, he was now glad they were surrounded by people. He suspected it would take all of his concentration—and their interference—to keep his self-imposed vow.

"There. All done. Can you give me a hand?"

When Wyatt covered her small hand with his own and tugged, he felt the roughness of a callous against his palm. The creeper rolled smoothly across the concrete. Kasidy jumped nimbly to her feet and stood before him, her cheeks flushed, her eyes sparkling.

Wyatt grinned at her obvious enjoyment. "Something tells me that's not the first time you've repaired a brake line."

Her cheeks turned a bit darker. "Um, no. My dad's a mechanic. He taught me everything he knows."

His brow shot up to show that he was impressed. "Yet you were working for the phone company when I met you."

She held out her hands, palms up, to show him the grease stains. "If you were a woman, which job would *you* choose?"

"The one with the biggest . . . tools?" Wyatt said suggestively, wiggling his eyebrows for effect.

Kasidy laughed and grabbed a grease rag to wipe her hands. "You're bad."

"Baby, you ain't seen nothing yet," Wyatt promised her. He took the rag from her and threaded his fingers through hers, tugging her closer. "Come here, my little grease monkey, and let me kiss you."

She held back, a half-serious smile playing about her beautiful mouth. "You don't mind the grease and the sweat?"

"I'm strangely turned on," Wyatt admitted, yanking her close and fastening his mouth on hers. Her lips were hot, and soft and a little salty. The shy touch of her tongue against his own sent a jolt of heat right into his groin.

They were both breathless when they broke apart. Wyatt leaned his forehead against hers, staring into her darkened eyes. "We'd better get out of here before I forget myself."

"I wouldn't mind if you did," she said boldly, squeezing his hands when he tried to pull away.

Wyatt was tempted. Very, very tempted. After a moment of struggling with his conscience, he let out a short sigh and said, "I don't want to run the risk of you hating me in the morning."

"I wouldn't."

Again he hesitated. He could see the want in her eyes, feel her trembling, and knew that he could take her here and now, in the garage. But something had changed between them, and Wyatt was reluctant to screw that something up. He needed time to analyze it.

He'd told Mrs. Scuttle that Kasidy was special.

Until now, he hadn't realized that he'd meant it. She *was* special, somehow. He wanted to find out the how and the why of it.

She shrieked as he suddenly lifted her into his arms and began striding to the garage door. He tried to lighten his rejection by joking, "I carried you in here, I can carry you outta here."

Instead of answering, she stuck a very wet, very stimulating tongue in his ear.

Wyatt groaned.

Wyatt had paused on the threshold to punish Kasidy with a kiss.

Before his mouth could find hers, the front door opened and Dillon bellowed, "She's stuck in the toilet!"

In his shock, Wyatt nearly dropped Kasidy. She grabbed his shoulders on the way down to steady herself as he set her on her feet and confronted the lunatic before him. Obviously, the stress of his separation from Callie had gotten to Dillon.

Very calmly, Wyatt asked, "Who's stuck, Dil?"

Dillon ran a distracted hand through his hair—which was already standing on end. "Mrs. Scuttle, that's who. Someone left the toilet seat up, and she um, fell in."

A cold chill ran down Wyatt's spine. He'd used the bathroom after his talk with the secretary.

"Mrs. Scuttle thinks Bridget did it on purpose," Dillon added.

Wyatt knew he should feel ashamed for letting that one slide . . . but he wasn't. This was Mrs. Scuttle they were talking about. "Well, we'll just have to get her unstuck," Wyatt said, taking Kasidy's hand and stepping inside. True, he wasn't looking forward to the task, but a man had to do what a man had to do.

His twin put a hand on his chest. "She won't let anyone in, bro. Says she's too embarrassed."

Dismayed, Wyatt stared at Dillon. "Not even Mom?"

Dillon shook his head. "Nope. Not even *Callie*."

"Then who?" Wyatt asked.

"She said . . . she said it had to be someone she didn't know."

"You're kidding."

"Nope. I wished that I was." Dillon looked frazzled. "I don't know what to do, or whom to call."

Kasidy spoke for the first time since Dillon opened the door. "How about 911? Don't they respond to this type of emergency?"

Both men looked at Kasidy, Dillon with abject gratitude, and Wyatt with admiration.

Fifteen minutes later, Wyatt and Dillon answered the door to the paramedics. Wyatt was still upset with his twin, but right now they had a crisis on their hands. Later, he would deal with his two-timing brother.

"First of all," Wyatt said, studying the two men. "You need to wipe those smirks off your faces. It's for your own good."

"Yeah," Dillon added seriously, "and you need these." He handed the two bewildered paramedics two pairs of earplugs still in their packages.

When Wyatt reached for the bicycle helmets Kasidy held, one of the paramedics attempted a laugh. "Um, what are these for? You did say on the phone an old lady was stuck in the toilet, right?"

Wyatt exchanged a worried look with Dillon. He turned to the paramedics. "Okay, let's start over. If you go up there unprepared, you could get hurt."

"Is this a joke?"

"No," Dillon said. "She's not an old lady. Her name is Mrs. Scuttle, and you have to say it with reverence."

"With reverence? Is she crazy, or something?"

Before Wyatt could start over yet again, Kasidy stepped forward. "Look, guys. Mrs. Scuttle is eighty years old, and she's very sensitive about her age. She's also very sensitive about the fact that she's stuck in a toilet. Wouldn't *you* be?" When they slowly nodded, Kasidy continued. "Okay, then. You remember that, and you should be all right. No smirking. No laughing, and no comments about her age or the fact that she's stuck in a toilet."

"Got it. Now, if you'll just show us where she is, we'll get this taken care of."

Wyatt saw one paramedic wink at the other, and feared the unsuspecting men were doomed. Well, they had been properly warned and coached. As they started upstairs, Wyatt remembered the scarves in his hand. He waved them at the paramedics to get their attention. "Oh, wait. You have to put on these blindfolds."

"No way, man."

"Uh-uh."

With a shrug, Wyatt slung the scarves over his shoulder. "Suit yourselves, but don't say I didn't warn you."

Kasidy tugged at his arm. "Are you going up?"

He grinned down at her. "I wouldn't miss this for the world. Shall we?" It wasn't Mrs. Scuttle's humiliation that he was dying to see; it was the smug paramedics' *reaction* to her humiliation that he didn't want to miss.

He and Kasidy joined Callie, Dillon, Greg, Isabelle, her two friends, the dogs, and his mother on the landing outside Mrs. Scuttle's room.

They all watched as the bedroom door shut behind the paramedics. Everyone fell silent. Even the dogs appeared to be listening for sounds from within.

Just when Wyatt had begun to fear Mrs. Scuttle had killed the cocky paramedics outright, the bedroom door opened abruptly. They came out onto the landing and quietly closed the door behind them, as if they'd been visiting an invalid.

Or royalty.

One of the paramedics asked, "Which one of you is Wyatt?"

Wyatt felt a familiar cold chill race down his spine. Not for the first time in his life, he wanted to shove his twin forward and run for the hills. His mouth was dry as he croaked, "I am. Why?"

"Because she wants to see you. Seems she remembered something while she was, um, stuck in the toilet. Said she wanted to thank you."

Double crap, Wyatt thought with an inward groan as he went to face the music.

Kasidy was the only person who hadn't defected by the time Wyatt emerged from the bedroom. He looked around at the deserted landing and lifted an inquiring brow.

Realizing that he didn't appear to be physically hurt, Kasidy let out a relieved sigh. "Thank God," she said. "I was afraid she'd brain you with the plunger or something."

Wyatt's mouth kicked up in a rueful smile. "Me, too. But it was worse. She lectured me."

"Ouch."

He laughed. "Yeah, ouch. I'm fairly certain I'll never forget, in this lifetime, to lower the commode lid. Where is everybody?"

"Mary said she couldn't stand the sight of blood—

especially when it belonged to one of her children, Dillon had an errand to run, Isabelle and her friends went for a swim, the dogs are napping, and Greg is waiting for you in the library." Kasidy had to take a deep breath before she could continue. Damn, he was hot. "I think Greg's having problems with Ramon."

"Dreams, again?" Wyatt asked shrewdly.

Kasidy's mouth fell open. "Yes. How did you know?"

"Just a lucky guess."

"He says that Ramon had a dream that Jaws was after him. Now he wants Greg to have the tattoo removed." Because she really was confused—and curious—she asked, "I suppose that makes sense to you?"

Wyatt nodded. "Jaws is a shark tattooed on Greg's butt. I wonder if Ramon knows how painful it is to have a tattoo removed?"

They began to descend the stairway together. "I take it Ramon takes his dreams seriously?"

"That's an understatement," Wyatt muttered. "A couple years ago, he kept having a recurring dream about catching Greg with another man. He nearly drove Greg insane with it."

Kasidy matched Wyatt step for step. "Hmm. Maybe Greg should give him a taste of his own medicine and have a couple of bad dreams himself, show Ramon how crazy it can make him." He stopped abruptly on the stairs, casting her a look of such admiration that she blushed.

"Wow," he breathed, sounding sincere. "That's a great idea. Maybe we should starting calling you Mrs. Doctor Love."

Mrs. Love. Kasidy had to look away, lest her girlish thoughts show in her eyes and embarrass her further. What would it be like to be married to a man like Wyatt? To be with him all the time, to wake up next to him in the middle of the night and—

"Are you thinking about sex?"

She stumbled on the stairs. Wyatt wrapped his fingers around her arm to steady her. They burned like a branding iron against her sensitive skin, and his husky, knowing chuckle made her toes curl.

"I was just teasing."

She pretended to glare at him. "Yeah, I know, and it's not very nice. How would you like it if I teased you?"

His smoldering look made her belly quiver with need. "You do tease me, every time you look at me with those huge, want-filled eyes."

Her face felt on fire. So did her insides. "Am I that obvious?"

Without hesitation, he nodded, and followed it with a slow, naughty grin. "But I'm definitely not complaining."

When her knees went weak, Kasidy gave up and sat down on the stairs. She put her face in her hands and groaned.

"What's wrong?" he demanded, suddenly concerned.

Through her fingers, Kasidy muttered truthfully, "You make my knees weak."

Wyatt sat beside her and slid an arm around her shoulders. His mouth nuzzled her ear as he said with a humbleness that nearly did her in, "I don't think I've ever been so flattered in my life."

She peeped at him through her fingers. "Really?"

Gently, he removed her hands and kissed her. Hard and hungry, showing her exactly what she did to him.

"Oh, pu-lease," Isabelle cried from the bottom of the stairs. "Get a room, will ya?"

Kasidy thought it was an excellent idea. Now she just had to convince Wyatt that she didn't need time.

She needed *him*.

CHAPTER 13

The closet beneath the stairs was as big as the kitchen in Wyatt's apartment. It was filled with dusty hatboxes that resembled something out of a 1950s movie, and the wheelchair that had gotten Kasidy into trouble with Mrs. Scuttle. There were spiders, too, eyeing him belligerently from the dark corners of the closet.

It was as good a place as any for an ambush. People coming from the kitchen to the stairs had to pass by the closet, and he could possibly use the spiders as a form of torture, should his prey resist.

Wyatt heard voices, followed by footsteps. He tensed, easing the closet door open just enough to allow him to see the backs of the people passing by.

When he sighted his prey, he rushed out, clamped a hand over her mouth, and walked backward into the closet, quickly and quietly shutting the door.

Her friends wouldn't notice her missing until it was too late.

"Don't struggle," he hissed in his best bad-guy voice. "Or scream, and you won't get hurt. Okay?"

When the girl in his arms nodded, he slowly removed his hand.

Isabelle punched him hard in the stomach with her elbow, then stomped on his foot. She turned to glare at him beneath the bare bulb overhead.

Wyatt let out a silent yowl of pain, warding her off with his hands and trying not to laugh.

"You scared the shit out of me," she groused.

"I'm going to tell Mom you're cussing," Wyatt gasped, still attempting to catch his breath.

She propped her hands on her hips. "Go ahead. Then I'll tell her that you nearly gave me a heart attack. What's with the drama? Couldn't you just tap me on the shoulder and tell me you needed to talk to me?"

Wyatt leaned against the wall, his eye on the spider behind Isabelle. He was certain she wasn't aware of it. Could be useful. "I've been trying to catch your eye for the past two hours. The only thing I accomplished was to give Brandy the idea I was flirting with her."

Isabelle folded her arms. "So *that's* what that was about. She asked me if you were a pervert."

Offended, Wyatt frowned and straightened away from the wall. "I most certainly am not! Well, not with Brandy, anyway." Which reminded him. "The reason I separated you from your friends is because I didn't want the whole damned world to know what I was up to."

"Oh. So you're up to something." Isabelle tapped her foot and feigned surprise. "Imagine that. My brother up to something. I suppose poor Dillon is the recipient—again? Must get boring with me away at college so much. And by the way, I didn't appreciate the box of flavored condoms you put in my suitcase. Now Brandy thinks I'm a nymphomaniac."

"Don't mention it," Wyatt said, biting back a smile. Apparently she hadn't found the fake chastity belt he'd left in the zippered pocket. "And this isn't about Dillon, for a change. It's about Kasidy."

Isabelle perked up at that. "Kasidy? You want to play a joke on Kasidy? But I thought . . . um, I was getting the impression from the way you two were sucking face that you liked her."

"I do. Which is exactly why you're here, in the closet with me."

After a short silence, Isabelle heaved an aggravated sigh. "Would you pu-lease get to the point before the posse comes looking for me?"

"The point . . . oh yeah. I want you to have a slumber party, here, and invite Kasidy."

His baby sister gawked at him. "Have you lost your mind? I'm twenty-one years old, Wyatt. I don't have slumber parties. I have grown-up parties." She shot him a sly look. "With boys and beer, and pot if we can find it."

She was kidding, of course. Wyatt refused to believe otherwise, and he hoped to high heaven she knew better. "I'll pay you," he said. "And I'll furnish the food, the entertainment—"

"The male stripper? Why, how thoughtful of you, big brother!"

"Don't be a smart-ass. No male strippers. I want this to be a teenage type of slumber party. You know, the kind where you play Truth-or-Dare, and put shaving cream on people's noses when they go to sleep first. The kind where you eat junk food until you want to puke, and sneak outside in your jammies to play in the sprinkler under the moonlight."

Once again, Isabelle's mouth fell open. "You were spying on me?" she squeaked. "I'm so telling Mom!"

Wyatt flushed. "I wasn't spying. I was watching over you, making sure you didn't do anything you'd regret. Now, let's see. Yeah, do the makeup thing and the toenail-painting thing."

"You *were* spying on us!" Isabelle accused. "Oh my God, you really are a pervert!"

"Can it, Izzy," Wyatt growled, becoming uncomfortable with her accusations. "I told you, Dillon and I—"

"Oh my God! Dillon was in on this?"

She looked really angry, which baffled Wyatt. Why would she be mad about something that happened a hundred years ago? "Is this about the *Playgirl* magazines?" he asked. "Because if it is, I never told Mom about that."

Isabelle covered her face with her hands. She stayed that way for a long moment before she finally sighed and looked at him. "Okay. I'm an adult now. I'm going to do the adult thing and pretend that I didn't hear anything you said in the past few minutes." Her fist landed in the middle of his rock-hard chest.

Fortunately for Wyatt, he saw the blow coming and managed to brace himself. Still, it stung more than he cared to admit.

"But if you ever, *ever* spy on me again, I'm going to make you regret it, Wyatt David Love. Do you hear me?"

Wyatt knew when to cave. "Yes, I hear you. I

promise I will never spy on you again." He crossed his heart for good measure.

"That includes the slumber party you're paying me to have," she persisted, emphasizing her words with a pointed finger in his chest. That done, Isabelle folded her arms again and shot him a coy look that made Wyatt groan inwardly.

"Now, about the food."

"Pizza?" Wyatt supplied helpfully, hopefully, but Isabelle was already shaking her head.

"Nope. 'Fraid not. In case you haven't noticed, I'm all grown up now, with grown-up tastes." She tapped a thoughtful nail against her chin.

He hadn't gotten to the ripe old age of thirty without recognizing the nail-tapping thing as a bad sign.

"There's a new caterer in town that I'd like to try." Her grin widened, and Wyatt felt a jolt go through him as he realized that looking at that mischievous smile was like looking in the mirror. More so than when he looked at Dillon, if that made any sense. "And I think I'll make the theme something tropical. Yeah, that's it. Hula skirts, which we'll have to rent, of course, and piña coladas, and fresh lobsters . . . I'll have to check the yellow pages for a good deejay."

Wyatt saw his savings account dwindling as his clever sister listed the many items she'd need for this slumber party.

Thank God he had a third job. He was going to need it.

Suddenly, her words caught up with him. He frowned severely at her. "Piña coladas? You mean virgin ones, right?"

"No, I don't."

Not an ounce of give there, Wyatt noticed. Still, there were ways around that. Piña coladas were made with rum, and rum looked like water. "Okay. What else?" He could have bitten off his tongue for asking, for he got that sly smile again. The one he didn't like.

"You have to tell me what this is all about. Are you trying to catch Kasidy doing something naughty?"

He wished. He cleared his throat. "Um, no."

Isabelle merely lifted a perfectly plucked eyebrow.

He would have to tell her, and pray that somewhere inside the college demon she had become, she still possessed compassion. "Kasidy, um, has never been to a slumber party."

"Ever?" Isabelle whispered, sounding awed.

"Ever. Her parents were rather . . . strict." Crazy, was the word he wanted to say. Cruel crossed his mind. But then he remembered her passionate defense of them and knew he couldn't voice his suspicions.

Suddenly, his college demon sister melted before his very eyes, becoming the sweet, compassionate baby sister that he loved and cherished. Tears welled in her big blue eyes. She fell into his arms and pressed her face against his chest.

Her voice was suspiciously thick as she said, "How sweet, that you're doing this for her." She sniffled, and wiped her nose against his shirt as she'd often done— to his disgust—as a child. "This must be true love. I can't wait to experience it myself."

The idea of a man lusting after his baby sister as he lusted for Kasidy effectively squashed Wyatt's mellow feeling. He jerked her back, glaring at her. "Don't you even think it. Sex is not—"

Isabelle put her hand over his mouth. "Shut up, idiot! I wasn't talking about sex. I was talking about love."

And that, Wyatt thought with a rueful groan, was a good example of how a man put his entire foot into his mouth, shoe and all. To cover the awkward moment, he said, "We can't let her know this was my idea. She has to think it was spontaneous."

"You can count on me. I *was* in the school play, you know."

Wyatt tried not to laugh. He didn't succeed. He tapped her on the nose and said gently, "Izzy, playing a carrot in the third grade does not an actress make. Although," he added diplomatically, "you made a very fetching carrot."

She snorted and flung her hair over her shoulder, giving him a smug look. "You'll see. She won't suspect a thing."

Deciding the meeting was over, Wyatt reached for the doorknob. Isabelle stopped him.

"You know you can't be around for the slumber party, right? No boys allowed."

"I get it." He started to turn the knob, but her amazingly strong grip stopped him again. What in hell did the child eat? he wondered. Wheaties four times a day?

"So where will you be?" she asked.

Her question prompted a scowl as Wyatt remembered something he'd temporarily forgotten. "Beating the crap out of your brother," he said, and meant it.

"Shoot," Isabelle groused. "And I have to miss *all* the fun."

* * *

"Wyatt will never fall for it."

Outside the doggie room, Kasidy paused on hearing Wyatt's name on Isabelle's lips. When on a mission as important as the one she was on, eavesdropping was allowed, she reasoned.

"He's so darn strict," Brandy said gloomily.

"Yeah," Isabelle agreed, sounding even gloomier. "He'd never understand that I just need to talk to Rodney, find out why he dumped me. Planning a slumber party and hiring Rodney as the deejay is the only way I can get him to talk to me."

Kasidy's heart went out to the girl. She shouldn't be listening, she decided, and began to turn away. But what Natasha said next stopped Kasidy in her tracks.

"What if we invited Kasidy? He'd have to trust you then, wouldn't he? Everyone knows he's hot for her, and he thinks of *her* as an adult."

Every muscle in Kasidy's body froze as she waited for their response. Eavesdroppers never heard good about themselves, Nana Jo had told her. Kasidy feared she was about to find out firsthand.

"Hey, that might be fun!" Isabelle said. "She's pretty cool, and I'll bet *she* wouldn't think I was stupid for wanting to talk to Rodney."

Well . . . maybe just a little, Kasidy thought, secretly flattered by Isabelle's compliment. She hated the idea of Isabelle baring her soul to this Rodney person, exposing herself to more hurt. Why had he dumped her? Isabelle was not only gorgeous but had a sparkling personality that Kasidy envied.

"Yeah," Natasha was agreeing. "Kasidy *is* cool, but can you trust her not to tell Wyatt?"

Without hesitation, Isabelle said, "Sure I could.

She's a woman, isn't she? We have to stand united against the opposite sex. That's what Mom always told me. Besides, I think it would be fun. Kasidy's older, more experienced. Maybe she could give us some pointers on how to deal with men."

Okay, so that was a bust. But she couldn't deny that it *would* be fun. Her first slumber party. Kasidy bit her lip, remembering her conversation with Wyatt and how she had confessed that she'd never been to one.

If she didn't know better . . . but no, that couldn't be, because the girls didn't know she was standing outside the doggie room listening, right?

"All right. You talked me into it," Isabelle said. "Let's just go ask her. She can't bite us, can she?"

With the speed of lightning, Kasidy raced down the hall, stopped, whirled around, and approached the doggie room at a leisurely, innocent pace. She hummed for good measure, and managed to look properly surprised when Isabelle appeared in the doorway.

Isabelle let out a shriek and put a dramatic hand to her chest. Her blue eyes were huge. "You scared the tar out of me!" she exclaimed, then laughed. She grabbed Kasidy's hands and pulled her inside the doggie room. "I'm so glad you're here. We've got a favor to ask you . . ."

Kasidy pretended to be all ears. Inside, her heart beat with excitement. Her first slumber party, and if she had it right, there would be no men in the house.

A perfect time to snoop.

And yes, a perfect time to recapture a piece of the childhood she'd never had.

How could a girl be so lucky?

CHAPTER 14

"You can't go in there!" Fish hollered as Wyatt strode purposefully toward the office behind the bar.

"The hell I can't," Wyatt growled, hoping the giant of a man would try to stop him. Fish was his friend, but he was itching to hit someone. Preferably his lying, cheating brother. How could Dillon and Callie do this to his niece and nephew?

When he'd gone to Dillon's house to talk to Callie, he'd found her gone, and the babysitter determined to keep Callie's whereabouts from him. Wyatt could think of only one reason Callie wouldn't want him to know where she'd gone.

She was with someone other than his twin. Not that he could blame her, after what he'd witnessed in the pantry, but dammit, his brother and sister-in-law had to work this out! For the kids' sake. For *his* sake.

For everyone's sake.

The office door was locked. Wyatt stepped back and gave it one swift kick, knowing how flimsy the lock was, since he'd installed it. The door bounced back against the wall, startling the entwined couple on the desk.

Dillon quickly shielded his lady friend from Wyatt's furious gaze, so Wyatt didn't get a good look at her. It wouldn't matter if she were the queen of England, she was barking up the wrong tree.

His brother was a happily married man with two kids, and it was time Dillon came back to reality and fixed things with his wife.

Slamming the door shut, Wyatt stood in front of Dillon, breathing hard. "I've spent the last two days trying to think of a good reason you would be screwing around on Callie. Two days," he emphasized. "And not one answer. Now, I want to know what the *hell* is going on!"

The woman hiding behind Dillon let out a gasp that sounded suspiciously like a laugh nipped in the bud. The sound sliced through Wyatt like a knife. He clenched his fists, ready and willing to beat some sense into Dillon and throw the home-wrecking floozy out on her conniving butt.

"For Pete's sake," a muffled voice said from behind Dillon. "Tell him before he clobbers you and sees *me* naked!"

"Callie and I are working things out," Dillon said hastily.

Wyatt was dumbfounded. "Then who—" he ground to a halt as Callie stuck her head around Dillon's shoulder to offer him a quick apologetic smile. Wyatt muttered a four-letter word he'd never said in front a woman. "Why didn't you just say so?"

Dillon smiled devilishly. "I was having too much

fun watching you turn rabid, bro. Nice to know you care so much."

"Yeah," Callie piped up. "We love you, too. Now, would you please leave so I can get, um, dressed?"

"Oh. Yeah, yeah." His face hot with embarrassment, Wyatt started for the door. He reached it, then turned, allowing his curiosity to override his embarrassment. "Um, why are you guys doing this . . . here, instead of your own house?"

"Two answers. Kaden and Jada," Dillon said. "They've figured out how to get out of their baby beds. Until we can decide what to do about it, we have to be . . . inventive."

"Have you considered abstinence?" Wyatt asked, beginning to find humor in the situation.

"Have you thought about biting me?" Dillon countered. He made a shooing motion at Wyatt. "Get the hell out of here, will ya?"

Wyatt jerked open the door, but managed to have the last word. "Now you know how it feels to have your space invaded, especially when you're trying to woo a woman."

"You weren't trying to woo her," Dillon argued. "You were trying to bonk her on the hood—"

"So I made a mistake," Wyatt said through his teeth. When had the tables turned? For the first thirty years of their lives, *he* had tormented Dillon. He didn't like the change. Not one single bit. "I'm making it up to her now."

"Oh!" Callie said, sticking her head out. "I heard about the slumber party. It was sweet of you to do that for Kasidy."

Was he under the world's largest friggin' microscope? Wyatt wondered, exasperated. Shaking his head, he left the two lovebirds alone. He'd volunteered to help Lou at the bar, since he was barred from the Hancock estate until tomorrow. Isabelle had been very, very clear on the rules.

Too bad, too sad, Wyatt thought, taking a drink order from one of the waitresses and filling it automatically. When things slowed down so that he could leave, he planned on sneaking into the house through the study window, which he'd left unlocked for that specific purpose. He wanted to be there when Kasidy awakened in the morning. He wanted to be one of the first to see her happy, flushed face.

The anticipation the thought produced kept him smiling through happy hour.

It was the best time of Kasidy's life.

She'd been secretly glad when Isabelle announced they couldn't get the caterer she wanted on such short notice, and just as relieved to hear that Isabelle's ex-boyfriend Dee Jay had gone out of town.

They had nominated Natasha as their deejay for the night, much to Natasha's delight, and ordered pizza delivered, much to Kasidy's relief. Kasidy had been too shy to tell them she'd never tasted lobster.

Natasha had surprised them all by combining a crowd-pleasing mix of country, rock, and rap. Kasidy was a country fan, herself.

The party consisted of Isabelle, Brandy, Natasha, two other friends of Isabelle's from high school, Ronda and Alicia, and Kasidy.

Then there was the guest of honor, an unexpected participant who had at first put a damper on the party when she showed up looking lost and lonely. The damper was soon lifted, however, when the new guest proved to them she was a fun-loving party girl, too, by volunteering to join Kasidy in losing her virginity.

Kasidy, sitting in a chair beside her partner, reached for Mrs. Scuttle's frail, wrinkled hand. She gave it a light squeeze and tried to smile, but the clay mask that had dried on her face was more effective than Botox. "Are you ready?" she asked the secretary.

Mrs. Scuttle blinked rapidly several times, the only sign that she was nervous. "I'm ready."

"Are you positive you want to do this?" Kasidy persisted. She didn't want the secretary to have any regrets.

"At my age, honey," Mrs. Scuttle said dryly, "the only thing I can be certain about is the gas I'm going to have after I eat broccoli."

The other girls laughed uproariously.

The laughter died down and an expectant silence fell over the room as Isabelle removed the ice cubes from Kasidy's earlobe. Beside them, Brandy did the same to Mrs. Scuttle's ear.

Kasidy quickly closed her eyes. She didn't want to see the needle. Isabelle had promised her that if her lobe was frozen properly, she wouldn't feel a thing.

When she felt a pressure against her lobe, Kasidy held her breath, certain she was about to feel the sting of the needle. Just when she thought she would pass out from lack of air, Isabelle touched her shoulder.

"All done with this one."

"Me, too," Brandy said.

Her breath left her in a whoosh. She glanced at Mrs. Scuttle, feeling a little better when she noticed that the secretary looked a little green behind her clay mask, as well. Wearing a tube top, a grass hula skirt, and the green mask on her face, Mrs. Scuttle was nearly unrecognizable. Ronda, whose mother was a beautician, had also teased and sprayed Mrs. Scuttle's hair into a beehive that might have looked fashionable on someone younger.

Kasidy wore the same costume and clay mask, only Ronda had French braided her hair instead of teasing it. But Kasidy had drawn the line at hair spray. The stuff took her breath away.

"Are you okay, Kas?" Isabelle asked before she began to prepare Kasidy's left ear for the needle. "'Cuz we can stop if you want to."

"No, I don't want to stop." In fact, she never wanted the night to end. She'd eaten enough pizza to give her heartburn, was slightly nauseated from the five different flavors of ice cream she'd sampled, had a mild headache from the music, and felt a little dizzy from the frozen piña coladas Isabelle had whipped up.

It was great.

Mrs. Scuttle was obviously enjoying the party, too. "I wished I'd had the nerve to get this done a long time ago," she said, her voice filled with girlish excitement.

"Me, too." Kasidy smiled as Moe, also dressed in a hula skirt, pushed his head onto her lap, begging to be stroked. Curly was subjecting himself to a makeover from Ronda, who had managed to tease the dog's hair into a round ball of fuzz. When she reached for the hair spray, he scrambled under the bed to join his brother, Larry. Larry had been a champ about the hula skirt, but had balked at mascara.

Everyone laughed at Ronda's chagrined expression.

"Gimme another drink, will ya, Tasha?" Mrs. Scuttle said, holding out her empty party cup. She punctuated her request with a hiccup, followed by a giggle.

Kasidy tipped her head around to give Isabelle a worried look, but Isabelle shook her head and winked at her.

"Don't worry," Isabelle assured her in a whisper close to her ear—the one growing numb. "She's not getting rum in her drink. She's getting bottled water, with a dash of rum extract I found in the kitchen."

An hour later, Mrs. Scuttle announced that her party engine had sputtered and died, and that she was going to bed. Kasidy and Isabelle volunteered to help the elderly woman upstairs to her room. Kasidy was amazed how easily the mind could be tricked; the secretary gave a convincing impression of a woman who'd had one drink too many, and she smelled of rum. But Isabelle had said she'd added rum extract, so that explained the smell.

When they reached her room, Mrs. Scuttle blinked in confusion. "Thish isn't my room," she said, shaking her head.

"It's your room," Kasidy assured her gently. "Remember, you're staying with Wyatt at the Hancock mansion?"

Mrs. Scuttle blinked rapidly. "Oh, yeah. I remember now."

"Do you want us to help you into your pajamas?" Isabelle offered, sharing a grin with Kasidy over the way the secretary was acting.

148

"No, I want to keep my hul-hul-hula skirt on," Mrs. Scuttle declared. "Can I keep it?"

Again Isabelle and Kasidy exchanged a grin. Isabelle shrugged. "Sure. Why not?" She pulled back the covers on the bed and helped Kasidy get Mrs. Scuttle settled.

The elderly lady sighed with contentment, her eyes already drifting closed. "I had a wonderful time, girls. The best."

"So did I," Kasidy said, and meant it. She looked at Isabelle. "Why don't you go ahead? I'll sit with her a bit to make sure she doesn't get back out of bed and go wandering around. She might do further injury to her ankle."

"Good idea," Isabelle said. "I'll see you downstairs. Oh, and be thinking about what you'd like to do next. It's your turn to pick the game."

After she'd gone, Kasidy sat in a chair next to the bed, savoring Isabelle's words. Simple words, really. *It's your turn to pick the game.* But they meant more to her than Isabelle could possibly know.

It was a shame she had to concentrate on the *real* reason she was here, Kasidy thought, casting one last glance at the sleeping woman before she turned out the light and left her to her slumber.

Instead of heading downstairs, Kasidy veered left down the hall, in the direction of her grandmother's room. She figured she had a good half hour to sleuth before anyone came looking for her, and this was an excellent opportunity to go for the one room most likely to be hiding the evidence she needed.

She made short work of the lock using the small

tool she'd hidden in her tube top, then slipped inside, shutting the door and locking it behind her. It was very dark, so she allowed her eyes to adjust before she moved forward, heading for what she hoped was an open bathroom doorway. When she reached it, she felt around on the wall until she found the light switch. She blinked as light flooded the huge master bathroom.

Quickly, she grabbed a towel and went back to the door, placing the towel at the bottom so that light couldn't be seen by anyone walking by—a trick her father had taught her. Then and only then did she turn on the overhead light.

She sucked in a gasp, slowly scanning her grandmother's room. It was filled with pictures. Pictures on the dresser, the armoire, the nightstands, and covering the walls. The majority of the photographs were of her mother at various stages of her life.

But the pictures that shocked her the most were of *her*. There was a picture of her as a toddler, playing in the park with her mother. Another picture, this one taken at a distance, was of Kasidy getting on a school bus. She could just make out the Minnie Mouse figure on her blue backpack.

Her first day of kindergarten, in a small town in Oklahoma. They'd lived there six months before moving on. The next picture had been taken three years later, during her school play. Kasidy recognized the picture immediately, and it brought a rush of tears to her eyes. Her mother had made her costume, a huge sunflower that Kasidy had also worn for Halloween that same year.

When they'd moved that time, the sunflower costume had been left behind. Kasidy remembered crying when she discovered they'd left it. Her mother had promised to make her a new one, but she never had.

Kasidy's knees threatened to fold, so she stumbled to the huge king-size bed and sank onto it, her eyes glued to the next picture. It had been taken the day the stranger had asked her questions during her walk home from school. She had thought she'd convinced him with her imaginative story about being a preacher's daughter.

Apparently, she had not.

Her grandmother had known, at least part of the time, where they were. She had followed them from town to town—or had paid someone to—taking pictures of her granddaughter to frame and study.

She quickly scanned the room, looking for more pictures of herself. She relaxed slightly when she realized the four pictures she'd seen already were the only ones. Either her grandmother had decided to leave them in peace, or her parents had managed to elude her hired bloodhounds after that.

Nobody, she mused, would recognize her from the fuzzy picture of a twelve-year-old girl walking along a sidewalk with her head down.

Kasidy was dumbfounded by the implications of the photos. If her grandmother had found them, why hadn't she followed through on her threat to expose her father? Obviously, she'd had plenty of opportunities.

Questions continued to bombard her as Kasidy searched the room for the videotape, or a safe where Amelia might have kept it. After twenty minutes, Kasidy forced herself to face facts.

The tape was not in her grandmother's room, and neither was the safe. Which didn't make sense. Where else would her grandmother keep her safe, or valuable items she didn't want anyone else to see? Her jewelry box on the dresser was filled with costume jewelry; Kasidy was sure that the real stuff had to be somewhere in the house.

Wherever that jewelry was, Kasidy was confident she would also find the incriminating tape. She didn't care about the jewelry—she just wanted that tape!

Discouraged, Kasidy folded the towel and put it back in the bathroom, turned out the lights, and locked the door behind her. Later, while the rest of the girls slept, she would search the other upstairs bedrooms, starting with Wyatt's room. Wyatt called it the master guest room. What if *that* room had been her grandmother's original room, before her grandfather died? What if she had been unable to stay in that room after his death, so she had taken another room?

It made sense, Kasidy decided, skipping downstairs to rejoin the party. Her ears had begun to throb, but the pain put a genuine smile back on her face. She'd never dreamed that her sleuthing expedition would turn out to be so much fun. Wyatt and his gang of friends and family had already gotten under her skin, and Kasidy knew that leaving them would be painful.

You could always stay, and claim your inheritance.

Kasidy paused on the stairs at the sound of Nana Jo's wise voice in her head. She had to admit she was tempted. Oh, she wasn't tempted by the money, or the fine things wealth could bring, but by the people she'd met and the hunk of a man who made her knees weak and her heart somersault.

If she stayed, she could look forward to a continuing friendship with Isabelle, and Mary, and yes, even the endearing, loveable Mrs. Scuttle.

And Wyatt. Sexy, breathtaking Wyatt Love. Maybe their attraction would develop into something wonderful, or maybe it wouldn't. Maybe she would just have a steamy, incredible fling with him.

Slowly, thoughtfully, Kasidy resumed her way downstairs. *If* she decided to make Atlanta her home, she would do it on her own terms, her own way.

It wouldn't involve accepting an inheritance from a woman who had made it her life's work to keep her parents fugitives in their own country.

No way.

CHAPTER 15

The house was quiet when Wyatt crawled through the study window at one in the morning. Happy hour had stretched into crazy hour, and he'd been stuck behind the bar longer than he'd expected.

He paused in the doorway of the study, listening for sounds coming from Kasidy's room two doors down.

Silence.

He smiled, tempted to peek inside, certain he'd find the girls sprawled asleep on the floor, the room wrecked and reeking of pizza and God knows what else they'd eaten. With his little sister's warning ringing in his ears, Wyatt resisted temptation and continued to tiptoe upstairs to his room. He grinned, wondering if Isabelle had figured out that he'd switched the rum for bottled water, leaving enough rum in the original bottle to flavor and scent the water. The real stuff he'd poured into the empty water bottles, to replace at a later date.

When he reached his room, he sighed and relaxed, heading straight for his bathroom to take a quick shower before bed. He was exhausted from tending bar all night, but eager to get the night over so that he could relish the happiness he was certain he'd see in Kasidy's eyes in the morning.

Was this love? he wondered, shedding his clothes and stepping beneath the hot spray. Was this what it meant, ignoring your own wants and needs in favor of making another person happy?

Because he definitely had needs ... and wants, when it came to Kasidy. Wyatt glanced down at his growing erection and chuckled to himself. Big wants. Big needs. In fact, he hadn't been able to stop thinking about her all night, although it hadn't been *all* about making love to her delectable body.

In the garage, she had stood before him, her nipples hard and straining against her T-shirt, claiming she was ready for him.

Was he wrong to hold back, thinking she needed more wooing? Was he shortchanging himself—and Kasidy—by playing the gentleman?

It was almost laughable, Wyatt thought, rinsing the soap from his hair. Because he felt anything *but* a gentleman. In fact, he was tempted to sneak downstairs and carry her back to his bed, stop wasting time and get down to the business of loving her good and proper.

Okay, so maybe not *proper,* but definitely good.

Grinning at the wicked direction of his thoughts, Wyatt quickly toweled himself off and reached to turn out the bathroom light on his way to his bed.

He stopped abruptly, his hand on the light switch, his eyes straining in the dark to make out the shape in his bed, faintly illuminated by the bathroom light.

Definitely a womanly shape beneath his covers. His grin widened as he turned out the light. Had he conjured Kasidy from his erotic fantasies? Who the hell cared?

Naked and humming with anticipation, Wyatt moved around to the far side of the bed and quietly lifted the covers, just enough to slide in beside her. Gently, he touched the poof of hair sticking out from the top of the covers. He winced at the stiff feel of it, then grinned ruefully as he realized Kasidy had most likely been the subject of one of his sister's "make-overs." What a good sport she was, he thought, carefully moving his hardened body so that it spooned hers. He wished that she was facing him, so that he could awaken her with a long, hot kiss.

Instead, he settled for pulling back the covers a notch and nuzzling her neck. To his surprise, her skin felt rough and wrinkled against his lips. Hair products, he mused, sliding his arm around her waist.

The bloodcurdling scream that erupted from his bed mate's mouth coincided with Wyatt's realization that it wasn't Kasidy he was embracing.

He jumped back. "What the hell?" A sharp elbow collided with his chin, knocking him off the bed.

The screaming continued, assaulting his eardrums and surely waking the dead.

Or a slumber party.

Wyatt scooted across the carpet to the door, gathering carpet burns on his butt along the way. He fumbled for the light switch, horror engulfing him as the familiarity of that ear-piercing scream sank into his fuddled brain.

Light flooded the room, revealing a freakish sight.

Mrs. Scuttle sat upright in his bed, her hair a wild halo around her painted face. Her red mouth was a perfect O as she continued to scream the house down.

Muttering a string of curses, Wyatt jumped to his feet and raced to the bathroom to get his bathrobe from the hook on the door.

The secretary continued to scream.

Isabelle was the first to arrive on the scene, followed by Brandy. She looked from Wyatt to Mrs. Scuttle, then shouted over the screaming.

"See! I told you he was a pervert!"

"I'm not a pervert!" Wyatt shouted back. And then he looked helplessly from the screaming Mrs. Scuttle to his openly amused sister. "Can't you *do* something?" And what the hell was the secretary wearing? It looked like a tube top! He shuddered, fearing the image would be forever embedded in his memory.

To his relief, Kasidy appeared in the doorway, assessed the situation, then quickly went to Mrs. Scuttle's side. Wyatt watched as Kasidy took the woman's bare shoulders and shook her gently.

"Mrs. Scuttle! Mrs. Scuttle! Look at me. It's okay."

The screaming stopped abruptly. Mrs. Scuttle, bug-eyed and dazed, stared at Kasidy. "I think I'm going to be sick," she whispered, just before she vomited all over Wyatt's bed.

Kasidy managed to jump back in time to avoid the worst of it, but she quickly moved back in and put her arms around the elderly woman's shoulders. "There, there. You feel better now, don't you?"

The room reeked of the strong odor of rum.

Wyatt's jaw dropped as the implications sank in. Mrs. Scuttle was in the wrong room. She'd just thrown up on his bed, and the room stank of rum. He couldn't keep the accusation from his voice as he demanded, "Is she drunk?"

Isabelle shot him a quelling glare. "Of course not, dummy. What you're smelling is rum extract. I substituted bottled water for her rum. She never knew the difference."

"She probably just ate too much junk food," Brandy observed. "I felt sick to my stomach earlier, too."

"Me, too," Natasha said.

They all seemed oblivious to the fact that Wyatt had gone as pale as a ghost. "Hell," he breathed, and wiped a trembling hand down his face. "We'd better get her to the emergency room."

He was *so* dead.

Wyatt's lack of color—and the fear in his eyes— scared Kasidy. She'd never seen him so worried.

They were seated in the waiting room at the emergency center, hoping the doctor would come out and give them an update on Mrs. Scuttle. People arrived in an almost continuous flow. Some of them Kasidy knew, and some she didn't. She was introduced to Greg's life partner, Ramon, and Wyatt's boss and his wife, Luke and Lydia. She'd lost track of the many escorts, all gorgeous hunks, that filed in with their families. Mary sat with Isabelle, Callie, and Dillon on the other side of Wyatt. She occasionally gave Wyatt's left hand a reassuring pat.

Kasidy kept her hand in Wyatt's, wishing she knew

what to say to take that awful look from his eyes. She was confused as to why he obviously blamed himself for Mrs. Scuttle's condition, but hadn't worked up the nerve to ask him.

The pain in her hand alerted Kasidy. She looked up to find a man dressed in green scrubs striding their way. He was flanked by a stern-looking middle-aged woman carrying a briefcase.

The doctor halted at the entrance to the waiting room. He looked around with a frown. "I'm Dr. Maden. Who's waiting for news of Mrs. Scuttle?"

Everyone in the room stood, including Kasidy, since she was still holding Wyatt's hand.

With an impatient shake of his head, the doctor tried again. "Who is her next of kin?"

"We all are," Wyatt said, his voice deep and serious. "How is she?"

Dr. Maden exchanged a dubious look with the woman at his side. "She'll be fine, but I felt compelled to call Social Services about this matter. This is Mrs. Stonewall. Mrs. Scuttle's caretaker should be aware that at her age, alcohol could be lethal." He paused and frowned at the crowd staring pensively at him. "So, who *is* her caretaker?"

"We all are," Dillon said. "We're all responsible for Mrs. Scuttle."

"That's right," a voice from the back called out.

Kasidy turned to watch Luke make his way to the front of the crowd. His breathtakingly good looks should have made her heart go pitter-patter.

It didn't.

"She's my secretary," Luke continued. "We all watch out for her."

"Well, somebody's not doing a very good job," the doctor said. "This woman was intoxicated."

Isabelle looked as if she might burst into tears. Kasidy didn't think she would be far behind her. After all, Mrs. Scuttle had been in their care when she became intoxicated. She saw Isabelle take a deep, shaky breath, and sensed instinctively Isabelle was about to step bravely forward. Kasidy tried to break free of Wyatt's hand, intending to step forward with Isabelle and claim her own share of the blame.

But Wyatt beat them to it.

"It's my fault," he said, startling them all. "I didn't want my little sister drinking, so I switched the rum with bottled water." When Isabelle gasped, he shot her an apologetic look before continuing. "Isabelle believed she was giving Mrs. Scuttle bottled water, when in fact it was rum."

"Who's Isabelle?" Dr. Maden asked sharply, scanning the roomful of pensive faces.

"I am," Isabelle said, with only a slight tremble in her voice.

The doctor pinned her with a stern look. "Is it true?"

"Yes. It's true." The look Isabelle gave Wyatt promised retribution.

"Well." The social worker spoke for the first time. "I'll have to talk to Mrs. Scuttle, but I don't see any reason to launch an investigation, since it appears to have been an accident."

"Can we see her?" Wyatt asked the doctor.

"I don't see why not. She's on I.V. fluids, and she's just about sober, I think. We'll give her something for her hangover when we're sure the alcohol is out of her system."

"I should talk to her first," Mrs. Stonewall interjected.

Dillon cleared his throat before the social worker could leave. "Um, it might not be a good idea to mention the word 'caretaker' to Mrs. Scuttle."

There was a hum of mumbled agreement throughout the room.

Mrs. Stonewall gave them an asinine smile. "I've worked with the elderly for many years," she said a trifle condescendingly. "I think I know what I'm doing."

Kasidy bit her lip to keep from smiling. She was glad she wasn't in the social worker's clueless shoes.

Wyatt waited outside the secretary's room in case the stubborn social worker needed him.

He didn't have long to wait.

The first object hit the heavy hospital door with a thud.

With a sigh, he darted inside, snagged Mrs. Stonewall by her bewildered arm, and pulled her to safety. "We warned you not to mention the word 'caretaker'," he chided.

The poor woman was obviously dazed by her close call. She straightened her suit jacket and tried to look dignified. "It's not healthy for her to live under an illusion," she said defensively.

Casually, Wyatt plucked a Q-tip from the woman's hair and slipped it into his pocket. "Oh, believe me. In this instance, it's a *lot* healthier for Mrs. Scuttle to believe she's independent."

"Have you considered a nursing home?"

"Have you considered a career change?" Wyatt countered silkily. "There's nothing mentally or physically wrong with Mrs. Scuttle, so no, she won't be heading for the nursing home. In fact, she'll never have to worry about that. She's got family."

The woman plucked another Q-tip from her hair and held it out. "She's dangerous."

"She's harmless," Wyatt argued smoothly. "Have you ever heard of anyone getting a concussion from a Q-tip?" When she didn't answer, he bared his teeth in a smile. "I didn't think so."

He couldn't resist a chuckle as Mrs. Stonewall sniffed and walked away, her back rigid enough to use for a highway. Finally, when she disappeared around a corner, Wyatt knew it was time to face the music once again.

Only this time, he'd be lucky to get by with a lecture, he knew.

Bracing himself, he knocked and opened the door.

Scrubbed free of makeup and wearing a faded hospital gown—a vast improvement, in Wyatt's opinion, from the tube top and hula skirt—Mrs. Scuttle looked her age. She was propped up against a mound of pillows, her expression a mixture of bewilderment and fury.

When she saw him, she reached for the ice bucket beside her.

Wyatt held up his hand. "Don't. You're in a hospital, Mrs. Scuttle. They'll declare you insane and put you in the nut house, and there won't be a thing anyone can do about it."

"You're not my caretaker," she muttered darkly,

glaring at him. But she let go of the ice bucket and clenched her hands in her lap. "Nobody is."

Gently, he said, "We know that and *you* know that, but *they* don't know that." He came closer to the bed and shoved his hands in his pockets. He knew he was taking a risk getting so close, considering what he had to tell her.

"I'm eighty years old," she declared heatedly. "If I want to drink, I can drink. It's nobody's decision or fault but my own."

"I agree." He didn't, but he knew when to lie for the sake of preserving a loved one's feelings. "They don't know you like we do. They don't know that you're a strong, brave, independent woman who takes care of *us*, not the other way around. We couldn't do without you."

Mrs. Scuttle focused sharp eyes on his face. They narrowed behind her thick glasses.

Uh-oh. Maybe he'd carried it a bit too far.

"What did you do, Wyatt?"

Yep. He'd definitely poured it on a little too thick. Trying to appear casual about it, Wyatt took a few steps back and leaned against the wall. There was no easy way to say it, so he just blurted it out. "I switched the rum for water, to keep Isabelle from drinking."

The secretary's thin brows arched in question.

"Um, Isabelle didn't want to give you rum, so she substituted it with bottled water flavored with rum extract."

"That wasn't rum extract I was drinking," Mrs. Scuttle snapped. "You think I don't know the difference?" Her hand shot out, grabbing the handle on her ice water pitcher.

Wyatt stiffened, but held his ground. "No, you were drinking rum, alright. I put the rum from the rum bottle into the empty water bottles."

For a tension-filled moment, there was silence. Mrs. Scuttle stared at him without blinking. Wyatt stared back, wishing she'd say something—anything. Cuss him. Throw something. Spit at him.

And then she threw back her head and cackled.

Suspiciously, Wyatt waited for the other shoe to drop as she continued to laugh in that witchlike cackle of hers. He was very afraid she was trying to trick him into letting his guard down.

But she kept on laughing, until a nurse rushed into the room with an alarmed look on her face. "What's going on?" the nurse demanded, looking from one to the other.

Wyatt finally allowed himself to smile. Then he chuckled. After that, he couldn't have spoken a coherent word if his life had depended on it. He was so relieved that his knees were weak.

He was going to live!

CHAPTER 16

" 'Meet me in the garage,' " Wyatt read from the note taped to the front door of the mansion. He grinned as he checked his watch. It was almost four in the morning. When Luke and Lydia had volunteered to stay with Mrs. Scuttle at the hospital, he hadn't argued long. He'd hoped Kasidy would wait up for him, but he hadn't expected it.

This was a nice surprise.

His surprise turned into stunned amazement when he got to the garage and saw what Kasidy had done. She'd placed a dozen tea candles around the bed of his truck, creating a soft, romantic atmosphere. Lining the bed was a thick layer of blankets, covered by a satin sheet.

Kasidy, wearing a tight T-shirt and a smile, reclined against a pile of satin pillows. The soft glow of the candle light played over her features, causing Wyatt to catch his breath in wonderment. She truly was stunning, he thought, forgetting to exhale. He remembered when his lungs began to burn.

He let his breath out slowly, so he wouldn't disturb the candles. "You're beautiful," he said huskily.

"You are, too," she said. She crooked her finger at him and motioned him into the truck bed. "Won't you join me?"

Wyatt hesitated. "If I come up there, I can't promise you I'll behave."

Her smile widened, a wicked, naughty smile that made Wyatt's groin tighten. "The only way you're allowed up here is if you promise that you *won't* behave," she said boldly. Deliberately, she turned onto her back and put her hands behind her head. The motion emphasized her erect nipples and drew the T-shirt high enough to reveal that she wore a teeny pair of pale pink panties.

He swallowed hard. It was going to be tough to please this woman, he decided regretfully, because he'd be lucky if he lasted long enough to get inside her.

Inside her.

Wyatt's bones liquified. He grabbed the tailgate and hoisted himself up. Two hours until dawn. Maybe he'd have time to recuperate and show her what he could really do to satisfy her.

When he knelt beside her, she rose to her knees and began unbuckling his belt. Her hair, which she'd taken down from her braid, fell in silky waves around her.

He stared down at her, thinking how innocent and childlike she seemed as she struggled with her task. He'd never dated anyone so natural, so damned innocent. Most of the women he had known would never think of a T-shirt and a seduction scene in the same sentence, nor would they consider the bed of a truck a romantic place to make love. In fact, he was fairly certain the women he'd known would have laughed in his face at the mere suggestion.

Yet Kasidy had planned it as if she were fulfilling a fantasy.

His conscience prompted him to say softly, "Baby, we don't have to make love here. We can go to my apartment."

She paused and looked up at him, her eyes dark and gleaming with anticipation. Her lips glistened, and as he watched, helplessly, she slowly licked them. Wyatt went so weak he nearly fell forward. Her low, husky laughter stretched his erection to impossible lengths.

"We'll get to your apartment . . . eventually," she said, bending over to yank down his shorts.

Wyatt didn't have the chance to warn her he wasn't wearing underwear. He sprang free, proud and thick and trembling, and popped her right on the nose.

Kasidy yelped and fell back. Wyatt was sure he hadn't hurt her, but he had definitely scared the hell out of her, if her big, shocked eyes were any indication.

Groaning, Wyatt reached out and pulled her to her knees, staring into her wide-eyed face. Her eyes were still dark with desire, thank God, but now they also held a hint of trepidation. With his erection smashed safely out of sight between them, Wyatt asked in a low, concerned voice, "Are you okay?"

She nodded and licked her lips again, making Wyatt groan a second time. "I'm . . . I just wasn't expecting it to be so . . . so . . . big."

Okay. He was a man, and like any man, his ego swelled at her stammered words. But he was also realistic, and knew that he was only a bit above average. Which probably meant . . . "Just how many of these have you seen?" Or not seen?

"Um." She bit her bottom lip and dropped her gaze. "One."

"Damn."

Her gaze flew back to his. "Are you disappointed?"

He cursed at the anxiousness in her tone. "No, baby. Of course not." To prove it, he swooped down on her mouth and kissed her long and hard. She might have been inexperienced, but God had blessed her with a talented mouth, Wyatt thought, coming up for air before his lungs burst.

This time when he looked at her, the trepidation was gone. She was back to looking lustfully at him again, which maybe wasn't a good thing, considering how close he was to losing it. "We're going to take it slow," he promised, hoping he could keep that promise. Wisely, he drew his shorts back over his erection and zipped them, chuckling at her disappointed groan. "We're going to get to know one another's bodies first. How's that?"

Eagerly, she reached for his zipper. "Good idea. I go first."

He stopped her with a laugh. "Oh, no you don't. I'm afraid that's out of the question."

"Not fair. We should flip for it."

Cupping her chin in his hands, Wyatt nuzzled her full, soft lips with his own. "Baby, if we're going to make this last, I've got to be first. Okay?"

After a moment, she sighed and leaned back on the pillows. She put her hands behind her head and watched him through half-lowered, sultry lids. "You first," she said softly.

If looks could scorch, he'd be an ember by now, Wyatt thought, wondering what he'd done to deserve the banquet she presented. As he hooked his fingers in the elastic of her panties, Wyatt asked the burning question, "Why only one?"

"Once," she corrected breathlessly. "Because it wasn't that great, so I didn't see any reason to do it again until I really wanted to."

Wyatt felt his ego swell again. He edged her panties down, holding his breath as he uncovered her inch by inch. It reminded him of slowly opening a really great present, knowing you were going to get exactly what you wanted when you got it all unwrapped.

The build of anticipation was the best part.

She squirmed and whimpered. "Can you go a little faster?"

"Patience, baby." He moved his finger over her nub and watched her arch her back and moan. She was so beautiful, so earthy and sexy. He couldn't wait to slide inside her, feel her heat around him.

But first things first.

She thought he'd never get her panties off.

Kasidy felt shameless . . . wanton, and wonderful. It took a tremendous amount of willpower to let him touch her without participating, without touching him back.

Finally, her panties were off. Kasidy felt the shock of his hot mouth against her inner thigh, and drove her fingers into his hair as her body jerked in reaction.

169

He was very close to the part of her that throbbed and ached the most. What if he . . . ? She wasn't completely naive. She'd watched movies, had seen magazines. She knew that it was done.

And then he did. He put his hot mouth right against the core of her, and thrust his tongue against her. Liquid heat rushed to the spot, glorying in his heated, talented touch. She felt a delicious tension began to build as he thrust his tongue in and out. Her hips began to move to the rhythm, shamelessly. She was twenty-five, so she wasn't a stranger to an orgasm, but she soon found out there were orgasms . . . and then there were *orgasms*.

When he drew her swollen nub into his mouth and began to suckle, Kasidy exploded. She lifted her hips off the truck, a cry bursting from her throat. The intense waves went on and on. Wyatt was relentless in his quest to give her the maximum pleasure, refusing to settle for less.

He took.

And she gave.

Finally, when the waves began to recede, Kasidy lay, gasping for breath. Her limbs felt boneless, so she could hardly resist when Wyatt rose above her and lifted her T-shirt over her head.

As if she *wanted* to resist. But she was afraid she'd never get her strength back, that she would remain boneless the rest of her days.

Wyatt proved to her that she had strength and then some.

He started at her belly button, kissing a hot trail along her stomach until he reached her breasts. Taking his slow, sweet time, he nuzzled and licked until

Kasidy was shocked to feel another wave of arousal building. When he took a pebble-hard nipple into his mouth, it reminded her of what he'd done before.

She gasped and grabbed at his head, pulling his mouth to hers. They kissed, tongue against tongue, devouring each other as if they couldn't get enough.

"It's my turn," she managed to gasp out against his mouth.

With a half-groan, half-laugh, he lifted himself up onto his elbows. He stared down at her, his eyes dark and luminous. "I was hoping you'd forget."

She frowned. "Really?"

His teeth flashed in a wicked grin. "No, not really. I'm just afraid it will end sooner than we both want it to, if I let you touch me."

She stroked his mouth with her finger. He drew it inside and sucked hard. Amazingly, liquid pooled between her legs. "If I promise to stop when you tell me to, can I?" She saw him hesitate, and couldn't deny that it gave her a feeling of power, knowing he wanted her that badly.

Instead of answering, Wyatt rolled onto his back. He lay there, stiff as a board. Grinning to herself, Kasidy lowered his zipper slowly, making sure her fingers brushed his erection as often as possible.

By the time she released him, Wyatt's eyes were closed and his jaw was clenched.

Kasidy relished her new-found power. She rose and straddled his thighs. Taking him in hand, she curled her fingers around his thick length and slowly began to stroke him. "Look at me," she commanded huskily.

"I can't," he said between clenched teeth. "Stop."

Pretending innocence, Kasidy stopped stroking him. "What? Stop stroking you? Stop touching you this way? Or that way?"

"Dammit, Kasidy. . . ."

"Okay, okay." She grinned at him when he opened one eye to scowl at her. "I know, I know. I promised." She let go so that she could finish removing his shorts. When that was done, she removed his shirt, as well, lingering over his puckered nipples and teasing them with her teeth.

"Stop."

With a sigh, Kasidy slowly rubbed her body along his, loving the feel of his hard, naked flesh against her own. Just as she had suspected, making love with the right person made all the difference in the world.

"Stop."

She was beginning to hate that word. With another sigh designed to distract him, Kasidy moved down again, and in one swift move, lowered her mouth over the tip of his erection.

"Don't!" he ground out, clutching her arms.

Kasidy lifted her head long enough to chide him. "Sorry, that's not the right word." With that, she lowered her head again, this time taking half the length of him in her mouth. His skin was like satin, and the way he pulsed inside her mouth made her clench her thighs in reaction. Was this how *he* had felt when he'd been loving her this way? she wondered.

"Stop, dammit!" This time Wyatt stopped her forcefully, lifting her up as if she weighed no more than a feather. His gaze burned into hers. "In my shorts pocket," he said raggedly. "Condom."

Trembling with anticipation, Kasidy found the

condom and discovered a new pleasure in sheathing him with it. "Hmm," she teased, unrolling the condom at a leisurely pace. "I'll bet you have to buy extra large, huh?"

"I'm going to make you scream for that," he threatened with a groan. Lifting her up, he positioned her so that she was poised above his erection.

Kasidy was panting, eager to feel him inside of her. She knew without a doubt that he was going to make her scream . . . again.

"Take it slow," he ordered roughly, his face taut with strain. "Lower yourself nice and easy. I don't want to hurt you."

"You won't hurt me," she said with conviction. She felt him pressing against her opening, and eased down over him. Her own juices made the passage easier, she knew.

With a half-hearted chuckle, Wyatt said, "Okay. What I really meant was, take it easy because you're going to be so tight I'm likely to explode before we get very far."

"I don't want that to happen."

"No, we don't want that to happen."

"Wyatt?"

"Hm?"

"This is really fun."

His helpless laugh thrust him upward, and Kasidy gasped as he filled her with his hard length. Incredibly, she felt her inner muscles begin to spasm.

"Oh, no," she breathed.

"Stop," he said, when he realized what was happening.

"I can't," she gasped, as her orgasm rushed upon

her. "Wyatt!" He grabbed her hips and held her still as the intensity of her orgasm shook her. When sane thought returned, she opened her eyes and saw that Wyatt's jaw was still clenched.

His gaze burned into hers, devouring her. "You didn't scream," he said softly, smugly.

Kasidy felt her eyes widen. "You mean . . . ?"

"That's *exactly* what I mean," he growled, flipping her over in one single move.

Remarkably, they were still joined. Rising above her, he began a slow, torturous stroking that left Kasidy with little choice. She clutched his shoulders and held on for dear life.

Wyatt bent close and kissed the corner of her mouth, teasing her into wanting more. She heard herself whimper, reaching for him only to find him frustratingly out of reach.

"You *will* scream for me, Kasidy," he whispered against her mouth, before satisfying her craving by kissing her until her toes curled.

All the while he brought her closer to her third climax with each slow, sure stroke. When he pulled her nipple into his mouth and sucked hard, Kasidy's orgasm peaked.

And she screamed, just as he'd ordered. But to her immense pleasure, Wyatt did a little screaming of his own.

Exhausted and completely sated, Kasidy snuggled up against his pounding chest and eventually fell into a deep, dreamless sleep.

CHAPTER 17

"Don't look, baby! Somebody ought to call the police! You'd think they'd have the decency to get a hotel!"

The outraged, unfamiliar voice pulled Wyatt out of a deep, exhausted sleep. He opened one gritty eye, then quickly closed it against the bright sunlight shining overhead.

Sunlight.

Overhead.

Disgruntled woman muttering about decency and hotels.

"But what are they doing, Mommy? Don't they have a home?"

The curious, concerned voice of a little girl.

Oh, shit. Something told Wyatt they were no longer in the privacy of the garage. Opening his eyes again, he rose slightly and peered over the side of the truck. He quickly scanned the heavily populated parking lot, then angled his head to read the sign over the building in front of the truck.

He groaned and fell back, closing his eyes. No doubt about it. They were not in the garage, or anywhere *near* the garage. They were parked in the parking lot of a grocery store, and he and Kasidy were lying stark naked beneath a blanket in the bed of his truck.

In broad daylight. With *people* walking by.

Knowing he had to wake her sooner or later and give her the bizarre, bad news, Wyatt gently shook Kasidy's shoulder. "Kasidy," he whispered urgently. "Wake up, but don't sit up."

"Huh?" She did exactly the opposite, sitting up and blinking in confusion as the bright sunlight torched her eyes. She rubbed them with her knuckles. "What? Where are we?"

From the corner of his eye, Wyatt saw a couple with two kids approaching. He pushed Kasidy back down and drew the covers over their heads. "Shh. Don't say anything."

Naturally, she didn't listen. "Wyatt? What's going on? Where are we, and why are we hiding under the covers? Am I dreaming?"

He wished! Isabelle was *so* going to regret this!

"Um, no, I'm afraid you aren't dreaming, baby." He kept his voice low, hoping the couple with the kids had gone into the store. Just to be sure, he took a quick look.

He threw the cover up over his head again. The couple had come and gone, but a whole group of senior citizens were heading their way. He knew—just as he was certain his soon-to-be-dead baby sister had known—that it would be next to impossible for him to get dressed and get into the cab of his truck without being seen by someone.

"Wyatt!" Kasidy hissed, obviously fully awake now. "Will you please tell me what's going on? How did we get here?"

"Isabelle," he ground out. "Can you find your clothes?"

He heard rustling, then a frustrated curse.

"I don't see them—can't feel them. Maybe they're outside the blanket."

Wyatt hated to give her more bad news, but if he knew Isabelle, there wouldn't be any clothes to be found.

"Oh, wait! Here's something! Oooh, yuk! Never mind."

He wasn't about to touch that one. "I think we'll have to wrap ourselves in these blankets, Kas."

"Yeah, it looks like it. Why would Isabelle do such a mean thing? She seems so sweet!"

"Payback, for switching the rum. And yes, she is sweet . . . most of the time." To be fair, he couldn't blame Izzy for being mad at him over the alcohol incident. His joke had backfired, and could have turned out even worse. He was still kicking himself.

"Okay," he instructed. "I'm going to lift myself up, and you grab the blanket out from under me." Kasidy did as he asked, but they were puffing and sweating by the time they got wrapped up separately in the blankets.

"Why don't I just stay here?" Kasidy ventured in a voice thick with embarrassment. "You can stop somewhere more private and let me in the truck."

"Good thinking. Okay, here I go!"

Wyatt dared not look around as he tried to hang

177

onto his blanket while slinging himself over the side of the truck. He didn't quite make it, as he soon found out.

"Nice ass, sugar," an amused, female voice drawled.

Suspecting his face was flaming red, Wyatt quickly opened the truck door and climbed behind the wheel. He fought the blanket from his legs and began to search for his keys. If he knew his baby sister, she wouldn't make it easy for him.

Ten sweaty minutes later, he found them tucked into an envelope in the glove compartment, along with a note for Kasidy from Isabelle. He was tempted to crumple the note and throw it away, teach Isabelle a lesson, but his conscience wouldn't let him. This wasn't Kasidy's fight, and as mad as he was at Isabelle, he wanted Kasidy and Isabelle to get along.

Just why that was so important to him, he had yet to figure out.

He needn't have worried about Kasidy. When he found a place mostly free of people, he stopped to let her into the truck. She was laughing as she climbed inside with her blanket and shut the door.

Laughing hard enough to make tears stream down her eyes. He doubted she realized that she had raccoon eyes, he mused, watching her with an alarming rush of warmth.

He tried to look fierce as he growled, "What's so funny?"

She laughed harder, clutching her middle and doubling over. When she could finally talk, she was still chuckling. "Your face! You should have seen your face!"

Instead of answering, Wyatt twisted the rearview mirror in her direction. He grinned at her squeal of horror when she saw herself.

"Oh! You're mean!" She punched him playfully in the shoulder, rubbing at the black circles under her eyes from the many coats of mascara Wyatt suspected someone other than Kasidy had applied.

It was the moment Wyatt realized that he loved her.

Kasidy was still chuckling when she picked up Isabelle's note and read it.

"What did the brat say?" Wyatt asked, looking gorgeous and sinfully sexy driving bare-chested. The blanket had fallen around his waist and he hadn't bothered to do anything about it.

Which was fine with Kasidy.

"She called me a regrettable 'casualty of war.'"

"That's all she said?"

"Well, she also said she was sorry."

"Oh, well," Wyatt drawled sarcastically. "That makes it all better."

"And that she would make it up to me." Kasidy folded the note, then turned to study Wyatt as she said, "She's already made it up to me, you know, by inviting me to her slumber party. I had the absolute best time." She saw Wyatt's eyes flicker, and her suspicions about his involvement deepened. "Thank you, Wyatt."

He jerked the wheel in surprise. "What?"

Kasidy rolled her eyes. "You know what I'm talking about. I might not have figured it out if it hadn't been for Truth-or-Dare. That was a little *too* coincidental."

"Oh." The sheepish smile he threw her way

warmed her from the inside out. "I just thought . . . well, you'd never been to one, so I thought—"

She reached out and touched his arm. "You don't have to explain. I'm glad you did it."

"Yeah, me too. I just wished I hadn't switched the liquor." He shuddered. "That little prank backfired on me."

"Yes, it did," Kasidy conceded. "But in the end, it didn't do any real harm. Mrs. Scuttle's going to be fine."

"Louise is back," Dillon announced the moment Wyatt and Kasidy walked through the door.

Since his twin hadn't batted an eye at the sight of a blanket-clad Kasidy scurrying to her room, or at his own blanket-clad form, Wyatt figured Dillon had known about Isabelle's prank. He glanced at the sports bag Dillon held in his hand. "Going somewhere?"

"Well, you *did* throw me out," Dillon reminded him dryly. "But yes, I'm going home. Callie and I made up."

Wyatt rolled his eyes. "I know. Remember, I was there?"

"Oh." Dillon blushed. "Yeah. I remember." He checked his watch. "Oh, I guess I should tell you that Mom and Isabelle have already gone home, too."

"Stop. I don't know if I can handle the excitement after the night I've had." He wasn't lying; just the thought of knocking around in the big old mansion with Kasidy—alone—made his heart kick into overdrive.

Dillon snorted. "Well, maybe I shouldn't tell you

that Mrs. Scuttle won't be coming back here when they release her today."

"Really?" Wyatt put a hand over his thumping heart. "What about her ankle?"

With a shrug, Dillon said, "I guess it's better."

Although he couldn't deny that the news was good, Wyatt got the strange feeling that his twin was lying. "Is there something you're not telling me, bro? Is it about Mrs. Scuttle? Is she really upset with me about the alcohol?"

"No, no. She's cool with it. Didn't she tell you?"

"Well, yeah, but—"

"Got to run. Have fun. See you later." Dillon reached the door, spun around, and snapped his fingers. "Damn, I forgot to give you this." He dug around in his backpocket and pulled out a tattered piece of leather.

Totally confused, Wyatt gingerly took it from his twin. "What's this?"

"I think it used to be your wallet. I found it on the kitchen floor."

His wallet. Which he'd probably left on the bathroom floor when he'd undressed prior to taking a shower, prior to getting the crap scared out of him by finding Mrs. Scuttle in his bed.

He felt the heat creep slowly up his neck as he thought about the contents of that wallet. Two hundred in cash. His driver's license, social security card, and a credit card. When he thought about how much time it would take to replace those things, he had to grind his teeth to keep from screaming.

Wyatt looked up and caught a smile on Dillon's

face before his twin managed to make it disappear. His eyes narrowed suspiciously. "You find this funny, Dil?"

Looking remarkably innocent, Dillon shook his head. "No funnier than *you* thought it was when those dogs trashed my cell phone. I seem to recall you were the last one to use it."

"So this is payback?"

"Not at all. I didn't have anything to do with this one."

He left Wyatt standing in the foyer, mulling over Dillon's last words. *This one*, he'd said, which would imply he'd been involved in other pranks. Could his brother have been the mastermind behind his unexpected guests? And what about the man-eating housekeeper? In fact, he'd never seen anyone recover from a sprained ankle as quickly as Mrs. Scuttle appeared to have recovered.

Wyatt stared at the pitiful remains of his wallet. Nah. No matter how much he tried, he couldn't imagine his brother behind his stream of rotten luck. Isabelle, maybe.

But not Dillon.

Kasidy felt like a new woman when she stepped out of the shower. Reaching for a towel, she caught a glimpse of herself in the mirror and let out a tiny squeak of dismay.

Love bites. Dozens of them. All over her body.

Recalling how she *got* those love bites produced an all-over body blush. What a night to remember! Wyatt had shown her just how much fun sex could be, while exhibiting a tenderness that had made it seem like so much more than sex.

Bonding. Romance. Maybe even . . . love.

She let out a soft gasp and clutched the towel to her chest. Love? Did she love Wyatt? Or was she just a little starstruck over the great sex?

Too early to tell, she thought, fighting panic.

But halfway to her closet, she stopped and forced herself to consider the possibility. What if she was? What could she do about it? Nothing had changed in her life. Until she found that tape, she couldn't be herself, and she knew she and Wyatt couldn't build a relationship based on lies and half-truths.

So now she had *two* reasons to get that evidence and destroy it. Her own future, as well as her father's, was at stake.

And possibly Wyatt's, if he felt the same about her.

Slowly, Kasidy grabbed a T-shirt from a hanger and began to get dressed. How would Wyatt take the news when she told him that she was Amelia's long-lost granddaughter? Would he be mad at her for keeping the truth from him? Would he understand her reasons?

Clad in panties and a T-shirt, Kasidy plopped onto the bed, dismay filling her as she realized something else. It wasn't just Wyatt who might be hurt by her betrayal. She'd made friends. Mary, Isabelle, Callie, and Mrs. Scuttle, to name a few.

She needed to talk to Nana Jo, she mused, padding to her backpack to retrieve her cell phone. Nana Jo always knew just what to say and how to advise her.

Nana Jo answered on the second ring, sounding breathless and more than a little irked. "Hello?"

"Nana?" Tears rushed to Kasidy's eyes at the sound of her grandmother's beloved voice. She hadn't realized how much she'd missed her. "It's Kasidy."

"Like I wouldn't recognize my only granddaughter's voice," Nana Jo chided. But she sounded pleased to hear from her. "How is everything going?"

"Good." Actually, it was going great, but Kasidy didn't want to throw her grandmother into a heart attack by telling her she'd spent the night having wild sex in the back of a pickup. "You sound irritated. Anything wrong?"

"Um, I just got another call from your father, wanting to speak to you. He's called three times since you left. I think he's becoming suspicious."

"Did you use the excuses I suggested?"

"I did, but I think he's starting to catch on. He's sharp."

"I know." Kasidy felt a pang of remorse for causing her father to worry, and her grandmother to lie. "It shouldn't be much longer."

"Have you had any luck finding the evidence?"

This time it was guilt that tweaked her tummy as she thought about all the good times she'd had, and how those good times had kept her from doing what she'd come to do. "Um, no. The house has been full of people, so I haven't had many chances to sleuth." Then, before she lost her courage, she said, "I'm thinking about explaining everything to Wyatt and soliciting his help."

"Are you, now."

Kasidy could almost hear the wheels turning in Nana Jo's mind as she absorbed the information.

She nibbled her bottom lip, waiting for Nana's sage advice.

"Do you think that's wise, Kas? I mean, what do you really know about this man?"

Boy, would she be very, very surprised at just how much I know, Kasidy thought, biting back a grin. "I don't think he knows anything about us, past or present." In fact, she was certain of it, especially after last night.

"Still . . . if you tell one person, that person will tell another, and so forth. It's human nature, honey. Before you know it, you'll be in the spotlight, and so will your father." Nana Jo paused before she added softly, "Or in your father's case, someone's crosshairs."

A cold shiver traveled down Kasidy's spine. As usual, Nana Jo had a valid point. After she hung up, Kasidy mulled over her grandmother's advice. Everything inside her urged her to trust Wyatt. With his help, they could make short work of her sleuthing and end her father's exile.

But on the other hand, Nana had made an excellent point. People were gossipers by nature, which was exactly why her mother had never gotten too friendly with her neighbors, and why they'd coached Kasidy not to entrust her school friends with secrets.

Besides, she'd witnessed firsthand how impossible it was to keep a secret from anyone in Wyatt's odd assortment of friends and family.

In the end, she compromised. She'd wait a couple more days. If at the end of that time, she still felt that she could trust Wyatt, she would tell him everything.

He'd be her first bonafide confidant.

Kasidy smiled at the idea. She liked it.
And she liked Wyatt.
Love?
Maybe.
Possibly.
Okay. Likely. Very, very likely.

CHAPTER 18

"See anything?"

Dillon lowered the binoculars and glanced at his wife. It was impossible to look at her and not laugh.

When he'd told her about the mission, she'd begged to come along. Because he hated saying no to her, and loved spending time with her, he'd said yes. She had immediately started to plan what she would wear.

She'd found a camouflage jumpsuit at an army surplus store, a pair of heavy boots, and a black ski hat. As if that weren't enough, she'd used black shoe polish to paint her face.

Callie scowled at his laughing face now, yanking the binoculars from his hand and nearly strangling him before he could get the strap over his head.

"When the neighbors see *you* and not me, and call the cops, you won't be laughing," she promised. She cast him a look filled with disdain and pointed at his cream-colored polo shirt. "You stick out like a sore thumb in that shirt."

Dillon's jaw dropped. "*I* stick out?" he asked incredulously. "In case you haven't noticed, we're on a hill behind a mansion, in Atlanta's richest neighborhood, and *you're* dressed like one of those Green Berets. Thank God you didn't shave your head!"

"Don't be silly." Falling silent, she looked for a long moment through the binoculars. Finally, she lowered them.

He choked back a laugh at her disappointed expression. "See anything?"

"Nothing important. Just one of the dogs taking off with Wyatt's shoe."

"He's still in the hot tub?"

"Yep. You'd think he'd feel like a prune by now." She handed him back the binoculars. "Are you sure you can trust Louise?"

"I told you, she and I have a deal. I keep Mrs. Scuttle away, and she tells me everything that happens between Wyatt and Kasidy. That way, if things get sticky, we can do something about it."

"You mean, we can *try*, darling."

Callie stared at him so long Dillon began to squirm. "What?" he finally asked.

She shook her head, her mouth twisted in a faintly awed, rueful smile. "I just can't get over how much you've changed since the twins were born. I mean, who would have thought you'd someday be crawling on the ground, spying on your brother?"

Dillon felt a blush coming on. "All in the name of love, Cal."

She snorted. "The hell it is! You're having the time of your life!"

Now that stung, and it wasn't true. "I'll have you

know," he replied haughtily, "that the best time of my life was when I was courting you."

"You mean when you were pretending to like me just so I'd give your bar a good review?"

"You don't honestly believe that, do you?"

She let him suffer for a full thirty seconds before she laughed. "Of course not, silly."

Feeling a vibration against his side, Dillon reached for Callie's cell phone, which he'd appropriated, and read the text message displayed on the screen. It was Louise, letting him know that she was about to leave for the day. She had nothing new to report. When he put the phone away, he lifted the binoculars. "Now things should start heating up," he said.

Callie grabbed the binoculars and rose, ignoring his protest. "You know the rules, Dil. After Louise leaves, *we* leave. We are not spying on Kasidy and Wyatt when they're alone."

"Damn," Dillon grumbled, but rose with her.

He just wasn't happy about it.

"There's fresh chicken salad in the fridge, and turkey cutlets for the boys," Louise told Kasidy on her way out. "You should keep an eye on Larry, though. He's food aggressive when it comes to his turkey."

Kasidy leaned against the staircase and did her best to appear casual. Inside, she was a bundle of nerves. When Louise left, she and Wyatt would be alone in the house. Well, *almost* alone. They'd have the dogs. "Thanks for the tip, Louise. I'll separate them before I give them the turkey."

Louise shook her head. "Won't work. Amelia always made them eat together, as a family. They won't eat any other way."

"Bless their hearts," Kasidy murmured. She really did feel empathy for the poodles. They still hadn't gotten over losing their mistress, although Kasidy felt she was making headway in helping them forget.

The housekeeper looked suddenly sad. "They miss her. A lot of people do. She was a wonderful person. It's just too bad that . . . well, I don't expect you want to hear about it. You didn't even know her."

Something in the housekeeper's voice put Kasidy on full alert. She stiffened. "Um, on the contrary, I'm very interested. I've heard a lot of wonderful things about Mrs. Hancock. Did you . . . um, ever meet her granddaughter?"

"No, I didn't," Louise said, her voice rough with anger. "And neither did Amelia. That daughter of hers was stubborn and spiteful! Amelia begged her forgiveness, but she wouldn't budge."

Kasidy grabbed the bannister for support. She had to bite her tongue to keep from defending her mother. She wanted to tell Louise that her mother hadn't had a spiteful bone in her body, that Amelia had lied.

But she couldn't, not without blowing her cover. Diplomatically, Kasidy said, "I'm sure there's another side to the story. There always is."

Louise seemed to soften at her words. "You might be right, dear. You might be right. Amelia's daughter was gone by the time I came to work for her, so I only heard Amelia's version." She looked down at the car keys in her hand. When she glanced back at Kasidy, her eyes were bright with tears. "Amelia had a stubborn streak of her own, so I guess her daughter came by it honest."

Softly, Kasidy asked, "Did she make provisions for you?"

"Of course, but only on the condition that I would stay on for six months after she died, so I could be here when and if her granddaughter showed up."

The words nearly stuck in her throat, but Kasidy managed to push them out. "Do you . . . do you think she'll show?"

"I don't know. I don't think money meant much to Willow after she left. Otherwise she wouldn't have given it all up for that thug she ran off with."

It hurt, but Kasidy bit her tongue anyway.

"So I don't know how the girl feels. Either way, I'm to stay so that I can tell the granddaughter how much Amelia loved her."

Kasidy had to swallow hard again. "How could she? She didn't even know her."

Louise shrugged. "Maybe she didn't, but I don't think a day went by that Amelia didn't think about her granddaughter, and yearn to see her. She . . . she has a few pictures from when the child was young, before her private investigators lost track of them for good. Well, I should get going. See you tomorrow."

"Yeah, see you tomorrow."

It was several moments before Kasidy could move. She blinked tears from her eyes, angry at herself for believing—if only for a moment—that Amelia had truly been the woman Louise described.

No. It wasn't possible. To believe that, she would have to believe that her parents had lied to her, and *that* she couldn't believe. In fact, she was ashamed of herself for having a weak moment.

Dashing at her eyes, Kasidy resolutely pushed the disloyal thoughts from her mind and went in search of Wyatt. She'd left the dogs napping in their room with the door open, knowing they would find her when they got hungry.

Speaking of hunger . . . Kasidy grinned to herself. Wyatt had certainly awakened her appetite last night, because she could scarcely think of anything else. Had it been real? Had she really experienced not two, but three earth-shattering orgasms? Was that even possible?

And more important, had it been a fluke?

Only one way to find out.

The scent of coconut reached Wyatt's nostrils just seconds before he felt the water begin to move around him.

Hallelujah, he thought, smiling. If Kasidy was here, then that meant Louise had left.

They were alone in the house at last. Alone to do exactly as they pleased. When they pleased, how they pleased, and where they pleased. There was the billiard room, with a huge pool table. His bedroom, ten other guest rooms, her room, the kitchen table, the dining room table, the rug in front of the fire place . . .

"Are you thinking about sex again?" Kasidy asked, her voice husky with laughter and arousal.

Wyatt opened one eye to look at her. He was only slightly disappointed to find her in a swimsuit, the white one. But his disappointment was short lived; he could easily remove it, and have a lot of fun doing it. "What gave me away?"

Her laughter skidded over his nerve endings like a cattle prod, bringing them to electrifying life. When her hot little hand landed against his erection on top of his shorts, Wyatt sucked in a sharp, chagrined gasp. Was he a man, or a teenager? He felt like the latter around Kasidy, as if he might explode at the slightest touch.

For his own sake, as well as hers, he grabbed her arms and hauled her on top of him. He was debating on whether they should make love in the hot tub. The warmth of the water definitely heightened his sensitivity.

Which meant that it probably did the same for Kasidy, which meant that he could likely turn the location to his advantage. He reached for the straps of her swimsuit, intending to get that out of the way.

She giggled and squirmed against him. "Wyatt! What if someone's watching?"

His hands stilled. "Like who?"

"Like a peeping tom, or somebody."

He grinned. "Then let's give him something to see."

"Wyatt!"

He laughed at her outraged expression. "I'm only teasing. Seriously, nobody can see us."

"What if someone comes in?"

"I instructed Louise to lock the doors when she left."

"Don't they have keys?"

He knew whom she meant by "they." His grin widened to a leer. "Not anymore, they don't." This time she didn't resist when he went for her straps. Within minutes, her warm, slick body was sliding against his in the hot, softly pulsating water. He took her mouth in a hungry kiss, marveling at how naturally and whole-heartedly she responded.

If she had inhibitions, she had yet to reveal them.

The realization was erotic fodder to his massively hungry libido. Moving her slightly to the side, Wyatt unerringly found her swollen center with his thumb. He captured her moan in his mouth and began a rhythm with his hand that had her arching against him and panting for more.

"Stop!" she gasped, grabbing his shoulders for support.

He tugged her bottom lip between his teeth, stopping long enough to fool her into relaxing, before he slipped two fingers inside her and began a pivoting motion that quickly brought her to a peak. He replaced her lip with a rock-hard nipple, and sucked as she came, prolonging her orgasm until she went limp against him.

Wyatt held very still, both amazed and disgruntled to realize that he was perilously close to peaking himself, and without stimulation.

Amazing.

She was amazing.

"Now it's my turn," she whispered, still breathless. She wrapped her arms around his neck and kissed him slowly, teasingly, darting her tongue inside his mouth until Wyatt groaned and closed his arms around her.

"Stop," he said, his voice rough with the effort it was taking to hold back.

She pulled away and blinked innocently at him. "Stop? But I wasn't doing anything." Then her eyelids lowered seductively. "At least, not *yet*."

Wyatt let his breath hiss between his teeth and managed to get out, "Have mercy?"

She cocked a saucy brow. "Like the mercy you showed me just a moment ago? I think not. Now, come with me, and I don't mean that literally."

Just as Wyatt suspected; he'd created a sex monster. He watched her rise from the hot tub, water sluicing off her high, full breasts. When she held out her hand, he obediently gave her his own. He rose, but before he could make a move, she put a hand against his chest and stopped him.

In two quick moves, she had his shorts to his knees. "Step out of them," she ordered, her eyes dark and smoky. "You won't need them where we're going."

Wyatt's mouth went dry. "I won't?"

She shook her head and took his hand again. "Nope."

Lord have mercy, Wyatt thought.

CHAPTER 19

Kasidy pushed Wyatt onto the bed and watched his eyes widen with pleasure as he bounced gently to and fro.

"It's a water bed!" he said, glancing around at the cluttered room. "She must have used this as a storage room. How did you find it?"

She'd been prepared for his question. "I found it when I was searching the house for satin pillows." It was apparent in the sudden darkening of his eyes that he well remembered the usefulness of those pillows.

"Clever girl." He patted the bed beside him. "Won't you join me?"

"Oh, I'll join you, all right." Kasidy boldly straddled him, settling her heat against his erection and making him gasp and moan. She gave the bed an experimental jiggle, smiling when Wyatt clutched her hips in a vain effort to hold her still. Leaning forward to kiss him, she subtly shifted her body until she could slide him inside her.

She didn't stop until he had filled her to the hilt. Then she began to rock gently, ignoring his raspy

196

pleas for her to slow down. Kasidy didn't need to slow down. Her inner muscles had already started to spasm when Wyatt shouted her name and thrust upward, his hands digging into her hips.

Panting together, they lay side by side on the gently undulating mattress. Kasidy cuddled against his chest, and he responded by putting an arm around her and squeezing.

"If this gets out," Wyatt whispered breathlessly, "I'm ruined. I don't even think that lasted a full minute."

His joking comment aroused the green-eyed monster in Kasidy. She wondered idly—and half seriously—what it would cost for a full-page ad in the local newspaper. Out loud, she said, "I don't get it. If both parties are satisfied, what difference does time make?"

Kissing the top of her head, he said, his voice laced with amusement, "You have a valid point, baby. But you're one of a kind, I'm afraid."

"And that's a bad thing?"

"Hell, no! It's a great thing. A terrific thing." He turned on the mattress until he was facing her, their mouths inches apart. "A very, very excellent thing," he murmured thickly. He ran his hand down her body, and pulled her hips to his. "The quicker we finish, the quicker we can start on another round."

Kasidy liked the sound of that.

An hour later, at Wyatt's insistence, Kasidy was back in the hot tub. Although she hated to admit it, she *was* sore from lovemaking. Wyatt had assured her that the hot, soothing water would wash away her soreness.

She looked up as he approached with a plate of chicken salad sandwiches and two glasses of ice-cold milk. Balancing the platter, he lowered himself cautiously into the water beside her and handed her a sandwich. He set the two glasses of milk on the rim of the hot tub.

"I could get used to this life," he said, taking a huge bite of his sandwich. He chewed and swallowed. "How about you?"

"Maybe," Kasidy said, deciding it would be best not to look at him. The way Wyatt ate his sandwich made her think of the ravenous way he'd attacked her the third time they'd made love. "Did you feed the dogs?"

"Yes, and I gave Larry his turkey first, like you said." He took a big gulp of his milk, leaving a thick milk mustache behind. "I was hoping to score some points with those boys, but I don't think it worked. They looked at me as if I'd eaten half their dinner before I gave it to them."

Trying her best to keep a straight face, Kasidy lifted one inquiring brow and glanced pointedly at the pile of sandwiches on his plate. "Did you?"

He feigned outrage. "Of course not!" Then he flashed a wicked, gut-punching grin at her. "It tasted like rubber, without any seasoning. They can have it."

"You're terrible."

"That's not what you said earlier," he countered smugly.

Kasidy splashed water at him, hitting his sandwich. Wyatt didn't seem to mind or care. "If you were a gentleman—" she squealed as he threw his sandwich onto his plate and hauled her up against him.

"I told you before," he growled. "I'm not a gentleman. Would a gentleman do this?" He sucked the air out of her lungs with a long, drugging kiss. "And this?" Hauling her farther out of the water, he latched onto one of her puckered nipples and nipped gently, then suckled until she was whimpering.

She scrambled for a handhold in his hair. "Wyatt, please!"

"And this?" He lifted her, burying his tongue in her belly button.

She pummeled his head lightly with her fists. "Okay! Okay! I'm sorry! I take it back." Both relieved and disappointed when he lowered her back into the water, Kasidy leaned over and licked the milk from his upper lip, lingering far longer than necessary.

"You're insatiable," Wyatt murmured when she pulled away, licking her lips.

"I think I am," Kasidy happily agreed. She took a small bite of her sandwich. She wasn't hungry, but she knew she should eat if she was going to keep up her strength, because if that gleam in Wyatt's eye was any indication, the night was not over.

Which suited her just fine.

To take her mind off her new hobby, Kasidy asked, "So how do you feel about this long-lost granddaughter? Do you hope she shows to claim her inheritance?"

Wyatt frowned thoughtfully. "That's a tough one. On the one hand, if she doesn't show then all of this goes to the dogs—literally. On the other hand, I knew Amelia, and although she didn't confide in me, I'm sure this estrangement from her granddaughter hurt. If the girl couldn't give her grandmother the time of day when she was alive, why should she reap the benefits of her death?"

"Maybe she has her reasons for staying away," Kasidy mumbled, pretending a great interest in her sandwich. Beside her, she felt Wyatt stiffen. She did the same, cursing her loose tongue. She had to remind herself again that behind that Chippendale body and handsome face was a sharp brain.

Softly, he asked, "Do you know something about this granddaughter that I don't?"

Kasidy hesitated. Was this the right time to tell him the truth? Could she trust him? She was falling in love with him. She knew that now. But did that mean she could trust him with her secret—as well as her heart? Although love hadn't been mentioned, Kasidy sensed that Wyatt didn't think of their relationship as a fling any more than she did. They had something special. She was certain of it.

"Kasidy?"

Wyatt's soft prompt made her jump. She turned to him, praying that she was doing the right thing. Her father's life depended on it. "Um, Wyatt, there's something I want to—"

The doorbell pealed, interrupting her. Wyatt frowned. "I'll get it. You wait here."

She waited until he pulled on his damp shorts before she hurriedly slipped into her wet swimsuit. Whoever it was, she didn't want the visitor to find her naked in the hot tub. She wasn't *that* uninhibited!

Just as she stepped from the hot tub, she heard voices raised in anger. But it wasn't the loud voices that sent a shaft of fear through Kasidy; it was the absence of barking that sent her slip-sliding into the house.

She came to a stop in the hall next to the staircase. At the front door, Wyatt stood, flanked by two burly men in dark suits. They held him by the arms and appeared to be trying to drag him to the front door.

In the shadows outside their door, the poodles sat together, silently watching the display as if they approved of the way the strangers were manhandling Wyatt. "You guys are a lot of help," she muttered.

Gathering her courage, Kasidy stepped forward, keenly aware that she wore a wet swimsuit and nothing more. But then, Wyatt wore only his shorts. "Should I call the police, Wyatt?" she called out boldly.

The three men turned as one. Wyatt looked angry. The two thugs looked amused.

"So *that's* why you don't want to come along with us," one of the thugs said, giving Kasidy a creepy appraisal that left her with a rash of goose bumps. "Can't say that I blame you, but we've got our orders. Mr. Slowkowsky wants to talk to you."

Mr. Slowkowsky. Kasidy's knees almost buckled. Why would a known mobster—her father's enemy, no less—want to talk to Wyatt?

"Ever heard of asking?" Wyatt growled. To Kasidy, he said, "If I'm not back in two hours, call the police." When she continued to look petrified, Wyatt attempted a reassuring smile. "Don't worry. I know this Slowkowsky guy. He's harmless, as long as he's getting his way."

Rooted to the spot, Kasidy watched, helplessly, as they shoved Wyatt through the doorway and into a waiting limo. She rushed to the door, but could see nothing behind the darkly tinted windows. When they drove away, she memorized the license plates, then raced for the old-fashioned wall phone in the kitchen.

Once there, she was brought up short. She didn't know anyone's phone number! Her frantic gaze lit on the scrawled message board on the wall beside the phone. Among the numbers, she found Louise's, and quickly dialed.

She didn't wait for a hello. "Quick, Louise! I need to contact someone in Wyatt's family!"

There was a pregnant pause, then Louise, sounding extremely curious, gave her Dillon's phone number. "Is there something wrong?" she asked.

Kasidy finished scribbling the number down and said breathlessly, "Some men came and forced Wyatt into a limo to take him to see Mr. Slowkowsky." To her frustration, Louise laughed.

"Oh, him. He's harmless. They'll bring him back safe and sound. Mr. Slowkowsky likes to do things the old way, mostly for show."

Harmless? Were they talking about the same man? Kasidy wondered. "But-but-Mr. Slowkowsky's a mobster, isn't he?"

"Well, he used to be, but when his brother went to prison, he turned over a new leaf and became legit. Rumor has it that his brother was stealing him blind."

Was that the story they'd tossed about, hoping to lure her father into a trap? Kasidy blew an irritating lock of hair out of her face, thanked Louise, and hung up.

She was beside herself. What should she do? Was Wyatt working for Mr. Slowkowsky, or was it just a coincidence? No. Kasidy didn't believe in *those* kind of coincidences. The kind that could wreck your life or leave you dead. And Wyatt had admitted that he knew Mr. Slowkowsky.

Time to call Dillon. Maybe Dillon could enlighten her. Kasidy dialed the number. She wiped her sweaty palms on her swimsuit as she waited for someone to answer the phone.

Callie answered.

"Callie? Is Dillon around?"

"Yes, just a moment. He's playing hide-and-seek with the twins, but I think I know where to find him. He likes to keep it easy for them."

While she was gone, Kasidy bit her thumbnail to the quick. She felt sick to her stomach, and she didn't think it was the chicken salad sandwich. When Dillon came on the line, she told him what she'd told Louise.

This time, she got an alarming response.

"Damn. I thought Luke told the old man he'd have to find someone else to do his dirty work."

Kasidy's blood turned to ice. "What? Wyatt's worked for Mr. Slowkowsky before?" Her stomach churned at the implications.

"Against his better judgement, yes." Dillon sounded grim. "I'll have to call Luke, find out what's going on."

"What . . . what if they hurt Wyatt?" Kasidy hated the shameful squeak in her voice, but she couldn't help it. She'd grown up fearing the name Slowkowsky as much as she had learned to hate it. And though her

203

heart was slowly breaking at the thought of Wyatt being involved with the Slowkowskys, she couldn't bear the thought of him getting hurt.

"Hurt him?" Dillon's bark of laughter was devoid of humor. "They wouldn't dare. Wyatt's got too much on them. Listen, Kas. Don't worry about Wyatt. He's a big boy, and he can take care of himself."

His last word faded abruptly, and Callie got on the line. "Kasidy? Would you like me to come over and sit with you until Wyatt gets back?"

It was tempting, but she felt silly, so she said, "Um, no, no. I'll be fine." She glowered at the three poodles watching her. "I've got the dogs for company."

When she hung up, she placed her hands on her hips and regarded the trio. "I should trade you in for Dobermans, or Rottweilers. Shame on you!"

Moe, Larry, and Curly didn't look a bit ashamed. They thumped their tails and whined in response.

"I think I need to catch Wyatt before he gets back to Kasidy," Dillon told Callie after she hung up. Hearing the sound of bare feet against the kitchen tile, Dillon quickly darted behind the door. He peeped around it, adding in a whisper, "Kasidy sounded petrified, as if she knew the *old* Slowkowsky, not the harmless old man he is today."

Callie covered her mouth and spoke from the side as the twins came creeping into the kitchen, their eyes big with expectation. "Maybe this will shed some light on why she doesn't want anyone to know who she is."

"That's what I'm thinking." Waiting until his twins drew even with the door, Dillon roared and pounced, sending them into a screaming, laughing frenzy as they tried to turn around and run on the slick floor. They ended up in a giggling heap. Continuing to multitask—something he'd learned from Callie—he leaned over to tickle them. "Can you hold down the fort for a while?"

"Sure, as long as you know that means you get bath and bedtime later."

He tried not to look smug as he said, "Can't. Got a party tonight at the club. Lou'll need my help."

Proving she could have the last word, Callie said, "Fine. I'll leave the dishes and the laundry for you, then."

"You're so kind, Callie."

"I know."

"And a great mom."

"Thank you."

"Not to mention a tiger in the sack."

Callie shook her head and sighed, but she had to bite her lip to keep from smiling. "It's not happening, Dil."

He blinked innocently. "What's not happening?"

"You're not getting the last word."

"Was I trying to do that?"

"Yes."

"No, I wasn't."

"Yes, you were." She tapped her foot. "You're *still* doing it."

"Am not."

"Are too. Stop it."

"Why?"

"Because I've got all night, and *you* don't."

"Good point."

205

"Bye, Dillon."

"Bye, sweetheart." With his twins hanging from his legs, he pulled her tight and kissed her. "Mmm. You taste good."

"Thank you."

"You're welcome."

"Well, guess I'll go." He walked backward, sliding the shrieking twins with him as if he didn't notice their attachment to his legs.

Callie followed, offering him a sweet smile. "Have a good night."

"You, too, honey."

"I will."

"You do that."

"You, too."

"I will. Bye, now."

"Bye, Dillon."

"You're beautiful. Have I told you that?"

Laughing, Callie disengaged the twins and hauled them clear so she could physically push her husband out the door. "Shut up."

With the door between them, Dillon smashed his face against the glass and shouted, "Love you!"

He was nearly in his car when he heard his wife shout back, "Love you, too!"

CHAPTER 20

When Wyatt saw Dillon's SUV blocking the driveway entrance to the Hancock mansion, he depressed the intercom button next to his left hand. "You can let me out here," he instructed the limo driver, still irritated with the high-handed way Mr. Slowkowsky had requested an audience. He'd read the fear in Kasidy's eyes, and couldn't wait to get back to the mansion and reassure her.

But apparently his brother had other ideas.

Wyatt got out of the limo and walked the short distance to Dillon's vehicle. He slid into the passenger side, not in the best of moods. "What?" he barked at Dillon.

Dillon rested an arm across the steering wheel, staring at the limo as it sped away. "I see that Mr. Slowkowsky still revels in drama," he said. "What did he want?"

"And that's your business—how?"

"Luke sent me," Dillon said. "Not to mention the fact that Kasidy was petrified by the way they took

207

you. She's convinced we'll find you floating facedown in the river."

Wyatt let out a vile curse. "I told her not to worry. I see that she listened."

"Can you blame her? Two thugs dragged you out of the house into a dark limo with tinted windows. You see it on television all the time. So . . . is this about his ugly stepsister again? Because if it is, Luke says to tell you that you don't have to escort her. You have the right to refuse service, and she's definitely given you a reason to refuse. If you'd been a woman, you could have pressed charges of attempted rape."

It wasn't a story that Wyatt cared to dwell on. He'd much rather forget. "That wasn't it," Wyatt said shortly. And then, because he was dying to tell someone and he knew he could trust his brother, he added, "It was about Amelia's granddaughter. The old man wants to make sure that if she shows, I don't let her out of my sight until he gets a chance to talk to her."

"Why does he want to talk to her?"

Was his twin's voice a tad on the sharp side? Wyatt wondered, narrowing his gaze suspiciously at Dillon. Dillon blinked innocently at him, a look Wyatt was beginning to question. Watching him closely, he said, "You'll never guess in a million years."

"Do I *have* to guess?" Dillon asked irritably. "Kasidy's waiting, you know."

Wyatt closed his eyes, recalling how brave she'd been, standing in the hall in her bathing suit. She had certainly shown more courage than those lousy mutts of Amelia's. "Slowkowsky's her grandfather," Wyatt blurted out.

"The granddaughter's grandfather?"

"No," Wyatt drawled sarcastically, "Amelia's grandfather. Of course I was talking about the elusive granddaughter. Seems she stands to inherit more than one fortune, if she ever shows."

"Did he say why he thought she wasn't coming forward?"

Suspicion tugged at Wyatt again. "Is there a reason for this sudden interest in Amelia's granddaughter?"

Dillon shrugged. "There's a reward, isn't there? I would think that would interest anyone. I could use a little cash. I have twins, you know."

"Right." Wyatt wasn't completely mollified, but he didn't have the energy to pursue the matter. If Dillon wanted to keep something from him, he knew it would take a crowbar to pry it out of him. "The old man mentioned something about a threat to Amelia's son-in-law. It was mostly a bluff, but it backfired on Amelia. The couple never stopped running."

"What kind of threat?"

"The son-in-law turned state's evidence against Slowkowsky's brother. What the son-in-law doesn't know, though, is that Slowkowsky is *glad* he did it. Slowkowsky's no-good brother was stealing from him, had been for a long while."

His twin's low whistle filled the cab of the SUV. "Sounds like an episode from the *Sopranos*."

"Yeah." Wyatt tapped his fingers against the dashboard. "If there was just some way of letting the granddaughter know that it's safe to come forward. . . ."

"Slowkowsky could try posting an article in all the major newspapers. He's still got clout, doesn't he?"

Wyatt shook his head. "He tried that. Apparently, the guy thought it was a trap."

"So . . . this granddaughter. She thinks they'll come after her, and torture her into telling them where her father is?"

"That's one theory."

"There's another one?"

Again Wyatt hesitated. He gave his brother a hard look. "This doesn't leave this car, understand?"

"Understood."

"My theory is that she doesn't want the money. If her parents were constantly on the run, then they're bound to have told her why. They probably poisoned her against wealthy people."

Dillon whistled again.

The sound was about to get on Wyatt's last nerve.

"What kind of person turns down that kinda dough because of bad feelings?"

Wyatt had been unable to think of little else on the limo ride back to the mansion. Slowly, he said, "A woman with integrity, and a fierce loyalty to the parents who raised her. A woman with grit. Definitely not a materialistic woman."

"Sounds like a special woman," Dillon said. "By the way, that was a dirty trick our little sister pulled on you two."

"Yeah." Wyatt felt the corners of his lips twitch. "She made me proud. And Kasidy, she was a real trooper."

"Yeah, she's got grit."

"You could learn a thing or two from her, bro. Loosen up."

"Nah," Dillon said as he did a U turn in the road

and drove through the gate. "I'll leave the pranks to you kids." He braked in front of the mansion. "You look worn out, Wyatt. Maybe you should get some sleep."

There was that innocent blink again, Wyatt thought. Shaking his head, he opened the door and got out. He had the distinct, uneasy feeling that he had missed something.

He just didn't know what.

She had the first three numbers. Laying the pad and pen aside, Kasidy pressed the stethoscope to the safe again and slowly began to turn the knob.

Just as she had suspected, she'd found the safe in Wyatt's room, behind a painting of Little Boy Blue that hung over his bed. Concentrating on finding the safe and getting that video had kept her heartache at bay.

She had to finally admit the truth to herself. Wyatt was a traitor, working for Slowkowsky. Apparently Amelia had known exactly whom to hire to carry on her twenty-five-year-old grudge against her son-in-law. How bitter she must have been, Kasidy thought, to find out she was going to die without getting her way.

But she'd improvised, continuing to play her evil little game even from the grave by planting a drop-dead gorgeous man in her house as a spy.

And it had nearly worked. When Kasidy thought about how close she came to confessing to Wyatt, she broke out in a cold sweat.

"Damn," she muttered, realizing she'd missed the click. She resolutely pushed her dark thoughts aside and tried again.

211

"Lucy! I'm home!"

Wyatt's shout startled her so badly she lost her balance and fell backward on his bed.

He sounded close.

Scrambling frantically to her knees, she replaced the picture and shoved the notebook, pen, and stethoscope beneath the bed. She'd just struck a seductive pose when he appeared in the doorway.

She hoped he wouldn't notice her flushed face, sweaty upper lip, and guilty expression.

"You look pissed," he said.

Ooops. She'd forgotten to hide *that* emotion. "I'm furious at those brutes for manhandling you," she lied. Actually, she *had* been furious, until she'd figured out that Wyatt didn't deserve her loyalty.

Or her love.

Or any damn thing else that he'd been getting.

Traitor, she shouted silently. It didn't matter that he didn't realize who she was. She knew him now. By his own admission, he yearned for wealth. People like Wyatt wouldn't hesitate to turn on a lover or a friend, for the right money.

Thank God she'd found out before it was too late for her father.

As for herself, she feared that it was too late. She'd leave her grandmother's house with a broken heart and a more mature outlook on men.

They couldn't be trusted. It was as simple as that.

Cocking a sexy hip, Wyatt leaned against the doorway, a wicked smile curving his mouth. "So you were worried about me?"

"Of course."

"And that's why you're lying in my bed—in the middle of dog pee?"

Frowning, Kasidy looked down at the bed. Belatedly, she saw the wide stain beneath her hip. At the same instant, she got a whiff of dog pee. She jumped up with a curse of dismay. "Yuk! Why do they *do* that to you?" As if she didn't know! The dogs were the smart ones. They knew what a lying traitor he was. A man who would stoop to anything for money.

A man who would lie in wait for an innocent woman, only to throw her to the sharks for . . . how much? How much was Slowkowsky paying him, on top of what her grandmother had left him?

No wonder Wyatt was so jolly. He lived in a mansion, was making a fortune as a spy, and had a willing, nearly nymphomaniac woman at his beck and call.

A slow heat began to spread along Kasidy's body, and it had little to do with the hungry way Wyatt was eyeing her. She had to get away from him, before she gave in to the fierce desire to punch his lights out.

"I'm going to shower and change," she said, hoping to get past him without Wyatt touching her.

She didn't make it. She stood stiffly as he pressed his warm, hard body against her back and closed his arms around her. Despite her determination to remain unmoved, she shivered when his lips nuzzled her neck. Obviously, her body had yet to catch up with her brain.

"Want some company in the shower?" he whispered.

She forced herself to relax, not wanting him to become suspicious until she figured out her next move. "Haven't you had enough excitement for one day?"

His hand wandered up to her breast. He cupped her, fondling her nipple with his thumb.

The man had a magic thumb.

But she didn't care. She *couldn't* care. She could have sex with anyone, now that she knew it could be good.

Okay, so maybe she didn't want sex with anyone else. That was the slow part of her brain that hadn't caught up with the smart part.

"A man can't have too much excitement, can he?"

"I guess not. What did Mr. Slowkowsky want with you?" Unconsciously, she held her breath. She was going on the assumption that he didn't know who she was. What if she was wrong? What if this seduction was a form of torture? Maybe Wyatt wasn't one of Mr. Slowkowsky's grunt men. Maybe he used a different kind of torture to get his victims to talk.

It had almost worked.

"He wanted to talk about his granddaughter," Wyatt said absently, lifting her hair and nuzzling the sensitive nape of her neck. "About that shower . . ."

Kasidy tried to imagine an evil gangster like Slowkowsky with a granddaughter.

She couldn't. Men like him didn't have granddaughters.

When Wyatt pressed his erection into her back, Kasidy knew what she had to do. She pressed her fingers to her temples and moaned in feigned agony.

"Oh, no," she moaned. "Not a migraine! I haven't had one in months. I thought they were over."

Wyatt instantly dropped his arms and turned her around. He wore an expression similar to the one

214

he'd worn the night he'd discovered Mrs. Scuttle was actually drunk.

"What can I do? Do I need to take you to the emergency room?"

Though his concern was touching, Kasidy didn't completely buy it. "Um, no. I just need to lie down in a dark room. It will eventually go away." She frowned, squinting her eyes as if it pained her to look at him.

And it did, because he was still the hottest man she'd ever laid eyes on.

"Come on. Let's get you to bed."

She was led like a child downstairs to her room. As they passed the dog's room, Kasidy slowed down. Appearing agitated, she grabbed his arm. "The dogs . . . they have to be walked before bed."

"I can handle the dogs."

"And tonight is bath night." She put a hand over her eyes and swallowed, as if it hurt to speak. "Louise said they always get baths on Saturdays." If she hadn't been so furious with him, she might have laughed at the dismayed silence that followed her statement.

Finally, he said, "I can handle the baths, too. It will give me a chance to bond with them."

"You have to dry them with a blow dryer."

"Okay."

"And brush them so their fur won't matt up."

"Got it."

"The scissors are in the little basket on the bookcase in their room."

Silence again.

"Scissors?" he finally asked cautiously.

Kasidy moaned and swayed. When he steadied her, she whispered, "Yes. After you bath them, you have to trim their hair from around their, um, rectums, so their poop won't stick to their butts."

"You're kidding." He sounded as if he'd gladly pay her a million dollars if she was.

"If you don't, it will cause an infection. Then they'll wipe their rears all over—"

"I get the picture," he said hastily. He tried to move her forward, but she held back, peering at him anxiously.

"Are you sure you can handle this? Because I can try, if you don't think you can. I don't want them to feel neglected."

"I can handle it," he said firmly. "Is there anything else?"

She covered her eyes again, so that he couldn't read her expression. "Just one more tiny thing. You have to read *101 Dalmatians* to them at bedtime."

"Now I *know* you've got to be joking."

She shook her head, then winced visibly. "Sorry, I'm not. It's something Mrs. Hancock got started. They won't settle until you do it."

"Sweet Lord," Wyatt muttered. "I knew the old lady was eccentric, but I didn't know she was flat out crazy. Can I get you something before I . . . do all of that?"

"A cold washcloth, a dark room, and quiet."

"Shouldn't I help you out of those damp clothes?"

"I can do it," Kasidy said a trifle too hastily. She hoped he'd blame it on the migraine. "Just get me a washcloth, if you don't mind."

The moment he was out of sight, Kasidy shed her clothes in record time and crawled beneath the covers. She was moaning softly when he came back with the washcloth.

"I hate to leave you like this," he said, sounding helpless.

"Please do. Your voice hurts my head."

When she opened one eye again, he had gone, turning out the light and shutting the door behind him.

Kasidy let the tears flow.

"Damned ungrateful pigs," Wyatt muttered darkly, punching in the next number. So far, he'd called three of his coworkers, who were also his friends.

Or so he'd thought.

This time, he knew he'd hit pay dirt. Greg was always ready and willing to help a friend in need. Hadn't he been there for Greg many times?

"Greg," he said the moment Greg answered the phone. "I need your help." Quickly, he explained his list of duties. When he finished, he got a now familiar, stunned silence.

"That's funny, Wyatt," Greg finally said, busting into laughter. "For a minute there, I thought you were serious! Trimming a dog's butt . . . yeah, that will be the day. Ha!"

For the fourth time, Wyatt cursed the sudden dead silence on his phone, and Greg for good measure.

Will Tallfeather, then, he thought, scrolling through his address book. Will worked for Mr. Complete, and he and his wife, LaVonda, owned a dog. They would understand and surely help him in his plight.

His buddy Will didn't freak at the butt trimming part, but he howled like a banshee when Wyatt mentioned reading a book to the dogs at bedtime.

Growing desperate, he was just about to punch in his mother's number when he remembered that Isabelle was home from college. And she owed him big time, after that prank she'd pulled.

"Sure!" Isabelle said when Wyatt got her on the phone. "I'll read them a story, but you can do the butt trimming part. Vets don't do the grunt work, bro."

Wyatt was so relieved, he didn't argue. Maybe he could bribe her with money when she arrived, he mused as he hung up the phone. His mother had loaned him her old phone when he'd told her his new one had been eaten by the dogs.

Cautiously, he slipped it into his shorts pocket. It might be an old phone, but it was the *only* phone he had.

He wasn't letting this one go to the dogs.

CHAPTER 21

"Hold him still," Wyatt instructed. He carefully snipped the last curl while Isabelle held tight to Moe's collar. "Okay. That should do it."

The moment Isabelle let go of his collar, Moe shot through the doggie door Amelia had installed in the patio doors. Wyatt didn't blame him. He sighed and looked down at the fruits of his labor lying on the newspaper.

The things we do for love, he mused with a faint smile.

"Where did they all go?" Isabelle asked, rising from her crouched position and stretching. "They disappeared as if they had an agenda."

"I'm sure they do. I'm also sure that you'll probably find them in my room."

"Why your room?"

"Revenge." Wyatt pointed at the hair clippings. "Wouldn't you want revenge if someone held you down and clipped the hair from your butt?"

Isabelle wrinkled her nose. "You have a point.

Kasidy's right, though. If you don't keep it trimmed, they'll start dragging their butts—"

"Stop!" Wyatt shuddered. "I've already got the image in my head, thank you very much."

"Speaking of Kasidy . . . how is she?"

"I don't know. She went to bed."

"Maybe I should check on her."

"She wouldn't appreciate it, little sister. I've never had a migraine, but I've heard they hurt like hell." He gathered up the newspaper and carried it to a trash bin at the edge of the patio. "How's school, by the way? We haven't had much time to talk."

"Oh, that." Isabelle sounded alarmingly reluctant. "I, um, dropped out."

"You what?" Wyatt whirled, scattering dog curls to the four winds as they slipped from the newspaper he'd folded. He sputtered and batted at his face.

Then he caught sight of Isabelle's wicked grin.

"Damn. You got me."

Isabelle's eyebrows rose. "I did, which is scary. You're starting to remind me of Dillon."

Wyatt's jaw dropped in dismay. He loved his brother, but he wouldn't want to *be* him. Dillon wouldn't recognize a good prank if it bit him in the ass. "Do I?"

"Gotcha again."

"You little turd."

"I'd watch the name calling, if I were you." Isabelle gave her blond hair a saucy toss. "There's still the bedtime story."

"Oh, yeah." Wyatt immediately feigned a subservient expression. "Yes, my queen. Anything you say, my queen."

She laughed. "That's better. Now, why don't you pour me a tall glass of Diet Coke while I round up the boys for bed."

"Yes, O Great One." When Isabelle tried to walk past him, Wyatt snatched her in for a quick, brotherly hug and a knuckle rub on top of her head. But his voice cracked a little when he said, "I love you, little sister. Don't ever change, okay?"

She mumbled something indistinguishable against his shirt, then pushed at his chest. "Don't get sappy on me. I *hate* it when you get sappy!" But it was clear from the love shining in her eyes that she didn't really mean it.

Chuckling, Wyatt swatted at her head as she darted away. "I'll get your Coke, then I've got to wash this dog smell off of me."

Isabelle looked down at her damp clothes. "Me, too, but I'm gonna wait until I get back to Mom's house. I don't have any clean clothes here."

A few moments later, Wyatt carried a tall glass of Diet Coke to Isabelle in the doggie room. He paused on the threshold, unable to believe his eyes and ears.

His sister read softly from the teeth-marked book in her hand. Moe, Larry, and Curly lay on their respective pillows, heads resting on their paws, their eyes glued to Isabelle. They didn't even glance Wyatt's way.

"Just put the Coke on that table," Isabelle said, indicating a plastic table by her chair. "Oh, and Larry brought me this tablet. I think it came from your room. You can forget the pen. It was demolished."

Wyatt took the tattered notepad and glanced at it. The top sheet was still intact, but the cardboard backing had been chewed beyond recognition. See-ing the numbers written on the front, he frowned and brought it closer. It wasn't his handwriting, but the numbers were vaguely familiar.

When nothing came to him, he shrugged and pitched it in the wastebasket. "I'm gonna take that shower. Want to order a pizza afterward?"

Isabelle gave him an absent nod and continued reading. He silently withdrew, still amazed at how the dogs seemed to be listening to the story. Nah, Wyatt decided, laughing at himself. They were just listening to Isabelle's voice. They couldn't understand what she was saying.

As he passed Kasidy's closed door, he paused. He wanted to check on her, make sure she was okay, but he didn't want to disturb her if she was sleeping. He'd heard that sleeping off a migraine was just about the only thing a person could do. Poor baby. He wished there was some way he could help.

He was about to continue when his foot crunched on something on the floor in front of Kasidy's room. Frowning, Wyatt leaned down and picked it up. It was a stethoscope, obviously a little the worse for wear. Teeth marks along the rubber casing told their own story.

Where did the dogs get a stethoscope? And why had they left it at Kasidy's door? With another shrug, he hung the stethoscope over Kasidy's doorknob and continued upstairs to his room.

He was in the shower when all the pieces of the puzzle fell into place. With soap still in his hair, he reached out and turned off the water. He had to think, and he needed silence.

The numbers printed on the pad were the first three numbers to the combination of the safe in his room. He'd watched enough movies to know what the stethoscope had been used for.

Kasidy had been waiting in his bed when he'd returned from seeing Mr. Slowkowsky. That fact alone might not have triggered his suspicions, even with the notepad and stethoscope, if she hadn't been lying in dog pee. Apparently she'd been too distracted by something else to notice.

Such as . . . cracking a safe?

Holding a towel to his forehead to keep the soap from running into his eyes, Wyatt walked to the door of the bathroom and looked at the painting over his bed. Hoping he wouldn't see what he feared he would see. Praying desperately that he'd be wrong.

The painting was crooked, alright.

The idea was ludicrous. Unthinkable. Impossible. Crazy.

Striking a seductive pose on the bed, Kasidy had looked flushed and angry, he recalled. Angry because he had interrupted her burglary? Flushed because she'd nearly gotten caught?

Was his innocent little spitfire a thief? Cursing his gullibility, Wyatt leaned a soapy forehead against the door frame as other clues now came to mind. When he first saw her, she'd claimed to be from the phone company. It was obvious now that she had been in the process of scoping the place disguised as a phone technician. Then he'd offered her an easier way.

What a good guy he was. As a reward, Wyatt slowly beat his head against the doorjamb. He was a blind idiot, and he was getting dumber by the minute.

The phone receptor Dillon had claimed resembled a baby monitor? Must have been the real McCoy. That's how she had overheard him describing in lurid detail his imaginary sex life with Amelia.

Of course, it hadn't been true. He'd only wanted to shock and embarrass that narrow-minded lawyer. But *Kasidy* hadn't known that at the time, and she hadn't been able to ask him without revealing to him how she'd been eavesdropping.

He wasn't just a good guy. He was a very dumb good guy.

With a numbing fury growing in his heart, Wyatt turned the water on and stood beneath the spray until he'd rinsed his hair clean. Then he quickly toweled off and walked naked to his bed. He removed the picture and used the combination he'd memorized. The stuck-up attorney hadn't wanted to give him the combination, but it was Amelia's orders, so she had. According to Jacob, the safe was where Amelia kept her petty cash, her jewelry, and various important papers.

Because Wyatt hadn't felt comfortable snooping through Amelia's personal belongings, he'd only glanced briefly at the contents to take inventory before he'd slammed it shut.

Now he had to see what Kasidy was after, what she'd used her body to get. It was no secret that Amelia had loved her jewelry. Apparently Kasidy had also known. Was she working alone? Was there an accomplice?

Grim-faced, Wyatt pulled open the safe. There was a stack of velvet-lined boxes. He took them out, one by one, and looked at them. A fortune in jewelry, although he wasn't knowledgeable enough to make an estimate. He flipped through the banded stack of cash. At least five thousand, maybe more. Aside from the cash, there was an unmarked video, a stack of deeds, titles to the vehicles, and some personal papers Wyatt merely glanced at.

A good haul for a thief, he mused darkly.

He debated, studying the contents now lying on a dry spot on his bed. Odds were Kasidy had combed the entire house looking for the safe. The moment his back was turned, he suspected she'd be back to finish the job.

Migraine. Ha! Not bloody likely. No, it was obvious now she had invented the excuse to distract him.

After some thought, he replaced the videotape—thinking it was probably important to Amelia, but worthless to a thief—and the papers. He took the cash and the jewelry and stuffed them into a laundry sack. He added dirty clothes from his hamper, then slung the sack over his shoulder.

Isabelle was watching television in the living room. She saw the sack and immediately jumped from the couch. "Hey! Where are *you* going? I ordered pizza!"

Wyatt was too furious to pretend otherwise. "Go ahead without me. I have to take some laundry to Mom."

"But doesn't Louise do your laundry?"

Smart girl. Wyatt bared his teeth in a parody of a smile. "Not this load." This was one load of dirty laundry he was going to have to sort out himself.

"What's wrong? You look madder than a wet hornet." She followed him to the door, then jumped ahead to bar his departure. "Oh, no you don't! You look like you're going to kill someone. What's going on?"

Sometimes his little sister could be a pest. This was one of those times. "Move, Izzy. I'm not in the mood to play childish games with you."

But Isabelle didn't budge. She folded her arms and took a stance, her chin jutting out. "Give me a clue and I'll let you by."

Wyatt clenched his jaw. "You wouldn't believe me if I told you." And she wouldn't, he thought savagely. Kasidy had pulled the proverbial wool over everyone's eyes. They were all gullible fools. But he wasn't yet ready to blow the horn. No, he had other, more devious plans in mind.

Like catching her in the act, and seeing just how far she'd go to get her loot. And he wanted to know why. Was money that important to her? Was she in trouble? Was burglary her way of life?

He deserved an answer. He loved her, dammit!

To Isabelle, he said, "Can you stay until I get back? I don't want Kasidy to be . . . alone in the house." He might find the silver missing on his return. Or God knows what else.

"Fine," Isabelle said with a huff. "I'll stay, and you can keep your ole secrets." She moved to let him by. "And don't expect me to save you any pizza, either."

"I don't. I've lost my appetite."

"What should I tell Kasidy if she wakes up and asks for you?"

"Tell her . . ." Wyatt had to bite his tongue. "Tell her I had a couple errands to run."

"Anything else, Mr. Mystery?"

Ignoring her sarcasm, Wyatt hesitated. "Don't let Kasidy out of your sight. She might get dizzy and fall and hurt herself." He hated to lie to his little sister,

226

but he was afraid to trust her with the truth. He could hardly say, *"Don't let her out of your sight. I want to catch her trying to break into the safe myself."*

Isabelle would die laughing.

He found his mother sitting at her kitchen table, studying. Without ceremony, he hoisted the sack onto the table. "I need you to put this in a safe place."

Mary put down her pencil and frowned up at him. "You're afraid someone's going to steal your laundry?" she asked, eyebrows lifted.

"No." Wyatt's jaw worked. He fought to keep his temper in check. "This isn't laundry. It's a fortune in jewelry and cash."

His mother leapt to her feet, apparently realizing—belatedly—just how furious her son was. "Wyatt David Love! What in the world are you doing with a fortune in jewelry and cash? Have you lost your mind?"

"Maybe," Wyatt clipped out. "Will you do it?"

Hands on hips, Mary regarded him over the rim of her reading glasses. "Will I be breaking the law if I do?"

"No. I'm the trustee of Amelia's estate. As long as I don't sell her things or give them away, I can hold them all I want. I plan on returning everything."

With a sigh, Mary removed her glasses and put them on the table. She pushed Wyatt gently into a chair. "Son, I gave birth to you. I can tell when you're furious. You don't get mad often, but when you do, you're not very rational."

"I don't get mad without a reason," Wyatt said defensively. His mother, as usual, had a calming effect on him.

"Of course you don't." Mary sat down again, leaning toward him. "But the last time I saw you *this* mad, was when that drunk you threw out of the bar keyed your truck."

"And kicked out my headlights."

"Yes."

"And my taillights, and broke my side mirror."

"I remember."

"He also pissed on my tires. But I didn't hit him."

"No, you didn't." She smiled to show that she was on his side. "You took him to court and he had to pay for the damage. And you banned him from the bar. *And* you called his wife and told on him."

Wyatt felt a vein in his temple start to throb. It matched the throbbing in his chest. "This is different," he said. "This is worse."

"Is it about Kasidy?" Mary asked gently.

It was impossible, even as a grown man, for Wyatt to resist his mother's warm, persuasive voice. She had always been able to get the story out of him. Now was no different. Swallowing a huge lump in his throat, Wyatt said, "Kasidy tried to break into Amelia's safe."

His mother jerked back in shock. "Are you certain?"

He nodded miserably. "I nearly caught her red-handed." Quickly, he related the story and told her how he came to his conclusion.

Mary frowned. "That does sound incriminating, but . . . it just doesn't sound like Kasidy. I realize that we don't know her that well—"

"Obviously, none of us really knows her," Wyatt said harshly.

"Now, Wyatt—"

"Don't 'now Wyatt' me, Mom. I may be a gullible fool—in fact, after today, I think that's a given—but I'm not blind."

"I'm sorry. You're right." Mary sighed, still frowning as if she couldn't quite get her mind around the facts.

Wyatt knew exactly how she felt. Only he had a heartache to go with it. Kasidy's betrayal was a double blow to his ego.

"Maybe . . . maybe she has her reasons?" Mary suggested. "I mean, I know it's never right to steal, but sometimes people make wrong choices for what they believe are the right reasons."

He wanted to think his mother could be right. He wanted it more than he'd ever wanted anything in his life. But he didn't want to be a fool a second time. "If she's got a good reason, I'll find out."

Mary nibbled on her bottom lip, a sure sign that she was worried. "You're not going to do anything you might regret, are you, son?"

Amusement flashed in Wyatt's eyes, then was gone. "For the sake of my very tender feelings, I'm going to assume you're not talking about anything physical?"

His mother looked horrified. "I most certainly wasn't suggesting my son might get physical with a woman! At least, not *that* type of physical." She laid a hand on his arm, her expression earnest. "All I'm suggesting is that you don't let your temper blind you to reason, and cause you to ruin the special relationship you have with Kasidy."

Wyatt made a face. "How do *you* know how special our relationship is?"

229

Mary chuckled. "Honey, I'm your mother. I know everything."

If he believed that, Wyatt didn't think he could ever face his mother again without blushing. He left, his heart heavy and his anger somewhat abated.

Not gone by any means, but abated.

CHAPTER 22

Kasidy was talking to her grandmother when she heard Wyatt's truck roar up the drive on the way around to the garage. She'd heard him leave earlier, and had taken advantage of the situation to call Nana Jo from her cell phone. She'd cracked her bedroom door just long enough to hear the blaring of the television.

Wyatt had left, but someone was still in the house, she'd deduced.

"Nana, I've got to go. I hear Wyatt returning."

Nana Jo was obviously worried. "Honey, I know you said you were close to finding the evidence against your father, but I really have a bad feeling about this."

"He doesn't have a clue, Nana. I can't quit when I'm this close. Surely you understand that?" Kasidy cocked her head, listening. She didn't want Wyatt to find her in the bathroom and think her migraine had gotten better. She needed more time to plan how she was going to enter his room again—without getting caught.

"Your father would have a fit if he knew what you were doing," Nana Jo said for the fifth time.

Kasidy smothered a sigh. "That's why he can't know. He'd come after me, and you know we can't let that happen. After finding out that Wyatt is in cahoots with Mr. Slowkowsky . . . well, I don't have to finish that sentence, do I, Nana?" She crossed her fingers, counting on her grandmother's mothering instincts to kick in.

She hit pay dirt.

"No, no. We can't have your father showing up." There was a short, agitated silence. "What if they catch you, Kas? What will happen then? I won't know if you get into trouble."

"Even if I'm caught—which I won't be—they can't prove that I'm Amelia's granddaughter." She mustered an off-hand laugh. "What can they do, haul me in for DNA testing?"

"Hey, don't joke. It could happen."

"You watch too much *CSI*, Nana," Kasidy chided. "Unless there's a criminal act involved, they can't force me to give something for DNA testing."

"Criminal, such as burglary? Safe cracking?"

"Everything that's in that safe legally belongs to me," Kasidy reminded her.

"But you can't own up to that without placing your father in jeopardy," Nana Jo shot back.

Kasidy was relieved when she heard the front door slam. "I gotta go! He's back." She hastily closed the phone, shoved it beneath a pile of towels, and raced to the bedroom door. Carefully, she opened it a crack and looked out. She heard muffled voices, but the television prevented her from understanding what was being said. She had started to close the door when she heard something knock against it. With a frown, she quickly stuck her head around.

That was when she saw the stethoscope hanging from her doorknob.

Her heart stopped.

She had shoved the stethoscope beneath Wyatt's bed.

Now it was hanging from her doorknob.

The implications were devastating.

Or maybe not.

She grabbed the stethoscope and hauled it inside before quietly closing the door. With her heart now racing full speed, she hightailed it back to her bed, jumped beneath the covers, and closed her eyes.

The stethoscope bit into her side as if to taunt her.

What did it *mean*?

Or did it mean anything at all?

If Wyatt had found the stethoscope—and obviously *someone* had—did that mean he'd connected it to her and its purpose?

"Not necessarily, Kasidy Raeann," Kasidy whispered out loud to herself. "Don't jump to conclusions and give yourself away."

But if Wyatt *had* found it, and had brought it back, how had he known it belonged to her?

Good question.

Brilliant question.

Damned *scary* question.

Holy crap. She was toast. There was no way Wyatt could have known it was hers unless he'd figured out why she'd have a stethoscope in the first place.

She wasn't a doctor.

She wasn't a nurse.

Moments ticked by, with her heart thundering in the silence of her room. The sound was enough to add to her panic. In desperation, she grabbed a pillow and placed it over her chest, hoping to muffle the telltale sound.

It didn't work. She could still feel it pounding against her chest, taunting her with the knowledge that she was caught. Her father would be disappointed. He'd feel as if he'd failed in passing on his rather unconventional talents. She'd have to leave and her father would continue to live the life of a fugitive.

Unless . . . unless she could think of another damned good reason she'd have a stethoscope in her possession, and a damned good reason to have it with her in his room. She squeezed her eyes shut and concentrated.

An idea came to her. Her eyes flew open. She inhaled a gasp, then blew it out in a slow, shaky, triumphant sigh. She had it.

Sex games.

She could convince Wyatt she had intended to play nurse with him. Yeah, that was the ticket.

Her bubble burst with an almost audible *plop*.

To convince him, she would have to use the stethoscope, prove to him that she'd planned to all along.

She'd have to sleep with the enemy.

Well, hell. It wasn't as if she'd suddenly stopped loving him after finding out he worked for Slowkowsky. To give a low-life scum-sucking worm his credit, Wyatt didn't know who she really was. In order to sleep with him, she could cling to the very fragile, flimsy fact that if he *had* gotten to know her as Amelia's granddaughter, then he might have fallen in love with her anyway, and changed his mind about selling her out.

Okay, so maybe "fragile" and "flimsy" were laughable exaggerations.

But they were all she had.

Despite the fact that he was exhausted both physically and mentally, Wyatt wasn't asleep when he heard the creaking of his bedroom door.

He turned his head, safe in the knowledge that it was dark and she couldn't see that his eyes were open.

So she'd come back, he thought, as that last flicker of hope he'd been unconsciously clinging to evaporated.

It was showtime, whether he was ready for it, or not. The trouble was, he still hadn't decided what to do when he caught her red-handed.

Scold her?

Lecture her to tears?

Strangle her into a confession?

Interrogate her until she told him something he could live with?

Not a single one of his answers gave him any peace.

With his battered heart steadily sinking, he waited. A tiny part of him admired her grit. The safe was above his head. It wouldn't be easy to remove the painting and finish cracking the safe without making a sound.

Was she that good, or was she just that arrogant?

Or was she that desperate? What was her story?

Wyatt was dying to find out. But he doubted anything she told him would completely heal his broken heart. She'd played him, which meant her appealing innocence had most likely been a sham.

Damn, she was good. Even now, much to his disgust, he was growing hard just thinking about how good she was. How incredibly tight. Refreshingly uninhibited.

The covers at his side rustled.

Wyatt stiffened. Alarm streaked through him as he thought of something he hadn't allowed himself to think of before now. How far was she willing to go? Was she desperate enough to kill him? As bizarre and painful as the possibility sounded, Wyatt forced himself to consider it. The Kasidy he thought he knew wasn't the real Kasidy. He had to remember that.

When he felt cold steel against his chest, Wyatt's heart stopped its mad pounding. His hand shot out, closing around a slender wrist.

"What the hell are you doing?" he heard himself growl incredulously. Because, as hard as he tried, he couldn't convince himself she'd really harm him.

He loved her still.

Cursing his own stupidity, Wyatt kept his crushing grip on her wrist and reached out with his free arm to tap the touch lamp next to his bed. Why didn't she just shoot him and put him out of his misery? Perhaps that was exactly what she had intended to do.

Soft light flooded the room, revealing Kasidy's wide-eyed face leaning over the bed.

Wyatt glanced down, his eyes bulging at the sight of the stethoscope pressed against his chest.

Not a gun, but the stethoscope he'd found outside

her room. His gaze flew to her face again. Perched on top of her blond head was a nurse's hat, crudely fashioned from a paper towel; he recognized the fruit basket design from a roll in the kitchen. She wore a T-shirt and panties, this T-shirt even tighter than the one she'd worn the night of her seduction in the garage. It was dark green and matched her eyes, with the name of a major brand of oil drawing attention to her perky, generous breasts.

Last night, he mused dazedly. Had that actually been only last night? As he looked at her beautiful face, she smiled seductively. Her lashes dropped down to fan her cheeks. Without makeup, he could clearly see the half a dozen freckles scattered across her nose and cheeks.

"My headache's all gone," she whispered huskily. "Now it's time to check *you* out, like I was planning to do when that migraine stopped me."

He had to wet his dry lips before he could speak, much to his chagrin. "You—you were?" He didn't believe her, of course.

Not in a million years. Hadn't he put all the pieces of the puzzle together? What about the numbers, the ones that matched the safe combination written on the pad?

The cold metal of the stethoscope moved lower, then lower still. Wyatt sucked in a sharp breath when it reached his belly button. He couldn't take his eyes from her face, so flushed and erotic. So beautiful and deceptive.

Deceptive.

He clung to that thought with the sheer desperation of a drowning man mere feet from the boat.

Between the lips of that seductive, mind-drugging smile, a knee-weakening, pink tongue darted out. She slowly swiped her lips, leaving him breathless.

The stethoscope dropped lower.

It bumped into the head of his erection, then settled firmly against it.

"Ah . . ." she crooned. "I hear a heartbeat, but it's not very steady. I think you might need mouth-to-mouth resuscitation."

At that moment—with what rational thought remained—Wyatt knew he should have stopped her. Without the rose-colored glasses, he knew what she really was.

She was a common thief, a professional burglar.

But he loved her . . . and the heat of her mouth scorched him into oblivion.

He was a goner. He justified his lapse of sanity with the knowledge that this might be the last time he'd have with her. He was weak. He was desperate.

He was in love with a thief.

Lord have mercy.

"Mom, stop cleaning and sit down. The meeting is about to start." Dillon took the towel from her reluctant fingers and gently guided her to a seat where the others were waiting.

After she'd called Dillon and told him about the loot Wyatt had dropped off at her house, Dillon had decided it might be prudent to get another opinion.

Or a dozen.

So he'd called friends and family into the bar for a meeting to discuss how they should proceed. Now he leaned against the bar, waiting for the low murmur of voices to subside. His gaze roamed over the crowd, impressed with the turnout.

Luke and Lydia sat at a table with Casey and her husband, Brett. Casey was co-owner in the spa that Lydia ran downtown, and Brett was a lawyer fast making his way to a partnership in the firm where he worked.

The escorts from Mr. Complete—Ivan, Greg, Jet, Tyler, Will, and Colin—sat at a table for six. Mary had taken a seat with Isabelle, Callie, and a very grumpy Mrs. Scuttle.

It was past the senior citizen's bedtime, and she'd made no bones about her displeasure at being called out at this time of night. Dillon hid his amusement, knowing the secretary had had the option to stay at home, but hadn't wanted to miss out.

A peanut whizzed passed Dillon's head, startling him.

Mrs. Scuttle bawled out, "Well? Are you going to say something, or are you just going to stand there like a bump on a log?"

Behind the bar, Dillon's bartender, Lou, and his bouncer, Fish, smothered guffaws of laughter. Dillon felt a flush rise along his neck. He wondered—briefly, and with obvious insanity—what Mrs. Scuttle would do if he threw something at *her*. But the thought didn't last long. He knew he'd never have the balls to find out.

He cleared his throat and glared pointedly at the grouchy secretary. "For those of you who are growing impatient, I'll bring you up to speed. Wyatt brought a sack containing a fortune in jewels and cash to Mom's house tonight, claiming Kasidy was attempting to crack the safe in his bedroom and steal the goods."

There was a collective gasp, just as he'd expected.

Mrs. Scuttle came to her feet, surprisingly nimble for her age. She raised a fist and shook it, as if she was participating in a controversial town meeting instead of an informal gathering among friends and family. "That's hogwash! Kasidy wouldn't steal a loaf of bread if her family were starving!"

Dillon closed his eyes and slowly counted to ten. When he opened them again, it was just in time to freeze Mrs. Scuttle in the act of throwing an entire handful of peanuts at him. With studied patience, he said, "I'm not saying I agree with Wyatt's conclusion, Mrs. Scuttle. And as far as I know, neither is anyone else in this room." He waited a beat to give someone the opportunity to disagree. When no one did, he continued. "I personally believe that Kasidy's looking for something other than jewels or cash, and that it has something to do with her father and Mr. Slowkowsky. I believe she thinks Wyatt is involved in a threat against her father."

"Hogwash, I tell you!" the secretary yelled.

"Right." Dillon dared to ignore Mrs. Scuttle. "So what we have is a bad case of noncommunication. Kasidy thinks Wyatt's a hired thug, and he thinks she's a thief."

"Why don't we just get them together and tell them the truth?" Will Tallfeather suggested.

The truth had worked in Dillon's case when he was wooing Callie. In fact, it had been Will's suggestion to tell Callie that he'd been switching places with his twin.

Dillon wasn't surprised when Callie stood to address the crowd.

"We can't tell them. They have to figure it out for themselves, just as Dillon and I did. If we interfere now, we could be cheating them out of some unforgettable memories later." Her gaze met Dillon's, and there was a tender moment of understanding between them.

"She's right," Dillon said, hoping the men wouldn't notice that his voice had grown huskier. "If Wyatt had told me that Callie wasn't a real reviewer, then our relationship might have ended before it had a chance to bloom into love."

Greg dashed a tear from his cheek. "That is so damned romantic, Dil. I get goose bumps just thinking about it."

Mary raised her hand. "But what happens if we do nothing, and Kasidy finds what she's looking for and leaves without confessing her love to Wyatt?" She bit her lip worriedly. "And what if Wyatt's stubborn pride keeps him from stopping her and confessing his love to her? If Kasidy disappears again, we might not ever find her."

"Good point, Mom." Dillon glanced over the crowd. "Anyone have any suggestions?"

Mrs. Scuttle didn't bother raising her hand. "I say we knock their heads together, rattle a little sense into them."

"Despite your firm theory on violence," Dillon drawled, "I don't think that would work, Mrs. Scuttle."

"I think someone should move back into the mansion to make sure Kasidy doesn't leave," Greg said.

"That person could also keep us informed of their progress."

The secretary immediately raised her hand in the air, waving madly. "I will! I will! I never did get to try out the pool, or that hot tub like I wanted to. Besides," she added smugly, "nobody can act as needy as I can when warranted."

Not a single person in the bar had the nerve to agree with her, or disagree. It was a damned if you do, and damned if you don't situation, and everyone knew it.

But Dillon had a big problem with Mrs. Scuttle volunteering for the job. "Um, I appreciate your help, Mrs. Scuttle, but I, um, can't let you do it."

"Why not?" she demanded, her huge owl eyes blinking rapidly behind her glasses.

Dillon, unfortunately, knew the signs of an impending tantrum. But there was no way out. He braced himself. "If you move in, Louise will quit again."

The silence was so absolute, a person could have heard a peanut shell hit the floor.

Finally, Mrs. Scuttle bawled out, "That pervert's back at work, after what she did to me?"

Sensing doomsday looming, Mary intervened. "Dil, couldn't you convince Louise to take a vacation? It shouldn't take long for things to come to a head between Kasidy and Wyatt, and Mrs. Scuttle is right. If anyone can guilt Kasidy into staying, it's Mrs. Scuttle."

"I could go along, too," Isabelle said. "To help with the dogs so that Kasidy and Wyatt have more time to work things out. I could be the snitch, and

Mrs. Scuttle could be the needy old—Ouch!" Isabelle put a hand to her ear where a peanut had nicked it. "I mean," she backtracked, keeping a cautious eye on Mrs. Scuttle, "needy *friend*."

"That's better," Mrs. Scuttle snapped.

The moment Mrs. Scuttle's back was turned, Mary snatched the bowl of peanuts and handed it to Greg at the table next to them. He passed it beneath the table to Collin, and Collin kept on passing it until it ended up in Luke's hands. Luke set it at his feet.

"Are we all agreed, then?" Dillon asked. When there was a show of hands, he nodded. "Okay. We'll place a buffer and a spy at the mansion, then hang back and see what develops."

"What did you call me?" Mrs. Scuttle demanded.

Dillon groaned and slapped a hand over his eyes.

Which was unfortunate for Dillon, since he wasn't able to see the shoe before it smacked him in the groin.

CHAPTER 23

"Wake up, Sleeping Beauty. Hope you like scrambled eggs and crisp bacon."

Kasidy jack-knifed so fast in the bed, she nearly knocked the tray from Wyatt's hands. She felt mortified and consumed with guilt. It was one thing to sleep with the enemy; quite another to actually *sleep* with him!

Wyatt lifted a brow at her, but said nothing as he settled the tray over her thighs. He moved around and arranged the pillows behind her as if she were an invalid.

"There," he said cheerfully, coming back around to perch on the bed beside her. "Comfy?"

Comfy? Kasidy blinked at his smiling face. Had she fallen into a silly sitcom? Had she been that convincing last night?

"By the way, thanks for fulfilling one of my fantasies last night." Wyatt smiled warmly at her, his gaze drifting to her mouth, which she promptly closed. "It was something else. How long had you been planning it?"

To cover her embarrassment, Kasidy took a hasty drink of her orange juice. It tasted fresh-squeezed. She forced herself to glance shyly at him; the all-over body blush she didn't have to force *or* pretend. "It was, um, kind of an, um, impulsive thing."

His fingers closed around her cover-clad thigh and gave it an intimate squeeze. "Well, just so you know, I love it when you're impulsive. I can't wait to see what you'll come up with next."

Kasidy nearly choked on her first bite of bacon. She really was starving, and who wouldn't be? After the night they'd had. She blushed again, hiking the covers over her breasts when they started to slip. She honestly didn't know how to respond to this intimate morning-after talk, because she hadn't planned on falling asleep curled against the warmth of his hard body.

She didn't have any regrets.

The realization both stunned her, and dismayed her. How could she *love* a man who worked for a mobster that had the power to make her father disappear forever? What kind of daughter was she?

A rotten one, that's what kind.

"Something wrong, baby?"

Oh, yeah. But nothing she cared to share with Wyatt. Her appetite fled, choked out by guilt. She wiped her mouth on a paper towel, then stared down at it in horror as she recalled the nurse's hat she'd made from the same roll. Her gaze flew to Wyatt's.

He was gazing at her with a lazy, innocent smile.

Well, she had one question answered. She had definitely fooled him last night. If he'd harbored any suspicions, she felt certain their lusty interlude with the stethoscope had washed them away.

"I-I should walk the dogs," she said, grabbing the tray and attempting to remove it from her lap. Before she could, however, Wyatt stopped her.

"No, no. You finish eating. I've already walked the dogs, and fed them their breakfast. After that butt-trimming thing last night, we've sort of bonded."

Kasidy's mouth went dry. "They-they let you do that?"

"Of course. Well, Isabelle helped hold them steady." He looked boyishly sheepish. "And I have to admit, it was touch and go with Larry. I heard him growl a time or two, and I was afraid he'd exact revenge the moment Isabelle gave him his head."

"He . . . didn't?"

Wyatt chuckled and squeezed her thigh again. "Yeah, he did, but not until later. I found him under my bed, chewing on my notepad. I would wonder how he got the notepad out of my nightstand if I didn't already know how clever he is. They can open *doors,* so I'm sure it's possible they can open *drawers,* right?"

"Um, right." Kasidy resisted the urge to put a hand over her quivering stomach. She knew she shouldn't feel guilty, but she did. "They're very smart." Lucky for her.

"I think they're growing on me," Wyatt confessed. "I'm even considering getting one when my job as trustee ends. How do you feel about that?"

How did *she* feel about it? Kasidy swallowed hard, unsure what he meant by that question. Was he . . . could he be hinting about a future together? And why in the hell was she feeling guilty over the possibility? He was a mongrel. A thug. So what if he really did love her? They had no future together, not as long as he worked for Mr. Slowkowsky.

The moment she got her hands on that evidence, she would tell him so, too.

Because she didn't know what to say, she stuffed her mouth with scrambled eggs and mumbled something indistinguishable.

She almost choked again when he said, "I've got to run a few errands this morning for Louise. Will you be okay here alone?"

Swallowing was difficult, but she managed. "Of course. I'll just play . . . with the dogs in the garden." And finish cracking Amelia's safe. For some perverse reason, the idea wasn't as appealing as it should have been.

"Good girl." He patted her thigh, then rose.

Kasidy soaked in the sight of his hard, lean body, unable to stop the searing regret that filled her heart. If she was successful, there would be no reason to remain.

She might be looking at Wyatt for the last time.

Downstairs, Wyatt put his carefully thought out plan into action. He handed Louise a list, a wad of cash, and his truck keys. "I really appreciate your doing this for me, Louise. You're a life-saver."

Louise pulled her brows together. "I still don't understand why I can't just take the Cadillac. It's what I always drive when I do the shopping."

"As I explained, I want you to see if you can hear the same tinkling sound I'm hearing from the engine."

"Tinkling?"

"Yes, tinkling . . . like wineglasses tipped together

in a toast." Wyatt feigned bewilderment. "I'm either losing my mind, or there's something weird going on beneath the hood. I just need another opinion."

"Oh. Well, if you're sure . . ." Louise, still frowning, gathered her purse and headed for the back door. "I just hope I don't wreck it or anything," she fretted.

"Full coverage," Wyatt called after her. "So don't worry, just listen and tell me what you think. Bye!"

He let out a huge sigh when the door finally shut behind her. His heart was heavy as he pulled out a chair and sat at the kitchen table, listening for the sound of his truck leaving. If his intuition was right, Kasidy would hear his truck, believe he'd left, and finish the job she'd started last night.

When he caught her red-handed cracking the safe, then he'd badger her until she told him why she'd turned to a life of crime. That was as far as his imagination had taken him. What happened afterward, he didn't know.

Maybe he'd forgive her. Maybe he could convince her to give up her life of crime to live happily ever after with him. But the question was, could he trust her? Or what if stealing was something she couldn't help, a sickness or something?

Then he'd get her the best help money could buy.

Time to face the truth, he realized with an inward groan. He still loved her, even if she was a thief. Loved her so much, in fact, that he'd rather live with a woman he couldn't trust, then live without her.

But what if she didn't love him? It was a question he'd been avoiding asking himself. What if everything that had happened between them had meant nothing to her? Wyatt had his share of ego, but he couldn't believe in his heart of hearts that she didn't feel anything for him.

Last night had been incredible, even better than before. And afterward, they'd cuddled and kissed and fallen asleep in each other's arms. Waking up next to her this morning had been one of the highlights of his life, and he'd realized that he most definitely wanted to continue waking up next to her.

The roar of his truck signaled Louise's departure. Wyatt reluctantly looked at his watch. He'd wait ten minutes, then sneak upstairs and catch her in the act. His stomach fluttered nervously as he waited.

Five minutes down.

Three minutes to go.

He was just about to get up when the doorbell rang. Cursing a blue streak, Wyatt rose and waited, undecided. Maybe if he ignored the summons, whoever it was would go away. Chances were, Kasidy would ignore it as well, if she was busy cracking the safe. She would assume that Louise would get it.

But the doorbell continued to peal, and more urgently each time until it became one long irritating ring.

"All right!" Wyatt growled, determined to give whomever it was a piece of his mind and then some. This was wrecking his plans to catch the woman he loved in the act of robbing him, dammit.

Jerking open the door, Wyatt took one look at the couple standing there and exploded. "For Pete's sake, Dil! What is it this time?"

Mrs. Scuttle hit him square in the gut with her humongous purse. "Don't you go sour on me, boy! Mind your manners or I'll have a talk with Mary."

Beside her, Dillon said in a weary voice, "Mrs. Scuttle, you promised."

"I did," she grudgingly agreed. Then she glared at Wyatt, who glared right back. "But then Wyatt had to go and be rude to an old woman."

It just wasn't fair, Wyatt thought savagely, that Mrs. Scuttle could say the word "old," but no one else could. Between clenched teeth, Wyatt struggled to sound civil. "I'm sorry, Mrs. Scuttle. I'm just rather busy right now." Not caring what they thought, he glanced at the stairway, wondering if Kasidy was at that moment opening Amelia's safe. Had she gotten that far? Had she heard the doorbell, and decided to wait? Or was she taking advantage of the situation to finish the job? When she realized the safe was basically empty, would she scream her frustration?

"Wyatt."

Wyatt jerked his head back around to stare at Dillon. "What?" he barked, then nimbly stepped back to avoid another gut-punching hit from Mrs. Scuttle's purse. Apparently promises weren't the secretary's forte.

"Mrs. Scuttle needs a place to stay."

Wonder of wonders. Was that supposed to surprise him? Wyatt clutched the door until his nails bit into the wood. "Why is that, dear brother?"

When Mrs. Scuttle opened her huge purse and pulled out a hanky, Wyatt felt a jolt of alarm. She dabbed at her eyes, and he noticed her bottom lip quivering.

"She's been kicked out of her apartment," Dillon informed him quietly. He put a protective arm around the now weeping secretary.

"Hell," Wyatt said. They had his full attention now. Well, most of it. A small part of his brain was still working on catching Kasidy in the act. "What happened?"

Dillon had to wait until Mrs. Scuttle finished blowing her nose before he explained. "The other tenants claimed she almost set the building on fire."

"I didn't!" Mrs. Scuttle denied tearfully, looking more pitiful than Wyatt had ever seen her. "I just burned a few cookies, and they got their drawers in a wad." She wept softly into her hanky.

Wyatt felt a wrenching of his heart, and reached out to pull Mrs. Scuttle into his arms. She wept on his shoulder as he patted her back and murmured reassurances in her ear. "Of course you can stay here," he told her when she wound down to an occasional sniffle. "I'm sorry for being so rude earlier. I had a few things on my mind."

Which reminded him. He shot a meaningful glance at Dillon over Mrs. Scuttle's head. "Could you take her into the kitchen and fix her a cup of tea, bro? I've got something I need to take care of." Although Dillon looked at him curiously, he nodded and led Mrs. Scuttle in the direction of the kitchen.

Taking the stairs three at a time, Wyatt hit the landing running and slid to a halt in front of his closed bedroom door.

He'd left it open earlier.

Without preamble, he grabbed the knob and swung it open.

Kasidy swung the safe open at the exact same moment Wyatt came crashing into the room.

She saw the tape, and reached for it.

"Don't!" Wyatt growled. "Just back away, Kasidy. It's over."

Tears of frustration burned her eyes. She was so close! The tape was there, right in front of her. Her father's freedom. Mere inches away.

"I know you're disappointed," Wyatt said.

He sounded sorry. Why would he sound sorry? Kasidy gulped back her alarm. Did he know? Was that why he sounded regretful? Slowly, she turned to look at him. She blinked her teary eyes.

Yes, he looked sorry. Sad. Regretful.

"If I could, I would give you the jewelry and the cash that was in that safe, Kasidy. But it wasn't mine to give. If you need money that badly, I could make you a loan. I've got a little in my savings account."

He wanted to loan her money. He had removed the jewelry and cash so she couldn't steal it.

He didn't know.

Wyatt thought she was a cat burglar? Kasidy swallowed a hysterical laugh. Too bad she couldn't just blurt out the truth, that she wasn't after the jewelry or the cash, that she wanted that stupid videotape. But she couldn't, because she didn't trust him enough. If she told him everything, she risked his going to Mr. Slowkowsky with that tape. Apparently, he and Wyatt didn't know what was on it, or her purpose here would be useless.

It was the one fact Kasidy could cling to. Since Wyatt didn't know she wanted the tape, and he'd removed the valuables, there was a strong chance he believed she was no longer interested in the safe.

Definitely better that he believe she was a thief

than for Wyatt to guess her true mission. Now all she had to do was find a way to hang around long enough to get another chance at that tape.

Kasidy opened her mouth to tell the man she loved one whopper of a story, but she didn't get the first word out.

Someone came thundering up the stairs, and long before Isabelle appeared in the doorway, Kasidy heard her sobs. Wyatt heard them, too. He turned just in time to catch his wailing little sister in his unsuspecting arms.

"Oh, Wyatt," she sobbed. "Mom and I had a terrible fight!"

Wyatt shot Kasidy a rueful smile that gave her hope.

"Let me guess," he said, smoothing Isabelle's blond hair down her back. "She kicked you out, and you need a place to stay."

Isabelle stopped sobbing in mid-stride. She reared back to blink at him incredulously. "Yeah. How did you know?"

He glanced at Kasidy again, but this time she couldn't tell what he was thinking.

"How do I know?" he asked, brows lifted. "Because I'm just beginning to realize that there's some hanky-panky going on around here. I guess you already know that Mrs. Scuttle has been kicked out of her apartment, and is at this moment downstairs drinking tea?"

His sister's eyes widened even further. "No! I didn't know. How could I have known? Dillon didn't say anything when he let me in just now . . . but then, I was bawling so hard I probably wouldn't have heard him."

Wyatt tapped Isabelle on the nose, still smiling in that endearing, lopsided way. "You're good, little sister. You're very good. But I'm on to you guys."

"What?"

"Who's behind this? Will? Collin? Or is it Tyler? Because I can see Tyler behind this. We all know it isn't Dillon."

Isabelle pushed away from him, frowning. "Are you losing it? I don't have a clue what you're talking about, Wyatt, and I don't appreciate your taking my fight with Mom so lightly. You're even *smiling* about it! It was an *awful* fight. She called me a selfish brat, and I told her she lacked compassion. . . ." Isabelle shuddered delicately. "It was just horrible."

"Fine. Whatever."

To Kasidy's amazement, Wyatt pushed his distraught sister toward the door.

"Go pick out a room before everyone else gets here."

With a huff, Isabelle flounced out of the room. After she'd gone, Wyatt turned to Kasidy.

She froze at the purposeful look in his eyes.

"You and me," he ordered. "In the waterbed room. It's the only place I can think of where we won't be interrupted." Slowly, he held out his hand.

Kasidy jumped down from the bed on wobbly legs, put her hand in his, and let him lead her to the slaughterhouse—er—waterbed room.

In the hall, they bumped into Dillon.

"Wyatt, I need to—"

Wyatt promptly held up his free hand. "Talk to the hand, bro. Whatever it is, I'm sure it can wait. Kasidy and I have some talking to do, then you and *I* have some talking to do."

To Kasidy's mystification, he ignored Dillon's protest and continued to pull her down the hall. Obviously, she wasn't going to be saved this time.

CHAPTER 24

"You didn't really work for the phone company, did you?"

In the few moments it had taken for Wyatt to lead her into the waterbed room and push her down onto the gently rolling mattress, Kasidy had decided to stick to the truth as much as possible.

Obviously, she'd made a terrible mistake in assuming Wyatt could be easily fooled.

She thrust out her chin, looking him square in the eye. "No." Keep it short. Don't volunteer more information than needed. Her father had taught her that. But he hadn't taught her what to do if she fell in love with the enemy.

Wyatt braced a hand on his hip, his expression inscrutable. "So you were scouting the place out, and I helped you along by offering you the job as dog-sitter."

"Yes."

"Am I correct in assuming, then, that you knew Amelia Hancock?"

"No."

"You didn't?"

Kasidy shook her head. So far, she hadn't had to lie. But she knew the time was coming, and she dreaded it.

"So you read about her in the paper, and figured since her attorney was offering a reward for information about her granddaughter, the old lady had to be loaded."

"Yes." Sort of the truth. Nana Jo had read it to her.

"Is this the first time you've attempted to rob someone?"

"Yes." Her father had taken her on a few dry runs, but he'd never allowed her to take anything.

Wyatt's voice softened. "Are you in trouble?"

Her body responded to the sheer pull of his voice with alarming ease. She fortified her defenses with a little sass. "It's too early to tell."

"Very funny." He didn't look amused. In fact, he looked deadly serious. "*Are* you in trouble, Kasidy?"

It was a tough question. She could tell the truth—she wasn't in trouble. But her father was, and now, because of her, his danger had increased. She had to protect him. She had to make this right.

So she lied. "Yes."

"Do you owe someone money?"

"Yes." She had a line of credit at a parts store. That counted, didn't it? Wyatt hadn't been specific.

He moved closer, and the sudden darkening of his eyes sent a chill through Kasidy. He was running out of patience, she realized.

"Okay. I'm done asking questions and getting short answers," he said tersely. "We're going to stay in this room until you tell me why you tried to rob that safe."

Damn. She liked it better when *he* was telling the
story and she was more or less agreeing.

To prove he meant it, Wyatt dusted off a sturdy
box and sat. He folded his arms, his penetrating gaze
boring holes into her.

"There's no bathroom in here. No food. No water.
No one to interrupt us."

She had never seen him so determined, she realized
with a sinking heart. Which meant she was going to
have to tell that whopper after all. And if that angry
tick pulsing in his jaw was any indication, she'd better make it a stellar performance.

She looped her arms around her knees, wishing she
didn't have to lie. Wishing he didn't work for
Slowkowsky. Although she felt she could trust Wyatt
with her heart, she couldn't risk trusting him with
her father's life.

Wetting her lips, she began her whopper. "Have
you ever heard of racing for pink slips?"

Wyatt nodded. "If you lose, they get your car free
and clear. If you win, you get theirs."

She took a deep breath. She had to make him believe her. "Well, I raced someone else's car . . . and
lost. I was so certain I'd win. You see, I souped up the
motor, and we were using nitrous."

"The owner didn't know you were racing his car?"

"No." She let her gaze fall from his as if she were
ashamed. "I was wrong, I know. But at the time I
truly thought I'd win and he'd never know."

"What was the car worth?"

The hint of sympathy in his tone made Kasidy
want to throw up. If she didn't love him . . . but she
did, and she didn't deserve his sympathy. "Thirty

thousand, maybe more, maybe less. He gave me three months to come up with the money. If I don't, he's going to press charges."

Now it was all about waiting. Had she convinced him? Would he swallow her incredible tale? And what would he do about it? Would he fire her and tell her he never wanted to see her again? Would he call the cops and have her arrested?

The last thing she expected him to do was fall to his knees in front of the bed. He put his hands on her feet, and shook her lightly, until she gathered enough courage to look at him.

She had to close her eyes against the infinite tenderness in his gaze. Her brain reminded her that he wasn't without flaws; her heart wanted to shrink into oblivion for lying to the man she loved.

"Kasidy . . . I don't have that much money, but I know how we can get the rest. We'll borrow the money from the bank. My credit is good."

He loved her. There was no other explanation for the sacrifice he was willing to make for her. Kasidy felt tears burn her eyes. Her flaws had just gotten a whole lot bigger, and his smaller.

Her hands were trembling as she held them out to him to take. "I can't let you do that, Wyatt. I appreciate it, but I've always been on my own, and I have to work this out by myself."

"Bullshit," he said softly, angrily. "You've got me, now. I love you." When her eyes widened, he smiled. "That's right. I love a thief. A safe cracker."

And a professional liar, Kasidy thought, feeling miserable. She discovered she much preferred shouting and cussing. He should have fired her, or threatened to call the cops. At the very least, he should have given her exactly fifteen minutes to pack her bags and get off the property.

Now she had to feel miserable and guilty and awful for lying to him, because he wanted to *help* her. Did he love her enough to help her father, too? Kasidy's throat worked. She wanted to blurt it all out and take a chance.

But she couldn't banish the image of her father lying in a shallow grave somewhere, killed by an aging mobster with a grudge.

She had to get that tape, and when she got it, she was going to stomp it to pieces, then set it on fire for ruining her chances of having a happily ever after.

"Will you think about letting me help you?" Wyatt asked softly.

Because she felt she had no choice, she said, "Yeah. I'll think about it." At the door, Kasidy heard a scuffling noise, followed by an urgent whine. She mustered a watery smile. "I think someone *did* find us." She was going to miss the trio when she left.

But not half as much as she was going to miss Wyatt.

Dillon hit the water facedown. He came up sputtering and cursing, his face burning from the impact. Glaring at his twin, he swam to the side of the pool and hauled himself up. Water ran from his clothes and shoes. He was soaked.

"What the *hell* did you do that for?" he shouted.

Wyatt wasn't smiling. "You may not be the mastermind behind this irritating deluge of visitors, but I'm pretty sure you know who is."

So his brother had finally stopped to smell the roses. Or in this case, the rats. It irked Dillon, however, that Wyatt refused to consider that *he* might be the mastermind. As a result he had no compunction about saying, "You're imagining things, bro. Nobody's out to spoil your little interlude with Kasidy." They were just trying to ensure he didn't totally screw it up.

He hit the surface of the water on his back this time, and discovered that it hurt as much as landing on his face. When he hauled himself back out of the water, he was mad. "You do that again," he warned his twin, "and you'll regret it."

"Oh, I'm sooo scared," Wyatt crooned sarcastically. He stood with his hands on his hips, daring Dillon to come closer. "I called the building manager where Mrs. Scuttle lives, so I know she didn't get kicked out of her apartment."

Dillon called his bluff. "The building manager knew nothing about it. The other tenants threatened to call the Division of Aging on Mrs. Scuttle. That's why she left." Hey, he was getting pretty good at this, he thought, resisting a taunting smile.

"Next you'll expect me to believe Izzy and Mom really had a fight. That one was a little over the top, don't you think, bro?"

Shaking himself like a dog, Dillon shot Wyatt a disparaging glance. "Mothers and daughters fight all the time, dumb ass."

"Bite me. Other mothers and daughters fight. Mom and Izzy don't."

"They did this time."

"Why can't she stay with you?"

At the risk of reminding him, Dillon jerked his head at the pool. "I don't have one of those." He shook himself off again. "I've had enough of this interrogation. I'm going to find a towel; then I'm going home. Good luck with the women."

Wyatt appeared to lose his bluster at that. "Hey! You can't leave me alone with them!"

Dillon pulled his wet shirt away from his skin, lifting a sarcastic brow. "You should have thought about that before you knocked me in the pool—twice."

"I still think something fishy's going on. What about that *Baywatch* babe of a housekeeper? You gonna tell me *that* was a coincidence?"

"Must have been, huh? Because the only person who could sound just like you on the phone—if someone did in fact call and change your preferences—would have been me." He allowed himself a tiny, taunting smile. "And I'm not capable of pranks, remember? I'm too uptight. Too boring. Too staid."

"Don't forget too much of an asshole."

"Go to hell."

"Lead the way, bro. Lead the way."

"No, I think I'll do better than that. I think I'll just *leave.*" He laughed all the way into the house, aware that Wyatt was glaring at his back.

When he reached for Callie's cell phone and encountered a soggy pocket, he stopped laughing abruptly.

Shit.

Forty-five minutes later, Dillon stepped from a hot shower into a warm towel his wife was holding out.

Since the twins' births, Callie's mothering instincts had spilled over onto him. Dillon didn't mind one single bit. Well . . . except for the time she leaned over to wipe his mouth in a busy restaurant. That one had been a little embarrassing, especially when the people next to them erupted into laughter.

"I just don't understand why Kasidy doesn't tell him the truth," Callie said, handing him another towel for his hair.

"I think she's scared. She doesn't know whom to trust." He toweled his head vigorously, then did his customary hop around the room as he pulled on his boxers. "You should have heard the tale she spun for Wyatt. Racing cars and pink slips, and he fell for it, hook, line and sinker." He chuckled, recalling how close he'd come to getting caught eavesdropping, thanks to the dogs. "If this works out, Wyatt will never have a boring moment."

Callie arched a challenging brow. "And *you* do?"

Dillon grimaced. "According to Wyatt, I do."

"That really smarts, doesn't it? That Wyatt refuses to consider you could be behind the pranks?"

He knew he'd be lying—and she would know it— if he said it didn't sting, so he didn't bother denying it. "It doesn't matter. He'll know soon enough. Right now I think we need to concentrate on how we're going to keep Kasidy from bolting. Since she lied to him, I get the impression she isn't going to get around to trusting him with the truth."

"What if you told her that Mr. Slowkowsky is her grandfather?"

"She wouldn't believe me," Dillon said with conviction. "I'm telling you, Callie. This woman has been brainwashed. If you had been told the same thing over and over by your parents, wouldn't *you* find it hard to believe any different?" He glanced up when Callie didn't reply, frowning at her expression. "What is it? Something wrong? Callie?"

"We need to do something drastic," she said. "Something that will force Kasidy to come clean about who she is."

"Exactly." His wife's comment sparked an idea. The idea quickly grew into an exciting possibility. Dillon sat heavily on the closed commode, his jaw going slack with wonder at his own imaginative thinking.

He was beginning to scare himself.

"Darling, I think you hit the jackpot," he said slowly, pulling her onto his lap. "And I think I've figured out a way to cash in."

"I'm all ears," Callie said, linking her arms around his neck.

Dillon tightened his arms around her. "Thank God you're sitting down," he muttered. "This is going to be a shocker."

"Ha! Rummy again!" Mrs. Scuttle crowed, laying her cards out on the bed. "Read 'em and weep!"

Kasidy smiled at the woman's obvious glee. She slapped her hands against her knees and tried to sound casual as she said for the third time in the last hour, "Well, I'd better go see if Isabelle needs help with the dogs."

Mrs. Scuttle's gleeful expression dropped like a stone. "Yes, dear, you should go. You're too young to stay cooped up with an old person like me. You should be out doing things."

On her way to the door, Kasidy faltered at the pitiful note in Mrs. Scuttle's voice. She sighed, determined to keep going this time. Wyatt had been gone for an hour, and she didn't want to miss an opportunity to get that tape.

Her hand was on the doorknob when she heard a sniffle.

Followed by another sniffle. She turned to look at Mrs. Scuttle, who offered her a watery smile over the edge of her hanky.

Kasidy felt a spurt of suspicion. Wyatt claimed there was hanky-panky going on, and she was beginning to believe there was merit to his suspicions.

The secretary had gone from laughing to crying in the space of a few seconds.

For the second time in an hour.

The first time Kasidy had tried to leave her, she hadn't made it to the door before Mrs. Scuttle burst into tears. It had taken her fifteen minutes to calm her down, and another fifteen of listening to the story of how her tenants had threatened a poor, defenseless old woman and forced her out of her home.

The first time Kasidy had heard the story, Mrs. Scuttle claimed she had been baking cookies when she set the smoke alarms blaring.

The second time, the secretary had said brownies.

An understandable slip, considering Mrs. Scuttle's age.

Yet . . . yet Kasidy felt something else was going on. Like Wyatt, she hadn't bought Isabelle's story about the fight with her mother. Oh, it wasn't that she was surprised they'd have a fight . . . it was Isabelle's dramatic show that Kasidy didn't quite swallow. Despite her Barbie doll appearance, Isabelle had proved to have a keen intelligence that would make her a popular vet one day. Isabelle was a little high strung, but she wasn't the hysterical type.

Yes, Isabelle had definitely overplayed her hand.

And now Mrs. Scuttle.

Kasidy could hazard a guess at Isabelle's intent; the young girl wanted to help out with the dogs in order to give Kasidy more time with Wyatt.

But the secretary's return . . . now that was something to chew on. She obviously didn't want Kasidy to leave her, but why? Mrs. Scuttle couldn't possibly know who she was, or what she wanted. Nobody knew, except for Nana Jo.

Right?

"I miss my goldfish," Mrs. Scuttle sobbed.

Resigning herself, Kasidy sat down and began shuffling the cards. Whatever her reason, she couldn't leave an old lady crying into her hanky, not even for her father.

She'd grown fond of Mrs. Scuttle.

CHAPTER 25

"I guess you've noticed I'm not very good at playing gin rummy," Kasidy told Mrs. Scuttle. She frowned down at her cards, wondering how she managed to deal herself such a crummy hand. "It's your turn to draw, isn't it?" When Mrs. Scuttle didn't reply, Kasidy glanced up.

She froze.

The secretary had fallen asleep sitting up, her chin on her chest. She was snoring softly.

Kasidy was afraid to move. She'd never witnessed a person falling asleep sitting up, so she was understandably skeptical. Was it a joke? The moment she tried to sneak away, would Mrs. Scuttle open her owlish eyes and start cackling?

Or worse, begin to cry again?

Precious moments ticked by. Finally, Kasidy knew she'd have to make her move, come hell or high water. Isabelle hadn't returned from walking the dogs, and Wyatt was still gone.

She might not have another chance.

Setting her cards aside, Kasidy carefully inched

from the bed, pausing often to study Mrs. Scuttle. Her heart was racing, and her palms had started to sweat. She slid another inch, and got her foot on the floor.

Her other foot landed with a soundless thud. Slowly, Kasidy used her hands to lift her butt from the mattress until she was standing. She crept to the door, wincing as she stepped on a creaky floor board.

She paused and looked back.

The elderly woman slept on.

Kasidy felt guilty leaving her sleeping in that position. It not only looked uncomfortable, it looked unnatural. Mrs. Scuttle was very likely to awaken with a painful crick in her neck.

Go on, you fool.

She started forward again. So far, so good. Another couple of feet and she'd reach the door. Opening it would be a little tricky, since Kasidy remembered that the hinges needed oiling.

Her sweaty palm grasped the knob. She turned it slowly, hardly breathing. She tried not to think about what Wyatt would say or do if he caught her cracking the safe again. There would be no lying her way out of it a second time, since there was nothing of value left to steal.

Nothing of value that *Wyatt* knew about, but something definitely valuable to Kasidy. So valuable that she couldn't wait to stomp it to pieces.

Just as she suspected, the door creaked as she opened it. She paused, looking back. The secretary continued to snore. Deciding to leave the door open rather than risk the creaking again, Kasidy tiptoed soundlessly down the hall to Wyatt's room.

She reached it without mishap, slipped inside, and locked the door. This time she would get the tape. If Wyatt came back before she got the safe open, he would have to knock the door down. She'd have the tape destroyed before that happened.

Moving quickly, she climbed onto the bed and removed the painting. She had committed the combination to memory, so it took her only a few seconds to open the safe.

She grabbed the tape and clutched it to her pounding heart, closing her eyes in sheer relief. Finally, she had the blasted tape.

And Wyatt hadn't caught her.

Kasidy stood kneeling on the bed, holding the tape. What should she do? Should she destroy it now, before Wyatt caught her? Or should she hide it and destroy it later, when she was certain not to get caught?

She held out the tape, fighting a growing curiosity to see for herself what incriminating evidence Amelia had guarded all these years. She was still undecided when she heard Isabelle scream her name.

Scream, at the top of her lungs.

Scream, hysterically, frantically. Like someone might if they were being murdered.

"Oh, for heaven's sake!" Kasidy muttered, exasperated with the endless drama generated by her newfound friends. "What the heck is going on now?"

"Kasidy! Where are you?"

Isabelle was still downstairs. Kasidy took note of this fact and raced to the door. Where could she hide the tape? she wondered frantically. She opened the door and peered left and right.

The hall was empty, of course. Mrs. Scuttle was hard of hearing, so it was unlikely she'd heard Isabelle screaming. Wyatt was obviously still gone, or he would have responded to his sister by now.

"Kasidy! Oh God, you'll never believe what happened!"

Kasidy rolled her eyes. With the Love family, she didn't think much would surprise her. Hearing Isabelle come pounding up the stairs, Kasidy took off running down the hall, away from the landing. She passed Amelia's locked room, another guest room, and yet another.

The room with the waterbed loomed ahead. Kasidy pushed against the door, opened it, and practically fell inside. She kicked the door shut with her foot.

"Kasidy!" Isabelle screamed again, closer this time.

Isabelle had reached the landing.

Wildly, Kasidy looked around the room. Boxes upon boxes stacked high. An old dresser, the mirror cracked and blackened with age. Her gaze lit on a folded stack of drapes piled on top of a matching chest of drawers. She hurried across the room and shoved the tape between the drapes.

She stood, breathing hard. Isabelle was still calling her, her voice steadily rising to an ear-piercing level. If Kasidy opened the door now, Isabelle would know where she was.

But Isabelle wouldn't suspect anything, she reasoned. Wyatt was the one she had to fool.

Taking a deep, calming breath, she walked to the

door and opened it. She stepped into the hall, almost in Isabelle's path.

"Thank God," Isabelle cried, launching herself at Kasidy. She grabbed Kasidy's T-shirt and shook her, her eyes wild and wet from crying. "They took them! They knocked me down and took them!"

Kasidy gently disengaged Isabelle's fingers before the girl stretched her shirt beyond repair. "Calm down, Isabelle. Take a deep breath. That's right."

But after one breath Isabelle resorted to hysterics again. "They took the dogs! I think-I think they kidnapped them!"

"Who took them?"

"Those-those men! They had ski masks on," Isabelle babbled. "Like they wear in the movies when they rob a bank and they don't want anyone to see their faces on camera!"

She wasn't joking, Kasidy realized, feeling the first stirring of real alarm. Before she joined Isabelle in complete hysterics, Kasidy demanded, "Someone took the dogs while you were walking them?" Isabelle nodded frantically. "But why would they do that?"

"I don't know!" Isabelle wailed. "Oh, God. It's all my fault! You trusted me to watch them, and now they've been kidnapped! Oh, God! Wyatt's going to *kill* me!"

Kasidy frowned, trying to sort out the facts and make sense of it all. "I don't get it. Why would anyone kidnap three dogs?"

Isabelle grabbed Kasidy's T-shirt again. "They said—they said they would call with instructions."

Her voice lowered to a dramatic whisper. "I think-I think they're going to demand a ransom, Kas. It must be someone who knows what the dogs are worth."

"What the blue blazes is going on?" Mrs. Scuttle demanded, startling a shriek out of Isabelle, and scaring a good five years from Kasidy's life.

In the midst of the ruckus, Kasidy hadn't heard her approach. Now she stood in the hall, blinking sleepy eyes at them and scowling, like a child woken from her nap.

"Well? Is someone going to tell me, or am I too old and feeble to be included?"

If the situation hadn't been so dire, Kasidy was certain Isabelle would have rolled her eyes at that one. She knew *she* wanted to. Mrs. Scuttle had the pity-me down pat. "It's probably nothing, Mrs. Scuttle. Just someone playing a joke."

"What?" Isabelle cried, sounding outraged. "You call this a joke?" She held up her hands briefly, revealing the red welts on her hands. "They jerked the leashes right out of my hands and knocked me down! If this is a joke, someone's in deep shit!"

"What?" Mrs. Scuttle echoed, looking sharper now as she shuffled closer. "Someone knocked you down, dumpling?"

Before Kasidy could warn her, Isabelle turned to Mrs. Scuttle. "That's right. They did! And they kidnapped the dogs!"

Mrs. Scuttle's eyes grew impossibly rounder behind her thick glasses. "They took the boys? Those adorable poodles? Kidnapped them, you say?"

"This is ridiculous," Kasidy snapped, unwilling to feed the drama. "Nobody kidnapped the dogs. It's a joke. Probably Wyatt paying Isabelle back for driving his truck while we were sleeping in the back. . . ." Kasidy's voice died away at Mrs. Scuttle's interested look in her direction. She felt heat creep into her face.

But Isabelle wasn't buying it. "No," she said, shaking her head vehemently. "Wyatt loves to prank people, but he wouldn't do anything that mean. He wouldn't *hurt* me."

Unfortunately, Isabelle had a point, Kasidy thought, her earlier alarm nudging toward panic.

"There you are. What's all the commotion?"

They all turned to look at Wyatt as he came striding down the hallway. Despite the situation, Kasidy sucked in a sharp breath at the sight of his hunky form. He was wearing a striped cotton button-down shirt tucked loosely into a pair of Khaki shorts, and a pair of new leather sandals.

The heated look he speared her with turned her knees to jelly.

"Someone kidnapped the dogs," Isabelle blurted out, then burst into tears. She went into Mrs. Scuttle's soothing arms and sobbed onto the elderly woman's shoulder.

"Is this a joke?" Wyatt asked, staring directly at Kasidy.

For no good reason that she could think of, Kasidy squirmed beneath his penetrating gaze. Was she imagining it, or had his heated look cooled a few degrees?

Since Mrs. Scuttle was occupied with comforting Isabelle, and Isabelle was occupied with crying, Kasidy was left to explain the bizarre story to him. "Apparently two men—"

"Three," Isabelle stopped sobbing long enough to correct.

"Three men took the dogs from Isabelle while she was walking them. They said they would call with instructions."

Isabelle flashed a hand at him, sniffling. "They ripped the leashes out of-of my hands and knocked me down!"

Wyatt frowned, but Kasidy didn't think he was buying her story—yet. Like her, he appeared to be having a hard time wrapping his mind around the possibility of a dognapping.

"Izzy," he said in a warning growl. "If this is another one of your pranks, it's a bad one."

His sister lifted her tear-streaked face to glare at him. "Me?" she squeaked. "How about you? Kasidy suggested *you* did this, to pay me back for parking your truck in the grocery parking lot!"

"What's this I keep hearing about someone parking a truck while you two were sleeping in the back?" Mrs. Scuttle asked tartly.

"Never mind," Wyatt and Kasidy said simultaneously.

Then Wyatt pinned her down again, and this time his gaze was definitely cooler. Cold, in fact. Kasidy shivered.

"If it wasn't Izzy, and it wasn't me . . . then who did this?"

He was staring directly at her, Kasidy realized. And with a jolt of shock, she belatedly figured out *why* he was staring at her so accusingly.

He thought she had masterminded the kidnapping

to get the money she claimed she needed. Okay, so maybe she had it coming for telling such a whopper and getting caught cracking Amelia's safe, but his accusation still stung.

"Can I speak with you in private?" Wyatt asked her softly.

Kasidy thrust her chin out, holding his gaze. "You certainly may."

He jerked his head toward the waterbed room.

She led the way inside.

He slammed the door shut.

She cooly walked over and locked it. When he lifted a questioning brow, she said, "So we won't be interrupted while I give you directions."

"Directions?"

"Yes, directions. Directions on how to go straight to hell, Wyatt Love."

Wyatt folded his arms over his chest. "You have to admit that I have justification for my suspicions."

"I'm not admitting anything," Kasidy said coldly. Inside, she was hurting. "I love those dogs. I would never do anything to hurt them."

"No, I don't think you would. But you might use them to get the money you need."

Kasidy mimicked his actions and crossed her arms over her chest. She was so mad she could spit. "Why would I do that when I could just accept your offer of help?"

"Pride?"

Her laugh was nothing more than a bark of disbelief. "How could you claim to love someone that shallow?" When he didn't answer, she huffed a sigh.

"Wyatt, I didn't kidnap the boys, and yes, I guess after what . . . happened, I can't blame you for considering the possibility."

Moments ticked by. The tension thickened between them. Finally, Kasidy saw him relax. He let out a sigh similar to the one she'd huffed.

"What the hell, then, is going on?" He ran a hand through his hair like a bewildered little boy. "Whoever kidnapped the dogs obviously doesn't know that I don't have the authority to pay them a ransom." He shook his head. "Dammit. This is ridiculous."

Kasidy agreed wholeheartedly. "Apparently someone doesn't think it is. Do you think we should call the cops?"

Wyatt gave it some thought before he finally shook his head. "I have a very strong feeling they'd laugh us off the face of the earth."

"What do we do, then?"

"I guess we wait for the dognappers to call and go from there."

"Okay."

"Alright."

"I'm sorry."

She looked at him and swallowed hard. "It's okay."

"No, really. I'm sorry." He held out his arms. "Come here, so I can show you."

Kasidy gave a moment's guilty thought to the tape buried between the drapes only feet away before she went into his arms.

He was irresistible.

* * *

"Aren't you worried they'll hurt the twins?" Dillon asked Callie anxiously as he watched Jada and Kaden climb all over the dogs. Jada had giggled so hard she had the hiccups. Curly and Moe appeared to be enjoying the romp with the toddlers. Larry, on the other hand, looked comically resigned.

Callie smiled ruefully. "I think maybe we should worry about the twins hurting *them*."

Dillon chuckled. "Yeah. I guess you're right." He cringed as Kaden exchanged slobbery kisses with Curly. "That's gross."

"Their mouths are supposed to be cleaner than humans'," Callie said.

Prudently, Dillon pretended he didn't notice the disgusted look on her face. He didn't think she was aware of it. "Wyatt and Kasidy should know about the kidnapping by now. I hope the Elmer's glue and the lipstick I used to make those welts convinces them."

"Yeah, and let's hope Wyatt doesn't call the police."

"He won't," Dillon said with conviction. "There's no way my brother's going to call the cops and tell them three poodles by the names of Larry, Curly, and Moe have been kidnapped. Absolutely no way." He gave a shout of alarm as Jada tumbled from Moe's back onto the carpet. He didn't breathe again until she burst out laughing. "I know I wouldn't," he added.

Callie picked up a tennis ball and pitched it into the ruckus to see what would happen. The dogs and toddlers ignored the toy in favor of each other. "You do realize that Wyatt might think Kasidy had something to do with the kidnapping? He believes she needs money, you know."

Dillon grinned at the thought. "Yeah, that would be cool. All the more reason for her to come clean and claim her inheritance, so that she can make him eat crow."

"You mean *when* and *if* he forgives her for lying to him about her identity."

"He will."

She punched him lightly in the arm. "You sound so smug. What will you do if Kasidy runs out on him, instead of saving the day?"

"She won't."

"I hope you're right, Dillon."

"Me, too, Callie."

"Don't start."

"Start what?"

"You know what."

"No, I don't." He blinked innocently at her. "What?"

"That."

"That, what?"

Callie closed her eyes and counted to ten out loud. When she was done, she said, "You're trying to have the last word again."

"No, I'm not."

"Yes, you are. Stop it."

"You stop it."

"Dillon!"

"Callie!"

"*Doggie!*"

They both jerked their gazes back to the mountain of dogs and toddlers. "Who said that?" Dillon demanded, looking from Jada to Kaden, then back again.

"I think it was Jada," Callie said in a hushed, excited voice. "Dillon, I think Jada just said her first word!"

Dillon sounded both disgusted and pleased. "Yeah, and it wasn't daddy or mommy. It was doggie. That's just great."

"Doggie!" Kaden crowed, hooking Moe around the neck and dragging him down to the carpet.

"It was Kaden," Callie said unnecessarily.

"Doggie!" Jada shrieked, grabbing a handful of black curls and hanging on for dear life as Curly tried to drag her around the room.

"They're geniuses," Dillon announced with fatherly pride.

"Yes, they are."

"Damned right."

"You know this means we're going to have to get them a couple of puppies."

"Damned—oh, no. No, no, no. After what these guys have put me through, there's no way I'm going to live with that."

With a dreamy smile, Callie said, "Maybe a couple of boxers. They're supposed to be excellent with kids."

"Collies are good." Crap. What was he saying? Dogs hated him. There was no way he was going to live with one. Been there, done that at the mansion, and didn't like it. Hoping she'd forget what he'd just said, Dillon changed his tune. "Dogs are destructive."

"So are kids."

"Kids are . . . kids. Dogs are optional."

"Maybe cocker spaniels would be better. Still cute, but not as big."

Obviously, she wasn't listening, Dillon thought. "I've got an idea. Let's bring about a dozen of your shoes into the living room and leave them. We'll take the kids to get an ice cream. When we get back, if you still want a dog or two, then I won't stand in your way."

Callie had to think about that one. Finally, she shrugged. "Okay. We'll try your test. If they don't chew up my shoes, I get to pick the breed. If they chew up my shoes, we don't get a dog right now and you owe me a dozen new pairs of shoes. Deal?"

Dillon thought about the vintage *Playboy* the dogs had shredded, and how he could have bought her at least two or three pairs with the money he would have made selling that magazine on eBay. "Deal."

Poor Callie, he mused, not without a fair amount of genuine sympathy. She was in for a shocker.

CHAPTER 26

They took up their vigil in the living room.

Wyatt fell asleep in the chair by the cold fireplace.

Mrs. Scuttle snored softly on the sofa, sitting upright.

Isabelle was asleep on the floor, her arm thrown over her tear-stained face to shield it from the lamplight.

How could they do it? Kasidy wondered with more than a little envy from her ramrod-straight upright position in another chair. How could they all just go to sleep, not knowing where the dogs would be sleeping tonight, or if they were even alive?

Kasidy glanced at the grandfather clock again. It was almost four in the morning. Chances were the kidnappers wouldn't be calling at this hour.

As if to mock her observation, the phone rang. She jumped. Isabelle moaned in her sleep. Mrs. Scuttle didn't stir.

Wyatt opened his eyes.

The phone rang again. It was a desk phone, one of the old-fashioned kind with a cord, an oddity in the modern world where portable phones were life-

281

lines for the busy mom multitasking her way through the day.

Her petrified gaze clashed with Wyatt's. He came alive, reaching over and snatching the phone from the receiver in one fluid motion. "Hancock residence."

What she wouldn't give for a speakerphone, Kasidy thought, watching Wyatt's expression with an intensity that made her head hurt. He looked so grim. And furious. And disgusted.

"Right." Wyatt's voice was raspy from sleep. "I've got it." He slammed the phone down and sat back. He massaged his temples, eyes closed.

Kasidy wished she'd been close enough to kick him. "Well? What did they say?"

He sighed and looked at her. "We've got twenty-four hours to come up with a hundred thousand dollars."

"They're insane!" Kasidy couldn't believe their gall. Normal people didn't hand over a hundred thousand dollars for a dog or three.

With the exception of her grandmother, she thought. Through others, she'd gotten to know enough about Amelia Hancock to know that her grandmother wouldn't have hesitated to pay the ransom to get her babies back. Kasidy loved them, too, but she didn't have that kind of money.

Unless . . . Kasidy threw her head back against the chair and closed her eyes. *Damn!* If she didn't know better, she'd think someone was trying to force her out of hiding. But she knew better.

Nobody knew she was Amelia's granddaughter with the exception of her family, and she knew they weren't talking.

Right?

Wyatt reached for the phone again.

"What are you going to do?" Kasidy asked. If he had a plan, she wanted to know about it.

"I'm calling Attorney Jacob."

"At this hour?"

He stabbed at the buttons and brought the receiver to his ear before he said, "I don't really give a rat's hairy ass what time it is." Into the phone, he barked, "Mrs. Jacob. Wyatt Love, here. Yes, I know what time it is. I wouldn't be calling you at all if it wasn't important." He shot Kasidy a reassuring look that did nothing to reassure her. "What do I need? I need a hundred thousand dollars by tomorrow this time. No, I'm not drunk. Someone has kidnapped the dogs. Yes, the poodles. Amelia's poodles."

Kasidy saw his face darken with color. His eyes narrowed, and the knuckles on the fingers twisting the phone cord turned white. What was that nasty lawyer saying to him?

"That's all you have to say?" Wyatt asked coldly. After a moment, he hung up. He looked at Kasidy, his color high and his eyes sparkling with anger. "What was I thinking?"

"What did she say to you?" For a long moment, Kasidy didn't think he was going to tell her.

"She said, 'Nice try, gigolo, but you'll have to do better than that.' "

"Meaning?"

"Meaning I'll have to come up with something more believable than a dognapping to scam money from the estate."

"She's evil."

Wyatt's teeth flashed in a humorless smile. "I agree, but knowing she's evil doesn't help us, does it?" He blew out a weary, disgusted sigh. "That was my only ace. I guess the kidnappers have themselves a trio of mutts."

Kasidy suspected that he'd meant to sound flippant, but he hadn't quite succeeded. Despite the hell the dogs had put him through, he'd become attached to them as well. And somehow, she didn't think the criminals who had them would keep them as pets when they realized they weren't going to get any money.

She thought about the tape upstairs, and jumped to her feet. To Wyatt, she said, "Give me fifteen minutes."

"For what?"

"I'll explain later." Taking the steps at a run, she jogged to the waterbed room and shut and locked the door. She took the tape out from its hiding place, cracked open the front, and began yanking the film out. Her hands were shaking.

She was sweating by the time the tape lay in a ruined pile at her feet. Her search-and-destroy mission was over, but she knew that her problems were far from ended.

Wyatt had been hired to watch for the granddaughter's return, Kasidy felt certain. Even if he didn't know about the tape—and she didn't think he did—it was still his job to alert Mr. Slowkowsky when Amelia's granddaughter arrived.

What Mr. Slowkowsky wanted with her wasn't hard to figure out. No doubt he planned on torturing her into telling them where her father was.

Kasidy stomped to the door, her jaw clenched with determination. If Wyatt truly loved her, maybe together they could figure out how to handle Mr. Slowkowsky. Otherwise, Kasidy would face him alone. He'd find out that it wouldn't be easy to break her.

Downstairs, Kasidy marched to the phone on the end table beside Wyatt and grabbed the receiver. She looked him straight in the eye and said, "Give me her phone number."

Wyatt looked confused. "Who?"

"The soon to be ex-attorney for the Hancock estate," Kasidy snapped. To show that she wasn't angry at *him*, she leaned down and planted a big kiss on his surprised mouth. Softly, she said, "I love you. Just remember that."

Looking more confused than ever, Wyatt gave her the number. Kasidy was keenly aware of everyone watching her as she dialed. Isabelle had awakened while Kasidy was upstairs and was now sitting cross-legged on the floor. Mrs. Scuttle didn't appear to have moved, but a quick glance told Kasidy that the secretary's eyes were open and blinking rapidly, a sure sign she was agitated.

She took a deep breath and punched in the last number. Her insides had turned to mush, and she could no longer meet Wyatt's gaze. He was going to be shocked. Possibly angry. No, *probably* angry. She'd deceived him. Tricked him.

Loved him like crazy.

The line on the other end began to ring. Kasidy bit her lip, wishing she could find a seat. Her legs felt rubbery, and there was a nasty taste in her mouth.

Fear, she realized, just as Mrs. Jacob growled into the phone.

"This better be good," the attorney said.

Kasidy's hand tightened on the phone. Oh, it was gonna be good. Or bad. Depending on which way a person looked at it, and right then only one person mattered to Kasidy.

Well, make that three. Isabelle and Mrs. Scuttle held a space in her heart as well.

"Mrs. Jacob? I need a hundred thousand in cash delivered to the Hancock mansion by noon today." Kasidy was proud of how strong she sounded. Strong and tough.

"This call is being traced," the attorney began coldly.

"Good. That's good." Kasidy resisted the urge to smile at Wyatt. "Is it being recorded, as well? Because that would be even better. You'd have a nice little record of this conversation to play back whenever you get grumpy about losing me as a client."

"Who the hell is this?"

Kasidy paused, knowing that what she said next couldn't be unsaid. There was no turning back. Was she willing to take the risk for three spoiled poodles?

Damned right she was!

"This is Kasidy Evans," Kasidy said in a firm, clear voice. "I'm Amelia's granddaughter."

She expected to hear nothing less than a scream from Isabelle, and a gasp from Mrs. Scuttle. Surprisingly, the only sound she heard was the sound of Wyatt choking. She couldn't muster the courage to look around. Had Mrs. Scuttle fainted? Why was Isabelle so silent? Was Wyatt really choking?

"If this is a prank—"

"If this is a prank," Kasidy said, "then you have nothing to worry about. If it isn't, then you're in deep trouble. It's your call." There was a long silence on the other end.

Finally, Mrs. Jacob asked, "Do you have proof of who you are?"

"I have my birth certificate, and pictures taken of me with my mother before she . . . died."

"We'll need DNA."

"Fine, but I thought you had to have something to match it to before DNA testing would prove anything."

"We have a number of DNA samples taken as you were growing up, *Kassandra Raeann*. Your parents might have lived on the run, but Amelia's investigators were always one step behind them. It's amazing what a little girl will leave behind when she's dragged out of her sleep in the middle of the night."

Kasidy took great pleasure in correcting Mrs. Jacob. "It's *Kasidy* Raeann. That's the name on my original birth certificate, the one my grandmother's investigators never saw."

Attorney Jacob made an amazing transformation. "I don't know what to say."

It was the first time Kasidy had heard the woman sound civil. But it was too late. She had already revealed her horns. "How about, 'I'll get that cash to you by noon'?"

"Well, I don't think I can do that, Ms. Evans. Amelia was very firm about that DNA testing."

Kasidy clutched the phone so hard she felt as if she were crushing the bones in her fingers. After putting

her life—and her father's—on the line, was she
doomed to fail to save the dogs after all? Her stomach rolled in a sickening lurch. Her voice sounded
high and squeaky to her own ears as she said, "Is that
your final answer?" Who was she, Regis on *Who
Wants To Be a Millionaire?* The irony of her
thoughts didn't escape her.

She was now, or was soon to be, a millionaire. If
there was some way to stall the kidnappers until she
was officially declared an heiress. . . .

For the first time, she turned to look at Wyatt.

It was like looking into the eyes of a stranger.

Her heart sank to her toes.

"Is it true?" Wyatt asked softly. He could feel the
muscle throbbing in his jaw, so he knew it was useless to pretend he wasn't angry.

Hurt. Flabbergasted. Confused.

Isabelle jumped to her feet and mumbled a hasty,
"I've got to go to the bathroom," before she fled the
room.

Mrs. Scuttle, with a comical amount of grunting
and muttering under her breath, struggled to her feet
as well. "I'm going to bed," she announced. "Don't
wake me until noon." She started to shuffle to the
door, but paused and added, almost as an after-
thought, "Unless you hear from those thugs who
took the doggies."

Wyatt was just as confused as Kasidy looked by
their reaction—or lack of one, rather. But he had
more important things on his mind.

Like getting answers.

"Kasidy?"

288

"I hear you," Kasidy said with a sigh. She plopped onto the sofa Mrs. Scuttle had vacated and put her hands over her face. She spoke between her fingers. "Yes, it's true."

"Why didn't you tell me?"

"It's a long, complicated story."

He absorbed her evasive answer for a few moments. Long enough to swallow a ball of temper before it exploded from his throat. "I've got all day," he said.

"We should get some sleep first."

She was definitely stalling, Wyatt decided. He laced his fingers together in his lap to keep from locking them around her lying little throat. Was she just a spoiled little rich kid having some fun? Had she been playing a game with all of them since her arrival?

Wyatt cracked his knuckles and bit his tongue.

Hell. He felt worse than stupid.

Deciding, for both their sakes, that getting some sleep was a good idea, Wyatt rose and headed for the doorway before he gave in to the urge to break the furniture and turn Kasidy over his knee.

"Did my grandmother have expensive jewelry?"

He stumbled at her question, he jaw dropping as he swung around to look at her. "What?"

She opened her eyes and gave him a weary look. "Did Amelia have any valuable jewelry?"

He clenched his jaw. "Yes. Why?"

"I could sell it, if there's enough. To pay the ransom. The DNA testing will take too long."

Admiration was the last thing Wyatt wanted to feel at the moment, but it sneaked in on him. "It's an idea, but I've got another."

She lifted her head. "What?"

Payback was a bitch, Wyatt thought with savage triumph. "We'd better get some sleep first."

"You're probably right. Wyatt?"

He braced himself against the vulnerability shining in her eyes. After the bombshell she'd dropped on him, how did he know what was real, and what was a game? "Yes?"

"Remember what I said to you before I talked to Mrs. Jacob?"

He nodded. How could he forget? She'd told him she loved him. Truth? Or lies? Who knew?

"I meant it," she said softly.

Two restless hours of sleep wasn't enough for Dillon.

He awakened slowly, feeling as if someone had poured sand into his eyes.

The first thing he noticed was that he couldn't move.

Not a muscle, with the exception of his head, and even that movement was limited.

He was lying facedown on the bed, arms pinned to his sides. Moving his head as far as he could, he tried to look over his shoulder. Jada lay sprawled on his back, sound asleep. Farther down, Kaden lay sprawled across Dillon's thighs, also sound asleep.

He looked down at his side, and found out why he couldn't move his arms. There was a big curly black dog taking up the left side of the bed. Dillon turned his face on the pillow to find Moe pinning his right arm. He didn't have to look—not that he could—to know that Larry lay across his feet. Who or what else could it be?

His entire body was weighted down with dogs and babies.

The moment Dillon turned his face back around, a blinding light flashed in his gritty eyes. He squeezed them shut, waiting for the light to die down behind his lids. When he dared to open them again, he saw Callie standing in the doorway, holding her camera and smiling.

"What was that for?" Dillon tried to mumble. It wasn't easy to move his mouth when he could hardly lift his head from the pillow.

"*Parent Magazine* has a photo contest this month. I'm thinking I should at least get first place for originality."

"Good for you. What are you doing up so early?" Callie had been up with him at four when he'd made the ransom demand using a voice disguiser. Shortly thereafter, the twins had awakened and joined them in bed, followed by the dogs.

All three of them.

"You got covered," Callie said too damned cheerfully. "I got knocked to the floor."

"Poor baby," Dillon mumbled. And then, just in case his wife hadn't been listening last night, he repeated himself. "We are not getting a dog."

"I know." Callie propped her hip against the door frame, smiling at him and giving him just enough time to think she had caved before she added, "We're getting two. They didn't touch my shoes. You, however, are going barefoot until we can get to the store."

Dillon didn't like the sound of that at all. "Why do I have to go barefoot?"

"Because there isn't a shoe of *yours* left that isn't chewed to pieces."

He groaned. "They hate me. I told you they hated me."

"Maybe they just don't like men."

"Oh, now I feel much better," Dillon drawled sarcastically. He tried again to move, and gave up after one grunt. "Can you help me, please?"

"But they look so cute!"

Through the covers on his back, Dillon felt a sudden rush of warmth.

"That had better be one of the twins," he growled.

"Oh, quit being a grouch. Of course it was one of the twins who peed on you." She knelt before the bed so that she was eye level with him. It was then that Dillon noticed the overly bright gleam in his wife's eyes.

"She told him," Dillon guessed, elation filling him. Finally!

"Yep. Got a text message from Mrs. Scuttle around five."

"Mrs. Scuttle sent you a text message?"

"She sure did."

"Callie, sweetheart?"

"Yes, darling?"

"Will you *please* help me up? Jada is not the only one who has urges, and with these guys on top of me pressing my bladder into the mattress. . . ."

Hastily, Callie rose from her squatting position and lifted the sleeping Jada in her arms. With Jada gone, Dillon was able to pull his legs out from under Kaden without waking him, and maneuver through the mountain of dogs out of the bed.

He was sweating by the time he found his feet. He tried to glare at the dogs, but ended up laughing instead.

"Two dogs," Callie said, chuckling with him.

"One."

"Two."

"One, and a very *small* one. A miniature Doberman or something."

"We'll see."

For once, Dillon was too weary to argue.

CHAPTER 27

As a bonafide night owl, Wyatt had never had trouble sleeping during the day.

But then, his mind wasn't normally so cluttered with things like dognapping and sneaky heiresses. From the moment he'd met Kasidy, he'd been on a roller coaster of mishaps, bad luck, fantastic sex, bizarre situations, and drowning in believe-it-or-nots.

Bedtime stories for dogs.

Making love in the back of his pickup in a dark garage.

Waking up naked in the back of his truck in a crowded parking lot.

Catching a safe cracker in the act.

Calling 911 to get an eighty-year-old woman unstuck from the commode.

And now, dognapping and surprising confessions.

Through it all, his mind kept coming back to the same mystifying, unbelievable yet undeniable conclusion: Dillon.

Wyatt knew he hadn't fallen down a rabbit hole, and he wasn't in Oz. So that left Dillon, because no way could he possibly believe everything that had happened to him in the past two weeks was based on coincidences or fate.

Uh-uh.

Somehow, some way, his twin had known from the start that Kasidy was Amelia's granddaughter. Using—or abusing—that knowledge, Dillon had set in motion a chain of crazy events that led to this moment.

A reluctant admiration bloomed inside Wyatt. Why, Dillon had nearly topped Wyatt's own crafty prank when Dillon first met Callie and believed she was a nasty reviewer.

But dognapping?

Maybe. Possibly. Wyatt couldn't swallow it—yet.

Because if Dillon was behind the dognapping, then Wyatt would have to admit that Dillon had trumped him. His clever maneuver had forced Kasidy to reveal herself.

And that was what stung the most, that it had taken a dognapping to force her into telling him the truth. If she loved him as she claimed, why wouldn't she tell him who she was? Was it because she didn't trust him? And what was there to not trust about him? Had she been making sure Wyatt loved her for herself, and not her money?

Another conceivable—but unproven—theory.

She'd lied to him about why she'd been trying to crack the safe. Obviously, if she wanted money she had only to come forward and claim her inheritance.

Unless . . . unless for some reason she'd wanted only a piece of the pie, and not the whole enchilada. Was her story about the pink slip and losing the car true? Was anything she'd told him or done true or real?

Wyatt snarled a nasty curse and glared at the ceiling. Maybe that's why she hadn't wanted to explain earlier, because she had suspected he'd have a hard time believing anything that came out of her sweet, kissable mouth.

Screw it. After what she'd put him through, after the lies she'd told him, she *owed* him the truth.

And he was going to get it from her.

The house was eerily quiet as he made his way downstairs to Kasidy's room. He hadn't realized how much atmosphere the dogs added to the mansion, with their playful romping and general mischief making. It just wasn't the same without them.

If Dillon was behind the dognapping, he was *so* going to regret it. Admiration aside, it was a sick prank.

Without knocking, Wyatt tried the door. The knob turned without resistance. He eased the door open, knowing he shouldn't care, but not wanting to startle her.

"I'm awake," she said. "I think I'm too tired to sleep."

He knew the feeling, and the hundred different questions zipping through his mind hadn't helped. Not that Miss Alias would know anything about that, Wyatt thought.

Kasidy pulled back the satin comforter as he approached the bed. She patted the spot she'd made. "Join me?"

No seductive smile. Just a simple invitation.

Which shouldn't have set his groin on fire, but it did.

Apparently, Wyatt mused, disappointment did not

cancel out lust. He told himself it was his own exhaustion that had him climbing into bed beside her warm, soft body. He told himself that it had nothing to do with the fact that he still loved her.

But he knew it was bullcrap.

He settled back against the pillows, propped his hands behind his head, and waited. With his eyes on her face, he asked, "How do I know I can believe you now?"

She didn't pretend not to know what he was talking about. "Because now I have nothing to hide."

"Why were you 'hiding' before?"

"Because I was afraid."

"Afraid of what?"

After a telltale hesitation, she said slowly, "That day Mr. Slowkowsky sent his men after you, I called Dillon. He said that you had worked for Mr. Slowkowsky before."

"Yeah?" Wyatt knew he was missing the point, but he was patient. Not exactly trusting, but patient.

"So I figured out why you were here. Mr. Slowkowsky sent you, hoping I'd show up. He wants my father dead, and he knows I can find him."

Oh. Wyatt could have kicked himself. He'd figured everything else out. But then, he hadn't known Kasidy was Amelia's granddaughter, so he'd had no reason to explain to her his unfortunate association with Mr. Slowkowsky.

He could explain now, but the part of him that was still pissed kept him silent. Let her squirm a little.

"It's okay, Wyatt. You didn't know who I was, and I'm sure Mr. Slowkowsky is paying you a lot of money."

Wyatt kept his mouth firmly closed. He was going to let her dig this hole all by her lonesome.

"I think you should know, though, that even if you turn me over to Slowkowsky, I'm not going to tell him where my father is."

His brave, brave girl. Wyatt was beginning to understand why she'd lied to him. But that didn't keep the knowledge from hurting any less. She *still* believed him capable of selling her out to Slowkowsky. After all they'd shared, she still didn't trust him.

He jerked when she put a hand on his thigh. He'd been hard and ready from the moment he slipped in beside her, but he didn't want *her* to know that. Not yet, anyway.

"Wyatt . . . I was hoping we could work something out. Unless you've told him, Mr. Slowkowsky doesn't know who I am. I could leave today and he'd never have to know I was here."

For the first time, Wyatt spoke. He had to ask the burning question. "What about the dogs?"

"I can sell the jewelry, then leave before Jacob gets the DNA evidence. You could tell everyone I robbed the safe and disappeared. Right now they have no proof I'm who I say I am."

Her hand moved higher, and Wyatt had to clench his teeth. He forced himself to relax and play along. It was hard to do when he was steaming inside. "What about us?"

"We . . . we could meet sometimes. Nobody would have to know."

So much for marriage and kids. Maybe she wasn't the marrying type.

And his mother, once again, was right, Wyatt

thought as he lunged for Kasidy and flipped her onto her back, covering her from head to toe. He sometimes let his anger blind him to rational thought.

Taking her hands in his, he pulled them above her head, rendering her helpless to the torture he had in mind. His mouth crushed hers, but instantly became tender when she kissed him back with the same innocent abandon that had endeared him to her in the first place. By the time he ripped her panties away, Wyatt knew that he was no longer punishing her.

She was punishing him, by responding in kind. She was showing him that she could be just as wild, as savage. And love doing it.

The knowledge inflamed Wyatt to a dangerous degree. He raked her T-shirt over her head, and she used her toes to scrape down the lounging pants he'd hastily pulled on before coming downstairs. When they reached his feet, he kicked them away.

Naked flesh met naked flesh. She panted against his hungry mouth, and he groaned when she surged her heat against his erection.

"Take me, Wyatt," she said.

"You want it, baby?" he rasped, reaching down and finding her wet and wanting. She scraped her teeth against his shoulder, and Wyatt nearly came undone. It was the first time he'd ever let the beast roar with such passion and abandon, and it scared him.

"I don't want to hurt you, Kas," he whispered in a guttural tone he barely recognized. "You're . . . you're driving me crazy." Her husky laugh spread goose bumps across his body.

"You won't hurt me." Her tongue found his ear. She nipped his lobe with her teeth, whispering promises he knew she could keep. "I want you inside me. Deep, deep inside me."

At least they agreed on something, Wyatt thought, just before he felt her tight heat envelop him. She arched her back, straining against him, and the action thrust her breasts into his face.

Wyatt took full advantage of her offering, nipping and licking and sucking until she wrapped her legs around him and brought him all the way home.

He went still, buried deep inside her. Tenderly, he kissed her, using his tongue to trace her lips, her teeth. He tugged on her bottom lip, and she playfully captured his. Restlessly, she moved against him.

And finally, she gave him what he wanted.

"Please, Wyatt. Move."

"Like this?" Wyatt slowly withdrew, then slowly buried himself again. He marveled that he could feel her inner muscles clenching around him, trying to hurry him along.

"Faster."

"Like this?" Again he withdrew, slowly. Teasingly. This time he held back, poised at her entrance.

"Wyatt . . . don't stop!" She was breathing hard and fast, and Wyatt already recognized the signs. "Inside . . . again!"

Because he couldn't say no, and didn't want to, Wyatt obeyed, gritting his teeth as he slowly entered her, then withdrew.

He picked up the rhythm slightly, sensing she was close, knowing he wasn't far behind. He loved her with savage tenderness, until she went over the edge, driving him deep with her hips and legs.

Wyatt locked his mouth on hers. She caught his

tongue and sucked hard. He buried himself deep and stopped, his entire body turning to molten lava as he followed her over the cliff. He let go of her hands. She buried them in his hair, her labored breathing music to his ears.

She believed it was the last time.

He was determined it would be the first of many.

"I want you to keep the dogs a while longer," Wyatt told Dillon the moment his sneaky, conniving twin answered the phone.

"Dogs? What dogs?"

Until now, Wyatt hadn't been one hundred percent certain. Just ninety-nine. His voice was soft and lethal. "The gig is up, bro."

"I don't know—"

"Give it up, Dil. I know you have them. You're the only nutcase that would attempt something this low."

"Are we talking about the same guy? You're referring to your brother Dillon. The boring, never has any fun, never participates in pranks, never lightens up, never laughs at jokes—"

"Go to hell, you freak. I'll deal with you later on the dognapping thing. Right now you can keep them." Wyatt smiled, imagining the dismay on Dillon's face. He suspected his brother hadn't planned on a long kidnapping.

"I think you've really lost your mind, little brother. Where's Kasidy?"

"She's asleep. When she wakes up, I'm taking her to Slowkowsky."

"So she knows he's her grandfather?"

301

"Nope."

Silence. Then, in a cautious voice, Dillon asked, "Wyatt, are you getting her back for not telling you she's Amelia's granddaughter?"

That was Dillon, Wyatt thought savagely. Concerned about Kasidy, when he should be worried about what Wyatt was going to do to *him*. "This isn't about revenge."

"Okay," Dillon drawled sarcastically. "This is about teaching her a lesson."

Wyatt knew his brother didn't deserve an explanation, but he gave it anyway. "She still thinks there's a chance I'll turn her over to him."

Dillon swore beneath his breath. "Why didn't you tell her that you don't work for Slowkowsky? Why didn't you tell her about his ugly stepsister who nearly tore off your clothes when you escorted her?"

Sometimes, silence speaks louder than words.

His brother swore again. "This is about your pride, your ego, isn't it?"

It was, but Wyatt wasn't proud of the fact. "She'll find out I'm not feeding her to the sharks."

"Yeah, *after* you give her a heart attack! I think I'm going to tell Mom."

"How old are you, three?" Wyatt taunted. "And don't think I don't know that Mom was in on this. Everyone was. I can see clearly now."

"Whereas before you were blinded by lust," Dillon said, revealing a dangerous amusement.

Wyatt grit his teeth. "Is Mom home right now?"

"Are you kidding? She's afraid to leave the house after you dumped the king's coffer on her doorstep."

"Very funny. I guess you've all had a good laugh at my expense."

"And about damned time, if you ask me."

"Screw you."

"Go to hell."

"Kiss my ass."

"Mark the spot and I'll pack a lunch."

With an aggravated explosion of breath, Wyatt effectively ended the argument by hanging up.

It was time to wake sleeping beauty, alias Kasidy Evans.

CHAPTER 28

Mary insisted on feeding them.

Kasidy knew she wouldn't be able to swallow a bite, but she didn't want to be impolite, so she followed Wyatt and Mary into Mary's big, bright kitchen. Textbooks were scattered over the table, along with paper, pencils, and about a billion Post-it notes.

Wyatt's mother began gathering the mess into a pile. She picked it up and shoved it into Wyatt's surprised arms. "You can put that in my room, and while you're there, you can pick up that laundry sack."

"She knows, Mom. She knows everything."

"Everything?" Mary's brow rose, and for the first time, Kasidy noticed a strange glittering in her eyes.

Like Nana Jo, when Nana Jo was mad and trying to pretend she wasn't.

Afraid that Wyatt was missing the clues and about to be ambushed, Kasidy blurted out, "Yes, Mary. I know everything, and I want to say I'm sorry for not announcing my identity."

With her gaze focused on Wyatt, who was beginning to squirm, Mary said, "Well, honey, I'm sure you had your reasons."

Although Wyatt was understandably uncomfortable with the daggers his mother was throwing at him, he maintained eye contact. "No need to apologize to Mom, Kasidy. She knew all along who you really were. Didn't you, Mom?"

To Kasidy's surprise, Mary folded like a poker player with an atrocious hand.

"I had *my* reasons, as well," she said. "Do you want mustard on your ham sandwich, Wyatt?"

"That's what I *thought*."

"Don't push it, son," Mary warned, the glitter back. "I'm sure you don't want me to ruin your punch line."

Bewildered, Kasidy looked from one to the other. They were at a Mexican standoff, and she didn't have a clue what they were talking about.

Mary folded her arms. "Are you sure you want to do this?"

"Mom . . . I love you, but you're putting your nose where it doesn't belong."

"Am I?" She thrust her chin into his face. To accomplish this, she had to stand on tiptoe. "I'm your mother, so as far as I'm concerned, my nose can go wherever it pleases. Now, considering what a horse's butt you can be when someone pisses you off, I'm going to ask you again. Are you sure you want to do this?"

Wyatt didn't blink. "Yes. Can we drop it?"

"Fine, but don't coming crying on my shoulder when it backfires in your face."

305

"Fine. I won't."

"Fine. Go get your jewelry and get back here and eat your sandwich."

"Yes, ma'am."

When Wyatt clicked his heels together and saluted his mother, Kasidy held her breath, certain Mary would sock him one. If she had smarted off to Nana Jo like that . . . well, she just wouldn't.

After he left to take the books upstairs and retrieve the jewelry and cash, Mary let out a huge sigh. She shot an apologetic smile at Kasidy. "I'll bet you can't guess which twin gave me the most trouble."

"It wouldn't be hard." Kasidy shook her head. "If I talked to Nana Jo like that I would be missing a few teeth."

Mary looked horrified. "She hits you?"

"No, no." Kasidy laughed. "The most Nana Jo ever did was slap my hands when I reached across the table."

The older woman relaxed. "Well, I like this Nana Jo already. I take it she's the grandmother on your father's side?"

Kasidy nodded, a little nonplused at how much Mary seemed to know about her. So much for incognito!

"Ah. You're upset because I knew who you were all along," Mary observed. She led Kasidy to a chair at the kitchen table and told her to sit. "And I guess you're curious as to *how* we all knew."

"Curious would be putting it mildly."

Taking out the sandwich fixings from the fridge, Mary began to prepare their meal as she talked.

"That first day you arrived, Dillon overheard you talking to your Nana on the phone."

"God. If that had been Wyatt. . . ."

Mary nodded in sympathy. "If that had been Wyatt, you would have packed up and left, never to be seen again. Am I right?"

With a shock, Kasidy realized she *was* right. The knowledge left her a little dazed.

"And if you had left, you wouldn't have made so many new friends and fallen in love with my son."

"I'm not—" Kasidy stopped. Mary was looking at her with a twinkle in her eyes. It would be silly to deny it when obviously Mary already knew the truth.

"So." Mary put a plate in front of her, smiling down at Kasidy. "Did you find what you were looking for? Because we all know you weren't after the cash or the jewelry."

Good thing Kasidy hadn't taken a bite, she thought, because she would certainly have choked. Looking around to make certain Wyatt wasn't in sight, Kasidy said in a low voice, hoping Mary would take the hint, "Yes, I found it."

"Good." Mary beamed at her. She, too, lowered her voice. "I don't think it makes much of a difference now, but it's smart to cover all your bases."

Mystified, Kasidy took a bite of her sandwich to cover the fact that she had no idea how to reply. She didn't even know if she and Mary were on the same page. And what was it that Wyatt planned to do that Mary disapproved of?

Glancing again at the doorway where Wyatt had disappeared, Kasidy swallowed her food and asked,

"Can you tell me what that conversation between you and Wyatt was about?"

"No, sorry. I can't." Mary sounded regretful. "I love my kids, but I'm a firm believer in letting them make their own mistakes."

Was *she* the mistake? Kasidy wondered. No, that didn't make sense. Wyatt's family and friends wouldn't have gone to all that trouble keeping Wyatt in the dark if they wanted her to disappear. At least, she *hoped* not.

"But I will say this," Mary said. "Wyatt loves you. Just remember that, no matter what happens in the next few hours."

One fact became crystal clear to Kasidy; the Loves loved their mysteries. Unfortunately, Kasidy didn't think her own love story was going to have a happy ending. Mary had said she knew everything.

Well, she didn't. She didn't know that Kasidy was going to have to leave. Destroying the tape had helped, but it hadn't solved the problem. The very nature of Wyatt's job proved that Mr. Slowkowsky apparently had other reasons for wanting to find her father. Her grandmother could have shown him the tape, or hinted that Kasidy's father was behind Mr. Slowkowsky's brother's indictment.

Kasidy realized she might never know for certain.

She couldn't wait around to find out, either. It was too risky. Wyatt hadn't actually said he would let her go, but after what they'd shared this morning, Kasidy had to believe he couldn't bring himself to turn her over to that monster.

Yet . . . if she stayed, eventually Mr. Slowkowsky would find her, or he might offer Wyatt more money.

Definitely too risky. For her father's sake, she had to go.

"Let's go."

Deep in her dark thoughts, Kasidy jumped at the sound of Wyatt's barked order. She set her sandwich down and shot Mary an apologetic look. "I'm sorry, Mary. The sandwich is good, I just can't eat anything right now."

"Take it with you," she said, shooting Wyatt a quelling glance before he had time to protest. She handed him a foil-wrapped sandwich. "And *you* eat this one. I know you two have been up most of the night, and you need to keep up your strength."

It wasn't until they were back in the truck that Mary's last comment caught up with Kasidy. "How did your mother know we'd been up all night?"

Wyatt started the truck and backed out of the drive without looking at her. "Good question. You're smart. You'll figure it out."

So Mary wasn't the only one to experience the bite of his sharp tone. Hurt, she rolled down the window and threw her sandwich to the birds.

"You should have eaten that," Wyatt chided.

"I'll eat when you eat," Kasidy said, keeping her gaze on the passing scenery. "Where are we going?"

It was a long moment before Wyatt answered. "I know someone who will give you the best price for the jewelry."

"A pawnbroker?"

"He's known to be on occasion."

Ah. Another mystery. The Loves should host their own show, Kasidy mused darkly.

The conversation didn't pick up again until Wyatt

309

turned into a gated entrance and stopped the truck. Beyond the gate Kasidy could see tall white columns and an immaculate lawn. A young guy with a receding hairline and a sour-looking mouth leaned out of a small booth.

Wyatt rolled his own window down. "Tell him Wyatt Love's here to see him."

The guy in the uniform tipped his hat. "Sure thing, Mr. Love. Wait just a moment."

A chill of premonition crept along Kasidy's spine. "This doesn't look like any pawn shop I've ever seen."

"It isn't a pawn shop," Wyatt informed her tightly.

Before Kasidy could ask him what he meant, the uniformed guard leaned out of his booth again.

"Mr. Slowkowsky says to let you through."

Kasidy felt the bottom drop out of her stomach.

The look of abject terror on Kasidy's face made Wyatt let out a string of curses and shove the truck into park. He reached for her, but she shrank back against the seat, her beautiful green eyes two round saucers of accusation. "For Pete's sake, Kasidy! I didn't think you'd be *this* scared! The old man's not who you think he is. He won't hurt you. He just wants to talk to you."

Kasidy fumbled for the door handle. Wyatt quickly hit the child safety lock button. Self-disgust made him sound harsher than he intended.

"Give him a chance, baby."

"You-you don't get it, do you?" Her teeth started to chatter. "My father put his brother in prison! He doesn't want to *talk* to me!"

"Your father did him a favor. His half-brother had been stealing from him for years." Wyatt gnawed his lip in frustration. He couldn't seem to get past her terror. "He's not harboring a grudge."

"My-my grandmother told my mother that if she married my father, she was signing his death certificate!"

It was a new experience for Wyatt to wish a dead woman to life so that he could wring her neck. "She lied, Kasidy. She lied, hoping your mother would come back to her." He hesitated, wondering if she was ready to hear the truth, if she would believe it. "Your mother was mad at Amelia for a different reason, baby."

Kasidy laughed hysterically. "You're feeding me to that—that shark, and still calling me 'baby'?"

Wyatt hit the steering wheel with his fist. "I'm not feeding you to the sharks!" he shouted. When she didn't respond, he shoved the truck in gear and left rubber on the asphalt. He flew down the long drive and braked sharply in front of the three-storey mansion. "Come inside with me. Let me prove it to you. Trust me, Kasidy." He held out his hand.

She stared at it as if he'd offered her a black widow spider. Then her huge eyes flew to his flushed, angry face. "You don't know, do you? He's fooled you into believing he just wants to talk to me."

"He went legit more than twenty years ago. Ask anyone."

She thrust out her chin. "My parents would have told me."

He hated to say it, but he knew that it needed to be said. "Maybe they didn't tell you. Maybe they had their reasons." None good enough, in his opinion. He was getting the distinct, and ugly impression that Amelia Hancock wasn't the only person he'd enjoy choking.

Kasidy had been brainwashed.

Furious at the realization, Wyatt opened the driver's door and got out. He kept his eyes on Kasidy as he walked around the hood of his truck to her door. "Come on." He grasped the handle and opened it, then took her arm. "This is getting ridiculous. Slowkowsky said he had a tape to show you that he and Amelia had made together. It should explain everything."

But Kasidy wasn't listening, Wyatt saw, catching her as she crumpled.

She'd fainted.

The instant Kasidy came to, everything came rushing back to her.

She was in Slowkowsky's house. Wyatt had brought her.

She jerked upright, looking wildly around. The sofa beneath her was pale blue and plush. A matching chair was on her right. In front of her was a marble-topped coffee table.

Two items graced the table: a videotape and a remote control.

Kasidy moaned and jerked her gaze away, forcing herself to check out the rest of the room.

It was obviously a living room. Dark paneling complemented the light furniture, and the room smelled of lemon wax and cigars, an odd mixture that tickled her nose.

One thing was certain: she was alone.

Adrenaline rushed through her veins. She leaped to her feet and raced to the double doors. They were locked. Damn! Then she remembered the handy tool she kept in her pocket.

It wasn't there. Belatedly, she remembered that she hadn't transferred it from her other shorts when she'd changed earlier. Damn, damn, damn!

Look at the tape.

Kasidy shook her head. She didn't want to look at the tape.

Look at the tape!

The voice inside her head sounded suspiciously like Nana Jo's, but why would Nana Jo want her to look at the tape? It was her son who was in danger, her son who had been running for twenty-five years.

Slowly, Kasidy backed away from the doors. Why not look at the stupid tape? She was here. Mr. Slowkowsky would do what he had to do whether she looked at the tape or not.

Apparently, that was what he *wanted* her to do, or he wouldn't have left her alone in a locked room with the tape and a remote. Where was Wyatt? Had he realized that Slowkowsky had tricked him into bringing her here? Was Slowkowsky holding him hostage, as well?

Look at the tape.

"All right, already!" Kasidy muttered beneath her breath. She wiped her sweaty palms on her shorts and approached the coffee table. Her hands shook as she picked up the remote and pointed it at the flat television taking up a good portion of one wall.

The screen flickered to life. Reluctantly, Kasidy picked up the tape and took it to the elegant cabinet to the right of the television. Inside was a VCR/DVD combination unit, a top-of-the-line stereo, and an impressive collection of DVD movies.

She slid the tape into the machine and pushed play. Slowly, she backed away, staring at the screen. It was obviously a homemade video, and the person holding the camera hadn't been very steady.

Kasidy heard voices as the camera made a sickening lurch around the room.

This room, Kasidy noted. Different furniture, but the same room.

"Will you focus the damned thing, you dingbat?"

It was a woman's voice, raspy with age. The voice and the tone reminded Kasidy of Mrs. Scuttle. But the woman who finally came into focus looked nothing like the secretary. She was classy, wearing pearls and a beige dress suit. Her hair was gray, but elegantly cut. Her eyes were a deep, piercing blue.

The man sitting beside her looked about the same age. He was grinning at the camera, and Kasidy could tell by the twinkle in his aging eyes that he was laughing silently at the woman beside him.

"I'm Amelia Hancock," the woman announced. "And this is Darth Slowkowsky, the man I have loved my entire life. He's also Willow's father, something I should have told her from the start."

Kasidy heard a gasp, and realized that it was her own. She'd seen pictures in the attic of her grandfather, and this man wasn't the one pictured.

Darth Slowkowsky. *Her grandfather?* Was this a joke?

314

"If you're watching this, Kassandra, then I'm dead and you're where you should be, where you should have been a long time ago."

As shocked as she was, Kasidy couldn't stem a surge of satisfaction at the realization that her grandmother had never known her real name.

Because her legs were weak, Kasidy sat on the carpet, her eyes glued to the screen.

"When I finally told Willow Darth was her real father, she said she'd never speak to me again." Tears glittered in the old woman's eyes. Kasidy saw her bottom lip tremble before Amelia stiffened her spine and went on. "She kept her promise, and I've never really blamed her. But she had my granddaughter, and I wanted the chance to know her."

"It wasn't right," Slowkowsky broke in to say.

Amelia shushed him, but the look she gave him was full of love and tenderness. Kasidy swallowed hard. She loved Wyatt, so she knew what it was like to love someone, yet live with the knowledge that you couldn't be with him. Was that what had happened to Amelia? Had she been forced into a loveless marriage, all the while loving Slowkowsky?

"Kas, when your father turned state's evidence on Darth's brother, he did it for your mother. She thought she was punishing Darth."

Kasidy moaned and closed her eyes. She didn't want to believe what Amelia was saying, but it was all beginning to make sense.

"Now, don't you go hating your mother," Amelia admonished as if she were right in the room with Kasidy. "She was hurt. She thought the man she'd loved all her life was her father. When she found out the truth, she hated me for it. She also hated the fact that her *real* father was Darth."

Darth leaned forward to add in a stage whisper, "Yeah, at the time I was a big-time thug."

To Kasidy's mortification, she felt her lips tug at the wicked light in his eyes. Grudgingly, she admitted to herself that she could see why her grandmother had fallen in love with the old rascal.

"When she ran off with your father," Amelia continued, "I fully believed she was doing it out of spite, and not love."

"Not true," Kasidy whispered. "They loved each other." She gave a start as Amelia echoed her words.

"But they loved each other. I know that now." Her grandmother sighed, looking sad. "There's blame on all sides, Kas. But the truth is, that's life. We only have a certain amount of control. The rest is left up to fate."

Then Amelia changed the subject and tone so fast, it took Kasidy a moment to catch up.

"Have you met my boys? Are they alright?" When Amelia rolled her eyes, Kasidy couldn't help grinning. "What am I saying? It's not like I can hear you if you answer me, wherever I am right now. I just hope they're doing okay, and that Wyatt took good care of them for you." The twinkle that suddenly appeared in Amelia's eye was very visible on the high definition screen. "What do you think of Wyatt? He's a hunk with a heart, isn't he?" She threw back her head and laughed. "God, what I wouldn't give to have seen his face when Mrs. Jacob read him the terms of the will!"

Kasidy put a hand over her mouth to stifle a laugh as Darth glowered at Amelia.

Amelia caught his look and giggled like a schoolgirl. She elbowed him sharply in the side, making him grunt. "You jealous bum. Wyatt's young enough to be my grandson. You know you're the only man I love." With that, Amelia leaned over and kissed Darth.

The kiss lasted long enough to embarrass Kasidy. She started to get up and turn off the tape, but Amelia finally came up for air.

"Sorry, sweety. I couldn't help myself. I just wanted you to know why I wasn't a part of your life. It's my biggest regret. My other regret is that I couldn't get Willow to forgive me. Why, I wouldn't have known about her death if your other grandmother hadn't called me and told me. It's a terrible thing to lose your only child, especially when you haven't seen her in eighteen years. I'm sure it was even harder to lose your mother at such a young age, Kas. I'm sorry that I couldn't be there for you."

Kasidy discovered she was sorry, too. Sorry for her mother. Sorry for Amelia, and sorry for herself. The woman she had hated and feared all her life turned out to be someone she knew she would have loved.

She couldn't blame her parents. Her life had been good, despite its ups and downs. And right or wrong, she knew her parents believed they had their reasons for keeping her from Amelia.

"Well, adios, Kas! Enjoy my money, and with any luck, you'll at least get to spend time with your grandfather, here. He can answer any further questions—and I'm sure you've got plenty. I loved you dear, even if I didn't know you."

Kasidy was turning off the tape when the double doors opened and in walked Mr. Slowkowsky and Wyatt. She lifted her brows and searched the corners of the room for cameras. She found none. "Psychic?" she asked.

Mr. Slowkowsky—her grandfather—grinned. "I see you've got Amelia's sassy attitude."

Kasidy slowly smiled back. "Yeah. I guess I have."

CHAPTER 29

"Are you very angry with Dillon?" Kasidy asked after they left. She'd spent an enjoyable few hours with her grandfather, and she couldn't wait to get back to her cell phone so that she could call Nana Jo and tell her everything that had happened.

The look Wyatt shot Kasidy revealed nothing. "I don't know what I feel. I think I'm still in shock."

Kasidy bit her lip, hesitating before she asked in a small voice, "Are you very angry with *me?*"

"For believing I would sell you out—even after I told you that I loved you?" Wyatt laughed shortly. "I should be."

"Is that a yes, or a no?"

"I don't know. I think I'm still in shock."

He was beginning to sound like a broken record, Kasidy thought. Wisely changing the subject, she said, "We still have to figure out what we're going to do about the dogs."

"The dogs are fine. Dillon has them."

She gaped at him. "What?"

With a rueful sigh, Wyatt nodded. "Yep. It was

319

Dillon all along, as much as I hate to admit it. He kidnapped the dogs to force you into revealing who you are."

"Clever. How long have *you* known about this?"

"Since this morning. I'm sorry. I shouldn't have put you through that, but I didn't realize just how terrified you were of Slowkowsky."

With a touch of bitterness, Kasidy said, "You didn't realize that I had been lied to my entire life. That's understandable. I'm having trouble believing it myself."

"Kasidy . . . I don't think your parents meant to hurt you."

"I know you're right, but the fact remains that they abused their parenting power. I should have been given a choice about my grandmother."

"Maybe your mother would have told you if she hadn't died."

"Maybe. I wonder what excuse my father will use?" Since she really didn't expect an answer, she wasn't surprised when she didn't get one. She looked out the window, realizing she'd never been in this part of Atlanta. It was a suburb, the tree-lined streets hiding driveways that led to neat, middle-class houses. "Where are we going?"

"To pick up the dogs."

"Good. I miss them."

The sound Wyatt made was half grunt, half laugh. "I never thought I'd say this, but I do, too. Besides, I don't like the idea of you staying alone."

His casual comment sent a shock wave through Kasidy. She'd been so dazed over the recent events that she hadn't thought about Wyatt not going home with her. The realization sent her mind into a tail-spin. Was he hinting that he couldn't forgive her? Or was he waiting for an invitation to stay, now that his job was over? She found she was too afraid to find out. "Mrs. Scuttle will be there to keep me company, and Isabelle."

"Something tells me they've already gone. When you confessed you were Amelia's granddaughter, they had no reason to stay."

She swallowed a ball of fear. "You . . . you don't have to go." Why couldn't she say she was sorry? Why couldn't she beg?

"My job is finished. The heiress has arrived." He tried to lighten the sting of his words with a dry laugh. "Although I have to admit I'm going to miss that hot tub."

The hot tub, but not her? Kasidy felt her world start to crumble. Wyatt spoke as if he never intended to use that hot tub again. What had changed? Was it because she was now wealthy? Or was it because she had lied to him, and now he felt as if he couldn't trust her? Less than four hours ago, Kasidy had believed she'd have to leave Atlanta and Wyatt. When she'd watched the tape and realized that she could stay, she couldn't have been happier. Maybe she *would* get her happily ever after.

Now Wyatt seemed distant . . . cool. She knew he had every right to be angry with her, for lying to him as well as for believing he was involved with Slowkowsky and willing to sell her out. Had she killed their love in the first fragile stage? Had she wrecked her chance at happily ever after?

She kept her eyes glued to the passing scenery to

hide the tears threatening. The enormity of what she'd done to him made saying I'm sorry seem puny and insulting. But somehow, someway, she had to convince Wyatt to give her another chance.

Life without him was unimaginable.

Larry, Curly, and Moe were ecstatic to be back home. They went racing into the kitchen, presumably to check out their dog food bowls. Louise had gotten into the habit of surprising them by putting a treat in their bowls when they're weren't around.

Wyatt hefted his laundry sack and glanced at Kasidy, who didn't know what to do or say to him. "I'll put the jewels and the cash back into the safe."

Kasidy stuck her hands in her shorts pockets, feeling awkward and bashful. "Thanks."

"I'd prefer you go with me, so there won't be any misunderstanding later about what I took out, and what I replaced."

Squashing a spurt of anger, Kasidy said, "I have no reason not to trust you, Wyatt."

His expression reminded her that only hours ago, she'd been certain he was about to feed her to the sharks. "Humor me."

"Fine." She followed him upstairs to his room, glaring at his back and wishing she could justify telling him where to stick his attitude. But she knew that she couldn't. She deserved every caustic comment he uttered, and then some.

She stood in the doorway as he opened the laundry sack, then unlocked the safe. When he pulled open the safe door, he froze. A chill crawled along her spine. "What is it?"

"Someone's been in here," he said. "The tape and the papers are missing."

"I took the tape," she said, frowning as she moved further into the room. When his brows shot up in question, she flushed. "I thought it was an incriminating tape about my father, so I took it and destroyed it. But I didn't take the papers."

"They're gone." His suspicious gaze lingered an instant longer than Kasidy thought necessary before he shoved the jewelry boxes and cash into the safe and closed it. "I think someone should stay with you tonight. I'll call Jet, one of my coworkers. He's done some bodyguarding."

"I don't want to stay with a stranger," Kasidy blurted out, then added softly, "I want *you* to stay with me."

"I don't think that would be a good idea."

"Why not?" Kasidy surprised herself by challenging. "Don't you trust yourself?"

His gaze grew heated as he slowly looked her over, until every inch of her body tingled. "No," he said bluntly. "I don't. But that's beside the point. It's a big house. Whoever took those papers could still be inside. Now you've got something for them to steal."

If not for his serious expression, Kasidy might have thought he was purposely trying to scare her. Whatever his motive, it worked. Drumming up a false bravado, Kasidy said, "I've got the dogs for protection. If there's someone in the house, they'll know it."

Wyatt laughed without much humor. "Yeah. They're real dependable, like the time your grandfather sent his henchmen after me."

Kasidy felt compelled to defend the dogs. "Maybe they could sense you weren't in any real danger."

"They're smart, but not *that* smart."

She was starting to feel the sting of his rejection. "Look, if you don't want to stay, then don't, but I don't need or want anyone else to stay with me."

In two strides, he was in front of her, invading her space. Kasidy didn't mind, but her pride was injured, so she pretended that she did. As a result, she thrust her chin out and refused to back down.

"I insist," he said softly, staring into her eyes.

She cursed the sudden weakening of her knees at that look. Hard to look tough when her insides were melting into a puddle. God, she loved him. She couldn't lose him. Didn't want to live without him. "You're not my boss." Childish words, but she was desperate. It was hard to think with Wyatt that close.

A tiny, smug smile curved his mouth. "That's not what you moaned earlier," he taunted.

A surge of elation further weakened Kasidy's knees. If he could remind her of their lovemaking, then maybe she still had a shot at forgiveness. Deliberately, she said, "A gentleman wouldn't remind a lady of what she says during a passionate moment."

To her joy, it worked like a charm.

He took her wrists and put her arms behind her back, holding them there. The action brought her flush against his hardening body. His voice was deep and husky. "How many times do I have to tell you? I'm not a gentleman."

Kasidy couldn't seem to take a deep breath. Boldly, she said, "Prove it." The air froze in her lungs as she waited to see what he would do. The bed was behind them. They were alone in the house.

Softly, sexily, he whispered, "I can feel your nipples growing hard against my chest."

Just as softly, she said, "And I don't think that's a pocket knife digging into my belly."

"Sex isn't always the answer to every problem, Kas."

"We can talk later."

His mouth hovered above hers, his lids lowered to half-mast. "I think I've created a monster."

She moved an inch, and their lips brushed. A thrill shot through her, jump-starting her heart into high gear. "I agree," she whispered. "It's all your fault." And then she laid herself wide open, giving him the perfect opportunity to attack, if that was what he wanted or needed to do before he could forgive her. "You make my knees weak, Wyatt, and I think I could have an orgasm just from kissing you."

He let go of her waist and brought her even closer. A deep moan rumbled in his chest, vibrating against her sensitive nipples and sending little arrows of desire straight to her belly and into her thighs. "You know just what to say, don't you?"

"I think that's only fair," she countered, nuzzling his chin. "Since you know just what to do to turn me on."

"We should be talking." But the words sounded half-hearted and weak this time.

Kasidy sucked in a sharp gasp when his hands came around and cupped her breasts. She began to unbutton his shirt. "Okay. You talk. I'll listen."

When she finished undoing his shirt, she moved to the button on his shorts, popped it open, and slowly drew down his zipper.

She dropped to her knees. He buried his hands in her hair and moaned again. Kasidy was beyond listening, but not above letting him believe otherwise, if it meant she could do what she wanted to do.

Needed to do.

The sudden muffled explosion of loud, angry cursing in the bedroom closet caught them both unawares. Wyatt quickly pulled Kasidy to her feet and shoved her behind him. She heard him zip his shorts, felt every muscle in his body tense.

Her heart was still beating like mad. She peeked around Wyatt, her eyes on the closet. "Who is it?" she hissed at him.

"I don't know," he hissed back.

The closet door burst open. Kasidy shrieked. Wyatt shoved her onto the bed and out of the way, bringing his fists up and ready to face his foe.

"I think we've caught our thief," he growled.

But Kasidy wasn't listening. She was staring at the livid man who'd burst from the closet. The man's chest was heaving. He held his fists at his sides, clearly furious.

"Kasidy," her father snarled. "I don't know why you're here, or what you're doing with this man, but I'll get your explanation later. Right now I'm going to beat the tar out of him for forcing my baby girl to-to—" Instead of finishing what he obviously couldn't bring himself to say, he let out a roar and charged Wyatt.

"No, Dad!" Kasidy leaped from the bed and

jumped between them, nearly getting crushed in the process. She had to brace her hands against her father's chest and dig her toes into the carpet to stop his charge. "Stop, Dad! He wasn't forcing me to do anything!"

Albert Evans huffed like a mad bull. His murderous gaze was on Wyatt. "I know what I heard. I'm not deaf, baby."

"No, but apparently you have selective hearing," she yelled back at him. In slow, cautious degrees, she relaxed her hold on him.

It was then they all heard the commotion on the stairs. All eyes turned toward the door just in time to see Larry, Curly, and Moe charge through the doorway and launch themselves at Albert. Their combined weight knocked him to the floor.

"Do something, Wyatt!" Kasidy shouted, grabbing the nearest poodle by the collar and hauling him away. She turned to see why Wyatt wasn't moving; he was obviously still in shock from discovering her father hiding in the closet. She suspected he was also shocked to see the dogs actually attacking someone.

Finally, he snapped out of his daze and waded in, grabbing Larry and Moe by their collars and hauling them off Albert.

Albert got up, cursing and wiping at the dog slobber on his face. He appeared shaken, but unharmed. He glared at the snarling dogs and Wyatt. "I should have remembered those damned mutts."

Kasidy's jaw dropped. "Remembered them? They've seen you before?" Her gaze met Wyatt's. She saw the light of remembrance dawn in his eyes.

"Amelia was burglarized last year," Wyatt said.

"Her attorney mentioned it at the reading of the will." He looked at Albert. "It was you, wasn't it?"

Without shame, Albert's head jerked in an angry nod. "Yes, it was me. I was looking for that damned tape."

Again Kasidy and Wyatt exchanged glances. "There was never a tape incriminating you, Dad."

"There was," he argued. He ran a hand over his short, greying hair. "I saw it last time before those mutts attacked me, and I heard you admit that you'd taken it from the safe."

"The tape wasn't about you. It was about Amelia and my grandfather, Mr. Slowkowsky." She waited, tense as a bowstring, to see if he would deny it.

His gaze fell from hers. He lost his bluster. "So you know." He looked at her again, his gaze narrowing. "But there *was* evidence, baby girl. Amelia held its existence over my head."

"She lied. They tried to tell you the truth later, but you wouldn't listen." She watched his face carefully, looking for signs that he was lying to her again. Would she even recognize them, since he'd obviously lied to her her entire life?

"It was a trick," he said with conviction. "Slowkowsky and your grandmother were trying to lure us out of hiding."

Larry strained against Kasidy's hold, whining and growling. She wanted to believe her father, she really did. "It wasn't a trick, Dad. At first, Grandma Amelia might have meant what she said, but she changed her mind when she realized Mom wasn't coming back. I've talked to Grandpa Slowkowsky. I believe him."

"She's telling the truth," Wyatt said. "I've known Slowkowsky for years. He's been legit for a long time. When you turned state's evidence against his brother, Slowkowsky found out that his brother had been stealing him blind. He wants to thank you, not kill you."

Albert hesitated, looking from Wyatt to Kasidy. Clearly, he wanted to believe them. Finally, he heaved a sigh. "I hope you're right, baby girl, because if you aren't, I'm a dead man." He pinned Wyatt with a stern look again. "Just who are you, and what are your intentions toward my daughter?"

"I'm going to marry her, if she'll have me."

Kasidy's knees tried to buckle. Joy swept through her, making her weak all over. Tears pricked her eyes as she looked at Wyatt. "Of course I will."

"Damned right you will," her fathered growled. "After what I heard in the closet, you should already be hitched."

The tension in the room popped like a balloon, and Kasidy began to laugh. Wyatt soon joined her. After what seemed like an eternity, Albert braved Larry's snarls and snatched her up for a rib-crunching hug.

She inhaled his familiar scent, hugging him back and crying and laughing at the same time.

Then she grew still as another mystery slowly unwound.

Her father's cologne. Wyatt and Dillon both wore something similar, if not exactly the same.

The dogs had recognized the scent. That's why they had tormented Wyatt and Dillon, destroying their things and generally making a nuisance of themselves.

She struggled free of her father's embrace. "Dad, what's that cologne you always wear?"

Albert blinked in bewilderment. "Forest something. It's what your mother always bought me. She loved it."

"Forest Deep," Wyatt said, sounding as confused as Albert looked. "Mom bought the stuff for Dillon and me last Christmas."

"Well, there you go!" Kasidy announced, tickled that she had figured it out. "The dogs caught Daddy breaking in last year. They remember his cologne."

"And that's why they chewed up my stuff, and Dillon's," Wyatt concluded. "That's why they hate us."

He sounded so relieved, Kasidy had to laugh. "We'll have to change your cologne, and yours, too, Daddy, if you're going to be visiting, and you are, right?"

Her father scowled. "If I'm still alive, baby. If I'm still alive."

Kasidy had let go of Larry's collar. He was still growling low in his throat, but the laughter had defused the dogs' fight instincts. "I'm going to take the dogs to their room. Wyatt, would you mind helping?"

"They have their own *room*?"

Wyatt laughed at Albert's incredulous expression. "Yep, and since you're going to be my father-in-law, I'll let you in on a little tip. Don't be around at bedtime, or you'll find yourself reading them a bedtime story."

"You're kidding me."

"Nope."

They left her father scratching his head in wonder as they took the dogs downstairs. The moment the door closed them inside, Wyatt let go of Moe and Curly and pinned Kasidy to the door. "Did you mean it when you said you'd marry me?"

Flushed and exhilarated, Kasidy nodded. She linked her arms around his neck. "I did. I love you. Why wouldn't I marry you?"

"I don't care if you're rich," Wyatt growled.

Kasidy burst out laughing, but sobered quickly when Wyatt didn't join her. He was serious, she thought. So that was what his change of attitude had been about. He was afraid she'd think he loved her for her money, and all because she'd first believed he was a gigolo.

Daring to tease him further, Kasidy dug some cash out of her shorts pocket and placed it in his hand. She closed her fingers around it, smiling seductively. "Tit for tat, lover boy. I was your nurse. It's only fair that you be my gigolo."

He tensed for an instant, then relaxed, chuckling at his own silly insecurities. Pulling her tight against him, he kissed her until she was breathless and hot. "Can I get a rain check? I'm a little uncomfortable playing sex games with your father in the house."

She took back her money and promptly stuck it in her bra. "Well then, you'll know where to find your fee when you get ready for it."

"God," Wyatt groaned, kissing her neck. "I can't believe how much I love you."

"I can," Kasidy said on a contented sigh. "Because I love you the same."

EPILOGUE

"I can't get it in the hole," Kasidy told her husband-to-be three weeks later.

Wyatt shot her a doubtful look. "Don't look at *me*."

"Will you please try? Just wiggle it around until it slips in. It's been almost a month, so I don't think it will hurt."

"But what if I *do* hurt you?"

"Believe me, if you get it in, it will be worth it." She turned to face him, hiding a smile at his terrified look. "I wonder if Mrs. Scuttle is having the same problem hitting the hole." Ignoring his expression, she lifted his hand and placed the tiny gold angel earring onto his palm.

He scowled down at it. "Couldn't you have gotten something bigger?"

Kasidy chuckled. "While I agree that bigger is better in *some* instances, earrings isn't one of them. Come on, Wyatt. The party's started, and since we're the guests of honor, I think we should be there. Besides, we have to stop by Mrs. Scuttle's room and escort her to the patio. You know she hates to wait."

Wyatt's face softened. He smiled, gazing at her with open adoration. "I can't believe you talked her into moving in with us."

"Lucky for us she swallowed that story about the boys being lonely when I moved into your room upstairs." She tilted her head and pulled back her hair. "Now. Put it in, please."

"You keep saying that, and we'll be skipping the party," Wyatt warned in a low growl. Cautiously, he began to insert the earring. He got it on the first try. Gloating, he said, "See? I haven't lost my touch."

Fully aware he wasn't referring to inserting jewelry, Kasidy laughed, then shrieked as he grabbed her up and lifted her high. She held onto his shoulders, looking down at him. Her heart felt as if it would burst from the joy coursing through her body.

"Have I told you how absolutely delicious you look in that dress?" he asked for the fifth time.

Without conceit, Kasidy knew the white backless summer dress looked good on her, complementing her honey-gold tan and emphasizing her curves. Isabelle had helped her pick out the dress during a frenzied, exhaustive shopping spree. Kasidy was now familiar with every strip mall within a ten-mile radius.

Breathless, Kasidy tried to squirm free before they both got into trouble. "Wyatt . . . Mrs. Scuttle, remember?" She laughed at his comic dismay. "We can finish this . . . later."

Wyatt let her slide to the ground slowly, making the most of every second. When she was on her feet, Kasidy leaned in to give him a kiss filled with seductive promises. "Later," she whispered before taking his hand and pulling him from the room.

Like happy children, they raced downstairs, pausing at the newly remodeled maid's room where Mrs. Scuttle now resided.

Kasidy knocked on the door. "Mrs. Scuttle? Are you ready?"

"Just a blasted minute!" Mrs. Scuttle bawled.

A loud crash from inside the room startled Kasidy and Wyatt. Alarmed, Kasidy knocked again. "Mrs. Scuttle, are you okay?"

"Yes!" she yelled, clearly furious. "I just knocked over the nightstand trying to put on these blasted panty hose!"

"Do you want—" Before she could finish, Wyatt had clamped a hand over her mouth. His eyes were huge and incredulous.

"Are you crazy? She'll eat you alive if you offer to help!" Slowly, he released her mouth.

She licked her lips, her heart tripping at how close she had came to making a terrible mistake. "Thanks. That was a close call."

"Go on without me!" the secretary shouted, making Kasidy jump. "And save me some of that homemade ice cream Vera's making."

Vera was the new housekeeper, and to everyone's surprise and delight, Mrs. Scuttle adored the tiny little Asian woman.

Arm in arm, Kasidy and Wyatt made their way to the backyard where their engagement party was in full swing. They paused in the open patio doors, gazing at the crowd of family and friends.

Dillon, Callie, and the twins frolicked in the pool. Isabelle and her circle of friends sat around the edge of the pool, dangling their feet in the water and gossiping. Kasidy followed Isabelle's intense regard to the new addition to Mr. Complete, Desmond Carter. He was young, he was gorgeous, and he was single.

He was also, Kasidy realized with amusement, just as intensely aware of Isabelle as she was of him.

Beside her, she felt Wyatt stiffen. She followed the direction of his gaze, her body going tense as well. But only for an instant. Mary and Albert occupied the hot tub, sharing shrimp cocktail and champagne. Deeply engrossed in conversation, neither seemed to be aware of the unruly crowd around them.

They made a handsome couple, Kasidy mused, wishing them the best.

Greg and Ramon manned the huge barbecue grill Wyatt had unearthed in the storage room in the garage. Greg had confessed to Wyatt earlier that he'd convinced Ramon the tattoo couldn't be removed without leaving a hideous scar.

Luke and Lydia sat at a patio table with Grandpa Slowkowsky and two of his sidekicks. It didn't surprise Kasidy that her grandfather had his audience in stitches.

Kasidy heard footsteps behind her. She turned in time to catch Nana Jo as her grandmother squeezed the life out of her and plastered her with kisses.

"Nana! You made it!" Kasidy felt a rush of happy tears as she pulled back to survey her grandmother. "You look hot and aggravated, Nana. Did you have car trouble?" Kasidy had offered to provide a plane ticket, or to send someone to get her, but Nana Jo had declined.

Nana Jo's brows furrowed slightly. "As much as I hate to admit it, I think my old Buick's about to lie down and die on me. I had to stop three times to let it cool off."

"I'm going to buy you a new car," Kasidy said in a tone that brooked no argument.

"I think that's a fine idea," Nana Jo surprised her by saying. "And while you're at it, what about one of those private jets? That way I could go to any island I wanted. Maybe I'll find me a hot Jamaican."

Realizing her grandmother was teasing, Kasidy laughed. Their reunion was interrupted by Mrs. Scuttle.

"Get out of my way," the secretary bawled, nearly knocking Nana Jo into the patio doors.

The noise began to die down as every eye focused on Mrs. Scuttle. When her shuffle took her in the direction of Greg and Ramon, they dropped their barbecue utensils and deserted their position with more haste than grace.

By the time Mrs. Scuttle reached the barbecue grill, it was nearly silent. Jada and Kaden, unaware of the drama, continued to shriek and frolic in their swim vests.

Her color high, her eyes glittering with anger, Mrs. Scuttle reached the grill. She lifted the heavy lid, pulled out an object from her dress pocket, and shoved it inside.

Kasidy and Wyatt realized at the same instant what she'd thrown into the fire.

Pantyhose.

Their gazes met. Laughter erupted, and to everyone's mystification, they had to hold onto each other to keep from collapsing.

COMPLETELY IRRESISTIBLE

Her voice laced with amusement, Nana Jo said, "I take it I just met the infamous Mrs. Scuttle?"

With tears streaming down her face and her sides convulsing with laughter, Kasidy could only nod.

COMPLETELY YOURS

SHERIDON SMYTHE

"Your Escort Will Be a Perfect Gentleman"

That was her sister's promise when Callie Spencer agreed to let one of the men from Mr. Complete squire her around town during her Atlanta business trip. But one look at her stud-for-hire makes Callie wish he'd break all the rules. And at first it seems the all-too-appropriately named Dillon Love will oblige. His burning gaze says he takes a very personal interest in their relationship. But his on-again, off-again seduction makes gun-shy Callie want to shoot herself in the foot. Her heart has already been broken once, by her ex-husband the underwear model, no less. Can she trust another breathtakingly handsome man, even when he promises to be completely hers?

Hot Number

SHERIDON SMYTHE

Jackpot! No one needs to win the lottery more than Ashley Kavanagh, and she plans to enjoy every penny of her unexpected windfall—starting with a seven-day cruise to the Caribbean. But it isn't until a ship mix-up pairs her with her ex-husband that things really start to heat up.

Michael Kavanagh hopes this cruise will help him relax, but when he walks in on his nearly naked ex-wife, everything suddenly becomes uncomfortably tight. Sharing a cabin with Ashley certainly isn't smooth sailing—but deep in his heart Michael knows love will be their lifesaver.

- -

JENNIE KLASSEL

IT HAPPENED IN SOUTH BEACH

If she's a beauteous, bodacious babe, gettin' down, gettin' it on, gettin' her man, she's definitely *not* good old Tilly Snapp. So what's the safe, sensible twenty-six-year-old Bostonian doing in Miami's ultra-hip, super-chic South Beach?

She's on the trail of the fabled Pillow Box of Win Win Poo—the most valuable collection of antique erotic "accessories" in the world. And she's after the fiend who murdered her eccentric Aunt Ginger. And while Tilly might not know the difference between a velvet tickle pickle and a kosher dill, with the assistance of the sexy yet unhelpful Special Agent Will Maitland, she's about to get a crash course in sex-ed.

Meet the new Tilly Snapp, Sex Detective.

South Beach ain't seen nothin' yet.